Weed in the Field

K. H. Leach

Contents

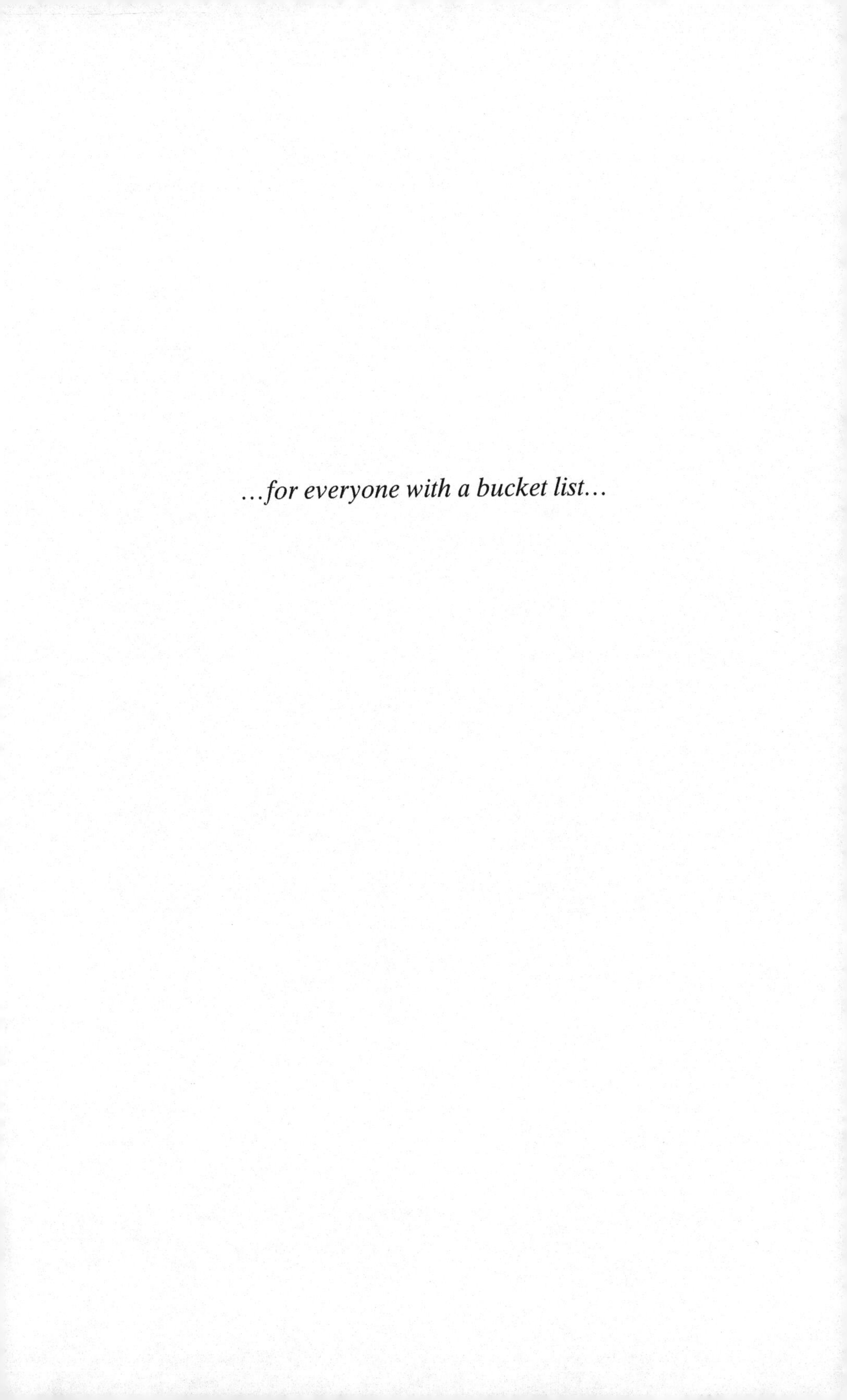

...for everyone with a bucket list...

The Parable of the Weeds

Matthew 13: 24-30

Jesus told them another parable:

"The kingdom of heaven is like a man who sowed good seed in his field. But while everyone was sleeping, his enemy came and sowed weeds among the wheat, and went away. When the wheat sprouted and formed heads, then the weeds also appeared.

The owner's servants came to him and said, 'Sir, didn't you sow good seed in your field? Where then did the weeds come from?'

'An enemy did this,' he replied.

The servants asked him, 'Do you want us to go and pull them up?'

'No,' he answered, 'because while you are pulling the weeds, you may root up the wheat with them. Let both grow together until the harvest. At that time I will tell the harvesters: First collect the weeds and tie them in bundles to be burned; then gather the wheat and bring it into my barn.'"

– The NIV Study Bible

Chapter One

Ophelia Hobart MacPherson Garrett walked down the dirt road toward the cemetery. She walked slowly, not so much because of her age or the stifling heat of the June day, but because of the high-heeled shoes she wore. The shoes were an ever-present aspect of her appearance, as were the pearls at her throat and the twist of brilliant blonde hair atop her head. She was an aristocratic woman, today wearing black for the funeral of her second son in as many years. She walked with dignified determination for she knew the eyes of the curious followed her.

She did not walk alone. Robert, his gentle brown hand supporting her elbow, walked on her left. Naomi Ruth, in a futile attempt to shade them from the blistering sun, held high a parasol on her right. The three moved through the heavy air in stately unity. The family trailed behind.

Ophelia passed first through the gate of the wrought iron fence surrounding this final resting place of centuries of Garretts. She moved across the small stamp of land that lived and breathed with timeless gravity. This earth was planted with tombstones. Ophelia wove her way between them intent on the funeral home tent standing at the far edge of the cemetery. Family followed, funneling through the narrow gate, picking their way across the graves.

As the procession approached the tent, the funeral home director stepped from its shade and led Ophelia to the front row of folding metal chairs. She took her seat. She was joined on either side by Robert and Naomi Ruth. Alice, Everett, junior, and Charlotte filled the row. The remaining family members gradually settled into seats behind them.

Those friends who had followed the hearse from the tiny church to the country for the Committal stood quietly outside the fence. They edged together in tight rows perpendicular to the recently planted rows of corn in the field behind them. They watched. They waited. They whispered.

The priest leaned over and spoke to Ophelia. He stepped back beside the casket of her son. His white vestments stirred wisps of dust. He opened the prayer book. Those watching moved in closer. They shifted, positioning themselves to see and be seen, cutting off any air that stirred, suffocating the family.

Father Matt began to recite the age-old Episcopalian rite of the dead. He spoke to ghosts for his voice dissipated in the haze of heat that lingered like an organza veil over the cornfield. Those assembled stared at the horizon of wavering long-leaf pines and planned the direction of their first steps after the final "Amen." Whom to talk to, what to learn.

It ended. The family stood. They silently made their way back to the road. There they were engulfed in hugs and air kisses. Their steps were hesitant as they moved through the crowd of friends. The attention and the heat were smothering. Robert and Naomi Ruth steered Ophelia back to her black Cadillac. It was too hot to tarry and talk. The family also moved toward their funeral home limousines. The friends followed suit, walking back down the dirt road toward their cars. They knew to go to the Garrett home where it would be cooler, conversations could be resumed and drinks could be had.

As Father Matt made his way back down the road to his car, he met two couples from his former parish paused beside the roadside ditch. After greetings he said, "I hope you are going by the house."

"No, we're heading back to Tarboro, God's country!"

"Oh, I don't know, it's actually pretty nice over here," Father Matt said.

"Over here they die too young."

***

Ophelia settled back into the coolness of her seat as Robert steered the big black car onto the county road and slowly accelerated.

"I hate to leave him here," Ophelia spoke.

Naomi Ruth, beside Ophelia on the back seat, reached over and squeezed her hand. "He's in good company."

"I suppose," was all Ophelia answered. She grew quiet once again, her faded blue eyes removed from the moment, staring blankly at newly planted fields as they passed. They rode in silence until they turned up the drive to Merrebanks.

"Looks like some folks preferred the cool of the house to the heat of the cemetery," Robert said, eying the cars that already lined the drive.

"Can't say as I blame them," Naomi Ruth said. "Eggie told me at the church she wasn't about to stand in the middle of a corn field in this heat…even for Everett. She said she would visit him later, when it was cooler. She was heading straight back to Merrebanks instead. I told her to take Mae Rose with her and, please, please, check on the church ladies when they got here and make sure they weren't destroying the kitchen."

Ophelia looked at the number of cars as they drove past towards the back of the house. "Eastern North Carolina does love a funeral and another Garrett funeral has them crawling with curiosity. Probably be right late before they all leave," Ophelia sighed.

"We'll manage," was all Naomi Ruth said.

Chapter Two

The house was a large white Greek revival with soaring columns and welcoming porches. It stood at the end of a long drive that wound through spreading live oaks and gnarled magnolias. Ancient English boxwoods wrapped the front of the house. On the east side a sweeping lawn rose up from the Chowan River. The smell of gardenias greeted everyone as they approached the porch, for large bushes grew near the walk. The bushes were laden with blossoms and the air was heavy with their scent. Ophelia always said gardenias reminded her of funerals and they bloomed profusely when each of her two oldest sons was laid to rest.

Ophelia stood in the entrance hall of her home, greeting everyone upon their arrival. She then steered them toward the spacious parlor with its doors open to the side porch and outside bar. Drinks in hand, people roamed at will in search of friends or family members. Eggie, the Garrett aunt and Ophelia's longtime friend, was ensconced with the elderly in the cool of the parlor. There they observed, spoke with and commented on the parade of friends moving through towards the bar. Alice, Everett's widow, was out on the lawn with their son, Everett, junior, and his wife Charlotte. They were surrounded by a host of those still in shock over the sudden loss of a friend. Julianna, the Garrett daughter, stood in the library with acquaintances from Raleigh. Hobart, the lone surviving brother and youngest of the family, was in the sunroom amusing a group of friends with his sardonic wit.

The ladies of the church circulated among them. They were the funeral food team. After a death in the family, they had the responsibility of nourishing the living. They passed platters of cucumber sandwiches and pitchers of sweet tea. They replenished the silver trays in the dining room with fried chicken, ham biscuits and deviled eggs. Their mission to feed family and friends was not a burdensome duty. This was being in the right place at the right time. This was that age old ability of making the most of a sad situation. This was a chance to observe, listen and collect information for discussion in the kitchen while they replenished the platters and refilled the pitchers. They especially enjoyed rummaging through Ophelia's silver for the proper serving pieces. They had been here just last year after Linus III's funeral therefore were well aware where everything was.

Two of these church women stood together by the sink in the kitchen. They were sisters. "He died too young," one said as she rinsed a Pyrex dish that had recently held fudge brownies.

"Hell, Mary Hester, anytime you die is too young, as far as I'm concerned. Don't raise your eyebrows at me."

"Your language...," Mary Hester said.

"Oh, pooh! Don't be such a prude," Athie answered her. "Where is Frances? She needs to quit socializing long enough to get back in here and help us...and what in the world is wrong with Hobart? His sarcasm is usually humorous but he's being downright mean this afternoon."

"He seems to have fallen into the bourbon bottle, poor thing. I guess he can't help but be a tad concerned about his mortality. He is a handsome devil, though. Dry this." Mary Hester passed the dripping Pyrex dish to Athie.

A well-rounded woman of undetermined age sailed into the kitchen. It was Frances. Her hair was an architectural masterpiece of delicate curls, piled artfully, if curiously, atop her hennaed head. She was draped in scarves and gold. She was a vision of powdered and perfumed confection.

"I didn't expect anywhere near this many people. I certainly adored Everett and from the looks of things I was far from the only one. I wonder if we need to call someone else to come help?"

"I really don't think so, Frances," Mary Hester quickly spoke up. "Betty Jean and India are out there passing trays and platters. Robert is tending the bar and Athie, Naomi Ruth and I are holding down the kitchen. I think everything is under control."

"Where is Naomi Ruth?" Frances asked, her back to the swinging door as she prepared to leave with freshly filled pitchers.

"She's gone to take off her wig. She said her head was hot," Athie replied. "Did you put mint in one of those pitchers of tea? You know Alice likes mint in hers."

"Oh, law, I forgot." Frances sailed back into the room just as the door to the back porch opened and Naomi Ruth entered. She was a tall, stately and, at the moment, very aggravated, woman. She paused at the door, her hand on the knob, looking to see what kind of mess these church women had made in the kitchen.

"Feel better, Naomi Ruth?" Mary Hester asked.

"I do." Naomi Ruth saw no need to elaborate. She was still taking stock of the kitchen.

"You know, Naomi Ruth, you're no spring chicken and if you want to scoot home for a spell and rest we can pretty much manage here," Frances commented as she dropped mint sprigs into the tea pitcher.

"I think not," Naomi Ruth replied. Athie and Mary Hester looked at each other and bit their lips. She continued, "*I* need to be *here.* Ophelia likes things done properly." She cast a jaundiced eye on Frances. "Folks seem to come out of the woodwork whenever there's a funeral…an invasion of the curious and hungry. Ophelia thinks it's too hot to eat but she's sure they'll all be expecting to be fed…so we'll feed them the food. They can feed their own curiosity." With that Naomi Ruth pushed through the swinging door into the dining room.

Frances shrugged and followed. She was nearly knocked down by a slight middle-aged woman pushing in from the other side.

"This door needs a glass, there's so much coming and going," India said as she made her way toward the pantry. "I'm going to refill the lemonade pitchers. They're emptied almost faster than I can fill them. I suspect it's being mixed with vodka. We also need some more pimento cheese sandwiches. Don't you think it's about time for everyone to be leaving? I guess since the Sheriff is out there drinking lemonade with the rest of them we don't have to worry about getting arrested on the way home. Wouldn't that be a hoot? Half of eastern North Carolina's finest spending the night in the county jail. Somehow I think Everett would get a kick out of that." She paused and sighed. "We're going to miss him."

"Amen," they all said together.

India left the kitchen with a pitcher of lemonade and the last of the pimento cheese sandwiches piled on a tray.

Mary Hester looked at her sister and took off her apron. "I see no earthly reason why we cannot have a drink. I'm going to go get us one." She wiped her hands and disappeared down the hall toward the library. Looking out the window over the sink Athie saw her reappear on the porch and pause to speak. Athie sighed as she realized it would probably be a while before she got her vodka tonic. She noticed Julianna standing with a group of people who were unfamiliar to Athie. Julianna certainly looked good for her fifty-two years... tall, thin, elegant, well-dressed...but pretty is as pretty does. They had all grown up together here in Hope Springs so Athie was well aware of Julianna's shifting disposition. Julianna could be warm and friendly or she could be cold and aloof. You just never knew which Julianna would show up. Their mother constantly reminded them that Julianna had thin lips.

"Mother says thin lips are a sure sign of a mean disposition," Athie said aloud as she stared out the window.

"Thin lips are mean lips," Naomi Ruth spoke beside her. Athie jumped. "Your mama is right about that, Athie. They're the sign of a little heart, a cold heart...or no heart a 'tall."

Chapter Three

Ophelia Hobart MacPherson first came to Hope Springs with her roommate from St. Mary's College, Eleanor Greene Garrett, known affectionately to everyone as "Eggie." The two girls had spent the previous evening in Rocky Mount staying with a cousin of Ophelia's and dancing into the early hours to the music of the bands of the June German. The next day Eggie's father sent the town car to pick them up and bring them back to their family home, Mayfield, just outside the tiny town of Hope Springs. They giggled and talked the entire way about their wonderful evening. Ophelia professed herself to be smitten with the young man who squired her to the dance. She talked about him so much that by the time they arrived at Mayfield, Eggie was rather tired of the subject and the young man, whom she privately thought rather a stuffed shirt.

As Ophelia followed Eggie from the car, her friend squealed with pleasure and ran toward a man who was just coming down the steps from the porch to greet them. When the two broke apart, Eggie turned to her friend and said, "Ophelia, this is my brother Linus. Linus, this is Ophelia, my best friend." Ophelia's and Linus' eyes locked and the young man from Rocky Mount was never spoken of again. Ophelia and Linus were married four months later.

That was in 1936. Ophelia was nineteen years old and full of life. The passage of time never changed that characteristic in her. Linus always said he was captivated the minute he laid eyes on her. Not only was she beautiful, but she possessed an irrepressible spirit.

Linus was ten years her senior, mature, responsible, and already fond of his established routine. Ophelia came into his life with an energy he badly needed, for, though he was one of eastern North Carolina's most eligible bachelors, he already had a reputation for being just a tiny bit dull. Ophelia changed all that. She brought out his quick wit and his undeniable charm. He gave her his heart and, in return, she gave him herself.

She also gave him four children. Linus III was born exactly nine months after the wedding night. Ophelia was devoutly thankful he did not come early and had hoped he might be a little late. Everett arrived two years after Linus; Julianna, six years after Everett; and Hobart, two years after Julianna.

They prospered. Linus inherited the Garrett family farmland. He also purchased acreage whenever it became available and grew to become the largest landowner in Chinquapin County. Linus loved the land. To him it was the place of family, the continuity of being. He was a gentleman farmer or, as he jokingly referred to himself, a "swivel chair" farmer. Linus made the decisions for the farms but it was his overseer and manager, Sam Jenkins, who made the decisions work. No callouses ever appeared on the pink palms of Linus' well-manicured hands.

The family lived in the beautiful ancestral home that previously belonged to Linus' Aunt Delia, his father's only sister. When she died Linus purchased the house and the surrounding farm from her estate. It was known as Merrebanks and there the family grew, aged like fine wine, nurtured by the soil, the sun, the rain, and the constant supervision of Ophelia and Naomi Ruth.

Each summer the family left Merrebanks and migrated to their cottage at Nags Head. When the bell rang for the close of school on the last day of each school year, Ophelia, Naomi Ruth and Robert drove the children to the beach. Ophelia and Naomi Ruth drove down together in Ophelia's station wagon. The station wagons changed over the years but the contents did not. There were Ophelia's prized African violets that she never trusted her husband or

Robert to tend properly over the summer months. There were the boxes full of clothing, never suitcases because they rusted in the salt air. There was whatever dog was beloved by the family at the time and there were Ophelia's art supplies. She loved to paint, though she hesitated to call herself an artist. Robert followed in the Cadillac with the children and a month's supply of comic books that were read before they reached the Pasquotank River.

Unfortunately summers spent at the cottage apart caused the one difficulty in Ophelia's and Linus' long and successful marriage. In the summer of forty-four, while Ophelia, Naomi Ruth and the two eldest boys were at the beach, Linus succumbed to the sultry wiles of Nellie Ormond down at Helen's Beauty Shop. His one affectation was his hands. He had a manicure once a week. Ophelia also frequented Helen's and never thought twice about her husband being there. That changed the summer Helen's rather unattractive sister, who did the manicures, amazingly found a husband and removed to Halifax County. Helen's pretty daughter, Nellie, came in to help her mother. Almost every woman in town went to Helen's so it did not take long for Ophelia to hear of her husband's infatuation with Nellie Ormond. It was one of the few times in her life that Ophelia left the beach in the summer and returned to Merrebanks. Unfortunately, Linus was not at home when she arrived nor did he return that evening. Poor Robert was caught in the middle of a bad situation. Ophelia took the keys to the car so that he could not drive to town to alert Linus of her presence. She also took the telephone off the hook so Robert could not call him. Then she waited.

Linus returned the next morning at sun-up, He parked his car out front so he never saw Ophelia's station wagon in the backyard. He came through the hall and back to the kitchen and with one look at Robert knew his life was about to change.

"Miss Ophelia is home," was all Robert said.

She heard him enter the house and when he came back into the hall she was standing at the foot of the stairs facing him.

"Please join me in the library, Linus."

No one knows what was discussed that morning. They were in the library the better part of three hours, according to Robert, who kept a watchful ear and eye. When Linus emerged he was pale. When Ophelia emerged she was placid. She returned to the beach that afternoon.

Shortly thereafter Nellie Ormond left town. Her mother, Helen, said she moved to Columbia, South Carolina, to marry a serviceman she was dating. Helen then hired another manicurist who could only be described as ugly.

Ophelia deeded the cottage to their children shortly after her Linus died. She said it held too many memories. Linus, III and Everett bought the others out. Linus, III willed Everett his share. Everett had his fatal heart attack there over Memorial Day weekend. Now it would be up to his wife, Alice, to face her memories.

Chapter Four

"My, aren't we pressing a call early this morning!" Athie exclaimed as Mildred came through the back door the morning after the funeral. "You're just in time for breakfast."

"No, thanks, I've already had mine. Don't you know all that stuff is bad for you?" Mildred eyed the eggs, grits and sausage sitting on the counter in the kitchen. "I only eat fruit and cereal for breakfast. Anything more and my stomach rebels during Stretch & Tone."

"Heaven forbid," Athie laughed.

The screen door squeaked its announcement of more company and Mary Hester appeared in the doorway.

"Well, obviously no one's going to church today." Mary Hester lowered her considerable frame into a seat at the kitchen table. "Saw you jog by, Mildred…a little early for a Sunday morning. What's going on? You sharing those eggs and grits, Athie?"

"I have plenty, Mary Hester. Erwin has left for the golf course and Mildred has already eaten her breakfast…all that grass and grain stuff she eats. She might as well be a cow." Athie cracked an egg into a bowl.

Mildred looked at her sisters. "I have news."

Athie was placing sausage in the hot pan. She stopped, spatula suspended in mid-air, and turned to look at Mildred.

Mary Hester also looked at Mildred.

Mildred was the youngest of the Hatcher sisters. She had the uncanny ability of being at the right place at the right time to learn the latest gossip. It was Mildred who called with the news of Everett's heart attack. It was Mildred who called when Linus III died of complications after gall bladder surgery. It was Mildred who called when Joe Lester Benton absconded with the bank payroll, leaving his wife and children waiting with the car all packed and ready to head to Six Flags Over Georgia, and he didn't leave alone! It was Mildred who called when she saw Bill Matthews parked in a car with Dr. Jeffrey's nurse in back of Belk-Tyler's kissing in broad daylight. It was always Mildred who called. How she knew everything before anyone was a mystery to everyone, but she did.

"What now?" Athie asked with a mixture of dread and curiosity. She sat down at the table.

Mildred began. "Well, after your food team left Ophelia's yesterday afternoon, our team got everything ready so the family could eat dinner whenever they wanted. Naomi Ruth wasn't too happy about all us being in the kitchen. She finally shooed us out, but thankfully, not before the big to-do." She grinned.

"It was close to eight-thirty. Ophelia and Naomi Ruth had gone upstairs. You could just tell Ophelia was bone weary. She said she was tired and it was just plain too hot to eat so Naomi Ruth helped her to her room."

"Who all was there?" Athie asked, trying to keep her younger sister on track.

"Let's see. There was Hobart. There was Julianna. Her children left for the beach earlier.

"There was Alice, of course, and Ev Jr., and that sweet wife of his, Charlotte. Ev's best friend, William and his wife, Gloria were there. "

"Who else?"

"Who else? Oh, Sam Jenkins and his wife, Estelle were there. I hear he's retiring soon so that's something else I guess Miss Phe will have to deal with, finding a new manager for the family farms.

"Alice's brother and his wife were still there. Alice's mother went on back to Tarboro. She isn't well, you know. And Carter and Minnie were there." Mildred paused. "I smell something burning."

Athie jumped up from her chair and rushed to the stove. She lifted a pan of blackened sausage from the eye. "Damn! Burnt to a crisp!"

"In case you weren't counting, that was thirteen who sat down to dinner. You know what that means, but what can you do? You can't say, 'One of you must come in the kitchen and eat with us.' So we just ignored superstition and went right on.

"Well, towards the end of the meal Hobart pushed back his chair and rose to his feet, rather unsteadily, I might add. He said he had an announcement to make. Then he launched into this rambling speech. He said that it was quite obvious he was swimming in a defective gene pool and since he himself was just a decade short of the deadly age of sixty he was going to enjoy what little time he had left. He was going back to Washington, D.C. and tell the museum he was quitting. He was going to sell his townhouse in Georgetown and move to Palm Beach...and Carter was coming with him!"

"What?" Mary Hester and Athie exclaimed in unison.

"You heard me. There was a silence so thick you could cut it. Julianna stood up, threw down her napkin, looked at her brother as if he had grown Medusa's own head and marched from the room. Everyone just sat there staring at each other, averting their eyes from Hobart and Carter and especially from poor Minnie who just sat there pale as a ghost. Then Minnie stood up and quickly left the room. Carter rose and rushed after her. Then everyone started hemming and hawing and shifting around in their seats. Then abruptly, everyone just got up and left the table, leaving Hobart just standing there. Very uncomfortable."

The sisters sat in silence, digesting this drama.

"Poor Minnie," Mary Hester finally said. "Are you sure you

heard right? Carter and Minnie have been married forever."

"I heard right, Mary Hester," Mildred said.

"Carter and Hobart. My goodness," Athie shook her head. "They grew up together."

"Poor Minnie. Whatever will she do? She has always been so dependent on Carter," Mary Hester continued.

Again there was silence, broken at last by Athie. "How embarrassing. Right in front of everybody."

"Poor Minnie," Mary Hester said again. Shaking her head.

"So Julianna was the first to leave the table." Athie looked up.

"Yes," Mildred replied.

Chapter Five

At Merrebanks the morning after the funeral Naomi Ruth tapped gently on the door of Ophelia's bedroom, then entered.

"Mornin', Ophelia."

"Mornin', Naomi Ruth," spoke a voice from deep within the covers of the bed.

"Blessed is the day the Lord has made," Naomi Ruth declared as she walked across the sunlit room with a tray in her hands.

"Rejoice and be glad in it," answered Ophelia as she pushed back the covers and sat up.

Sitting on the side of the bed she eased her feet into her high heeled slippers.

"I put a muffin on your plate this morning. Somebody brought them over here yesterday. They're probably store-bought but Robert ate one and said it was pretty tasty." Naomi Ruth placed the tray on the table beside the window while Ophelia made her way to the chair beside it.

The room was a large corner room overlooking the long lawn down to the river. Its buttercream walls and chintz covered chairs lent a warm and cozy feel despite the high ceilings and size of the room. It was the room she shared with Linus but its personality was hers. The room faced east and Ophelia never allowed the curtains to be drawn because she wanted to awaken each day to the light of the rising sun.

"I really have little appetite, 'Omi," Ophelia said as she settled into her chair. "From the looks of Hobart, though, I don't think he has that problem. Did you notice? He's getting a belly." She put on her glasses and reached for her hot tea.

"Well, I tell you, Phe, I think his weight is the least of Hobart's worries right now." Naomi Ruth began making up the high old canopied bed that had been in Ophelia's family for nearly two hundred years.

Ophelia peered over the top of her glasses at Naomi Ruth. "And just what is that cryptic remark supposed to mean? Obviously something went on downstairs last night that we missed out on but you have had the great good fortune to find out about this morning. Spill."

"Well, Robert said that over dinner last night Hobart made a rather startling announcement." Naomi Ruth continued to make the bed, never raising her eyes. "He said that seeing as how his brothers were dropping dead right and left, and as how he himself was just a decade away from the dangerous age of sixty, he believed it was time for him to do what he wanted."

"I never got the impression he did anything else," spoke Ophelia. "Go on."

Naomi Ruth continued.

When she finished Ophelia sat silently watching her. "Poor Minnie," was all she said.

"Yes," Naomi Ruth nodded. "I'll be back later to do something about your hair," she said over her shoulder as she went out the door.

***

Out of the corner of her eye Ophelia saw her door slowly nudge open. She smiled as a long wet nose appeared and two bright yellow eyes peeked at her around the corner. Maize, Ophelia's yellow Labrador retriever, padded into the room and over to her chair. She sat on Ophelia's feet and rested her noble head on Ophelia's lap.

"Good morning, my friend, did you sleep well?" Ophelia asked as she rubbed the dog's head and scratched her ears. "I fear we have some thinking to do this morning. You going to help me?"

As if in answer Maize sat back on her haunches and placed both paws on Ophelia's knees. When she did her eyes were almost on a plane with Ophelia's. They were wise and serious golden orbs and always a comfort to Ophelia.

Suddenly the bedroom door flew open and Julianna made her entrance, flouncing in the chair across from Ophelia. Maize dropped and turned towards her, a low, subtle growl growing in her throat.

Ophelia patted the dog's head in reassurance and Maize settled down at Ophelia's feet, never taking her eyes from Julianna.

"That dog has never liked me," Julianna observed, glancing at Maize.

"Yes, and it's odd because she's usually quite friendly," Ophelia said. "Did you sleep well, my dear? It was a long day."

"So, so, Mother. What about you?"

"As well as I could. Dr. Bisbo gave me a little something to help me relax."

"Mother, what are you going to do about Hobart?" Julianna abruptly changed the subject.

"What do you mean, Julianna?" Ophelia took a sip of her tea, watching her daughter over the rim of the cup.

"Oh, Mother, you know good and well what I'm talking about. There is no doubt in my mind 'Omi has already filled you in on what happened at dinner last night." Julianna stood up and started roaming about the room. Maize's head lifted and her golden eyes watched Julianna's every step.

"What concerns you, Julianna?" her mother asked, and if her daughter had listened carefully she would have noticed a subtle underlying nuance to her mother's question.

"It's embarrassing! We Garretts are now an item of gossip. It's downright tawdry. Carter Harris of all people! And, poor, simple, little Minnie. What will she do? Not that I'm overly concerned, other than her rather unfortunate connection now with us." Julianna sat down on the stool of her mother's dressing table. She turned to look at herself in the mirror, her back to her mother. She raised a well-manicured hand to smooth her golden hair, tugging a section behind her ear.

Ophelia watched her beautiful daughter. The little childhood ditty came to mind:

There was a little girl
who had a little curl,
right in the middle of her forehead.
When she was good,
she was very good indeed,
but when she was bad she was horrid.

"Hobart's timing is poor, I must admit, but he is a grown man, capable of running his own life without interference from his family." She looked at her daughter. "I'm sure there is more to this than we know so I suggest we see what he has to say before we judge."

"Well, do what you want, Mother, I'm not going to have anything to do with him. He and Carter can evaporate into thin air as far as I'm concerned. Personally I think Hobart should be removed from the Garrett Trust. He's made a mockery of the Garrett name. It's shameful!" Julianna picked up her mother's sterling silver brush and began to brush her expertly styled and colored hair. The brush, comb and mirror were part of a handsome antique sterling set once belonging to Ophelia's grandmother.

"That's not going to happen, dear. Hobart is my son…my only son now…," she paused and looked out the window. "He will always have my love and support." She looked back at Julianna. "Besides he is not to blame. Homosexuality is in the genes, not the water. If you want to blame someone, blame me."

Julianna turned from the mirror and looked at her mother. It was an odd look. She turned back to the mirror. "They're all disappearing," she murmured.

"Who?" Ophelia asked.

"The Garrett men." Julianna turned towards her mother, brush raised in her hand. "How will our name survive?" She turned back to the mirror and began to brush her hair with her mother's antique brush. "Maybe I should change my children's name to Garrett." She looked back at her mother in the mirror.

"Oh, I really don't think there's any need for that," Ophelia said.

Julianna sat quietly, studying herself in the dressing table mirror. Ophelia sipped her tea, watching her and waiting.

"What about Alice?" Julianna suddenly asked.

"What about Alice?" Ophelia echoed.

"Now that Everett is dead I see no need for her to get his share of the Trust or a share of your estate. The money should be divided among your remaining Garrett children. After all, Alice is no kin to us."

Ophelia looked down at Maize. Sometimes Julianna's self-absorption surprised her. After all these years, she ought not to be shocked when it reared its ugly head but she was. Ophelia had had enough.

"Actually, Julianna, I am seriously thinking of leaving everything to Maize."

"Oh, Mother, be serious."

"I am being perfectly serious. You will get your share and your siblings...and their heirs...will get theirs. It should certainly support everyone in the manner to which they are accustomed, if you are careful."

Naomi Ruth entered the room. "Do you need help getting dressed, Ophelia?"

"Yes, thank you, Naomi Ruth. Julianna was just leaving, weren't you, dear?" Ophelia stood.

Julianna rose from the dressing table stool. "'Omi, I declare, I think you were lurking outside the door."

Naomi Ruth just smiled at her.

"I will see you at lunch, Mother. I'll probably head back to Raleigh this afternoon." Julianna strode toward the door and turned, her hand on the knob, "Mother, I want great-grandmother's silver comb and brush set when you die. Please leave it to me. I don't think Maize will mind."

With those words she left the room.

***

"Was that our very own paragon of greed I beheld flitting down the hall?" Hobart cheerily asked as he entered his mother's room several minutes later. "Sometimes I wonder where sister dear came from. Was she a changeling left upon the doorstep?"

"Morning, 'Omi. Good morning, Maize," he added as he sat in the chair opposite his mother.

Maize wandered over to Hobart and placed her paw on his knee. Hobart slowly rubbed her ears.

"Will you be here for lunch, Hobart?" Naomi Ruth asked.

"Yes. I'll probably leave mid-afternoon. I'll certainly miss your cooking, 'Omi."

She smiled at him and left mother and son sitting together in companionable silence. "What am I going to do with you, Hobart?" his mother laughed.

"Love me like you always have, I expect, Mother. Though sometimes I guess it's easier than others. Sorry about last night."

"What in the world got into you?"

"Why, Mother, dear, Jim Beam got into me! Took my senses right away. Very poor taste, even I must admit but something just came over me. Everyone was sitting there wearing their long faces...

and rightly so…but all I could think of was getting on with life…not dwelling on death…so I proceeded to tell them how I was going to go about it!"

"But, Hobart, you placed poor Minnie in a rather embarrassing position. Did she know about all this or was it a bombshell for her?"

"She knew," Hobart answered his mother. "Actually Minnie has known for quite a while. And so have the children, by the way. Both boys are grown now. Carter and Minnie told them several years ago. Poor Minnie. At the time she was devastated. She told Carter he was the only man she could ever love and wanted to stay with him regardless. But I gather that's changed now. She has a beau, Carter said, though I haven't a clue who it is."

Chapter Six

Late that afternoon, when the oppressive heat had abated somewhat, Ophelia made her way to the kitchen. She asked Robert if he would drive her out to the cemetery. She wanted to check on the grave site and remove the flowers, surely withered or dead in the summer heat. He readily agreed and Naomi Ruth, Maize and Ophelia again found themselves being driven over the country roads of this small area of eastern North Carolina to the ancestral cemetery.

Ophelia sat in the back of the big Cadillac with Maize at her feet. She gazed at the newly planted fields of soybeans, cotton, and peanuts. They needed more rain. Maybe when she found a new farm manager she would consider adding more irrigation systems. She sighed. It was all up to her. Her biggest regret was the lack of interest her boys had in farming. She knew Big Linus worried about that, too. Neither young Linus, Everett nor Hobart inherited their father's love of the land. She thought of what Julianna said that morning.

"Julianna, for all the wrong reasons, of course, was concerned this morning about the Garrett line." She spoke into the quiet of the car. Robert glanced up at her in the rearview mirror.

Naomi Ruth turned in the front seat to look back at her.

"Julianna is only concerned with herself. Excuse me, Phe." Robert's eyes went back to the road.

"Yes, but she has a point. We do seem to be dying off. Son Linus died with no issue. Everett and Alice have Ev Jr. but he and

Charlotte insist they want no children. Hobart will not have any children. That's pretty much the end of us." She paused. "Of course, Julianna has a solution."

"I'll bet she does," Robert said.

"And what, pray tell, does Julianna suggest we do?" Naomi Ruth asked.

"She wants to change her children's name to Garrett."

Naomi Ruth and Robert were silent. It was obvious they were searching for words.

Ophelia smiled as she watched her two old friends struggle for an answer.

"How ironic," Naomi Ruth finally said.

Ophelia laughed. "Yes, isn't it."

They rode in silence the rest of the way.

When they arrived at the cemetery, Maize bounded from the car and ran among the graves. Naomi Ruth and Ophelia slowly wandered through the tombstones commenting on the various family members resting underneath. Robert followed with the large trash bags. Linus, III's tombstone still gleamed new. Everett's grave was mounded with flowers, most of which were sadly drooping and wilted. They began to fill the trash bags with the funeral foliage.

"Always seems such a waste," Naomi Ruth said, pushing withered gladioli deeper into the bag. "They don't last long."

"You mean the flowers or the people?" Ophelia asked.

"Both, I reckon," Naomi Ruth observed.

They worked in silence, picking and pulling and shoving into the bags. When they finished, Robert carried the heavy bags back to the car. Ophelia and Naomi Ruth took steps to follow him but both paused beside Linus III's grave.

"Wonder whatever happened to Miss Sarah?" Naomi Ruth looked down at the headstone.

"I often wonder myself," answered Ophelia. "I'm still surprised and very sad that we never heard another word from her after she left that October day."

"Do you think either Linus heard from her?" asked Naomi Ruth.

"If they did they never mentioned it," Ophelia said.

They grew quiet nursing their thoughts, which, truth to tell, were quite similar. They had been friends for a very long time.

Slowly they turned and made their way back to the car. Maize trotted at their heels.

***

That evening Naomi Ruth and Ophelia sat together in Ophelia's bedroom. Maize lay on the floor between them peacefully sleeping.

"Back to just us, 'Omi," Ophelia said.

"Seems mighty quiet. Nobody fighting," Naomi Ruth said. She picked up the well worn Bible beside her chair and opened it to Proverbs, the fifteenth chapter. She read the twenty-seventh verse then closed the Bible and looked at Ophelia.

"Oh, she 'troubleth,' all right; no doubt about that," Ophelia said. "And Lord knows it's usually 'cause she wants something."

"Yep. She has 'troubleth' in the past; she 'troubleth' now, and there is no doubt in my mind that she will 'troubleth' in the future." Naomi Ruth laid the Bible on the table beside the chair and stood.

"Come on, Maize. Bed time. Shame Ophelia done told Julianna she's going to leave you everything. I best be keeping your dog food under lock and key!"

Chapter Seven

"Hector! Yoo-hoo, Hector!" Mildred called out the back door trying to get the attention of the man tinkering with the lawnmower over by the shed. He looked up in exasperation at the interruption.

"Could you come here a minute?" Mildred hollered while beckoning with her arm. Hector couldn't, or wouldn't, hear sometimes. She went back into the kitchen. Clara was cleaning breakfast dishes. Athie and Mary Hester were seated at the breakfast table. They had arrived at their mother's home early for the sisters had a plan and it involved Hector. Athie and Mary Hester lived nearby. They had raised their families in homes within walking distance of their mother's. Mildred had moved back into the family home with her mother years ago when her husband ran off with the senior warden of the vestry. They were a close family in many ways.

Their mother, Margaret Elizabeth, known to all as "Bessie", was upstairs dressing for the day. If she thought it strange that her two married daughters appeared in her kitchen so early this morning she made no comment. Mildred waited for her to leave before she called to Hector. She really didn't see any need to stoke their mother's natural curiosity. Bessie would find out in time.

"What y'all girls up to now?" Clara asked from the sink. "Know it ain't good."

About that time Hector came through the door, wiping his hands with the bandanna he always kept in his pocket.

"What you need me for, Miss Mildred?" he asked as he removed his wide brimmed hat and wiped the beads pf perspiration from his wrinkled brow. The girls wondered silently how old he was. They could not remember a time in their lives when Hector wasn't there.

"Hector," all the girls spoke at once, then Mary Hester, the eldest, took over. "You've got to help us find out something. You have got to go into the front yard and act busy...weed or mow or something...right now and stay there all morning, if it comes to that... which I don't think it will," she added. "You must keep an eye on the Harris'. We need to know what's going on!"

"What in Pete's name y'all up to now?" he asked looking over at Clara. She raised sudsy hands in a shrug. "Carter Harris and little Miss Minnie grew up with y'all. Why I got to spy on them? I hope to goodness you're not trying to tell me he's robbed the bank or something." Hector looked at each of them in turn.

"No, of course not," answered Athie. "We would go out there ourselves but I think it would look funny, us weeding and all, "she murmured.

"Well, you got that right. Y'all don't know a weed from a rutabaga!" Clara commented as she wiped her hands and began to put up the dishes.

The sisters turned as one and glared at her.

"I've got things to do," Hector said. "Don't have time for y'all's foolishness. I declare, by now I would have thought y'all would have outgrown that consuming curiosity of yours. How many times has it gotten you in trouble? You always take it too far...just stirring the pot!"

Hector put his hat on his head and turned towards the door. "Oh, please, Hector." The sisters begged.

"We think Carter is leaving Minnie today and running off with Hobart Garrett," Mildred blurted out.

Before Hector or Clara could recover from this startling

announcement the door from the dining room swung open and the mother of Mary Hester, Athie and Mildred marched in. Miss Bessie was eighty-five years old and denying it with every breath. She was an aging dynamo. She had flaming red hair worn short in tight curls. She was of medium height but age had rearranged her body into what her daughters called "dessert." Indeed she did resemble a collection of marshmallows supported by toothpicks with a cherry on top. She was dressed for town, purse in hand, and ready to go.

"Oh, Hector, there you are. Thank the Lord. You must drive me to *Kut & Kurl* right this very minute. I have misjudged the time. The girls totally threw me off visiting so early this morning. Of course, I was thrilled to see them, and we had to talk, but now I'm late. I'm sure Norma Sue is wondering where in the world I am." She stopped to take a breath but continued to advance towards the back door.

"Hector is busy this morning, Mother," Mary Hester rose quickly from her chair. "I'm going to take you to the beauty parlor. We best hurry."

Mary Hester steered her mother out the back door with a beseeching glance at Hector as they passed. They headed down the walk to the garage. She helped her mother into the large old Lincoln and set off. As they passed the Harris' house Bessie turned to look.

"Why, what is going on at Carter and Minnie's? Is that Father Matt's car? Has somebody else died?" Bessie asked.

"I haven't a clue, Mother, but I am certain you will find out at the beauty parlor!"

***

Hector wasn't outside thirty minutes before he returned to the kitchen. He even beat Mary Hester back from *Kut & Kurl.* He removed his hat and sat down at the breakfast table. Clara brought him a glass of water and he alternately sipped and mopped his forehead. Mildred and Athie sat impatiently staring at him.

"No space in the driveway. Cars everywhere. Even Father Matt's car is there. Looks like a funeral. Guess it kinda is for poor Minnie if what y'all say is true." A hint of doubt was in his voice. He put his bandana back in his pocket and drank more water.

"It is. Did you recognize the cars? Do you know whose they are?" Mildred asked, leaning forward.

Hector thought a minute then said, "I'm pretty sure one of them belongs to Carter, Jr. I have seen it here right often…when he's visiting his folks. Holidays and such. He has those two small children so they need that big car for all the stuff you've got to cart around for kids these days."

He continued, "And I think one belongs to the other son…Wilson. He works in D.C. for some drug company. Oddly enough one car is Alice's but she and Minnie do go back a ways. This is rather awkward for her I would imagine but Miss Alice has always had an unusual air about her. She just kinda transcends things…situations… people. You know what I mean. She floats."

The last was a statement, not a question. Everyone nodded in agreement.

"That's four cars," Mildred said. "Anymore? What about Carter's car? Has he left?"

"No, Carter's car is still there. I walked to the end of the block," he admitted "and I could see it in the garage in back, as well as Minnie's." Hector continued. "There are two other cars but I have no idea whose they are. One is mighty fine, I might add. Big. Now, can I get back to work?"

He clapped his hat back on his head and walked out the door.

Mary Hester walked in as he walked out. She took the seat he had just vacated. A little over an hour had passed since she left.

"Where have you been?" Mildred asked. "It only takes ten minutes to get to the beauty parlor."

"Well, I dropped Mother off in front because she was having a hissy fit about being late. Then I parked and went back inside to see what time she wanted to be picked up. She had forgotten to tell me in her hurry. And, of course, the minute I walked in I could tell everyone was in a state. All they could talk about was Hobart, Carter and poor Minnie. The untimely death of poor Everett, last week's topic, has fallen by the wayside. So I took a seat and listened."

"So...what did they say?" Athie and Mildred leaned forward.

"I will tell you what I heard after you tell me what Hector saw," Mary Hester replied. "I saw for myself Father Matt's car. So did Mother, I might add. Her antennae went into full operating mode. But I didn't have time to identify the other cars. One was the biggest Mercedes I have ever seen."

"Hector said the boy's cars were there and Alice's but there were two cars he could not identify and one was mighty fine. That must be the Mercedes you saw. He saw no one coming and going from the house. He went back to work. I think he's perturbed with us." Athie finished and glanced over to see Clara nodding her head in silent agreement. Athie frowned at her then glanced back at Mary Hester.

"You're looking smug, Sister. What have you learned at the beauty parlor?" Athie asked.

"One of the unknown cars belongs to Minnie's sister, Martha Jane, if the beauty parlor gossip is correct, and it usually is," Mary Hester replied. "She came over from Raleigh this morning."

"Wonder who called her? Guess she's worried about her sister like everyone else," spoke Mildred. "Minnie is such a frail little thing, poor dear. She is pretty, though, in a quiet, reserved sort of way."

"I don't guess the ladies at the beauty parlor knew who belongs to the other car...the big Mercedes?" Athie asked.

"As a matter of fact, they did," Mary Hester answered and paused for effect.

"You gonna tell us or sit there like the aggravating Sphinx?" Mildred asked.

Mary Hester let another minute pass. "Drum roll, please." She grinned at her sisters, enjoying the moment. "The very big and very fine Mercedes belongs to Minnie's new beau."

"Minnie has a beau?" Athie asked in obvious surprise.

"Indeed she does," Mary Hester could hardly contain herself.

"Who?" Mildred asked.

"None other than…" Mary Hester paused again, clearly relishing the moment, "Grant Whitworth."

The sisters stared. The silence was deafening. "Grant Whitworth?" Athie was incredulous.

"Julianna's Grant Whitworth?" Mildred asked.

"One and the same," nodded Mary Hester.

The three sisters just sat there staring at each other. Then slow smiles of an identical nature began to turn the corners of the three sister's mouths. Clara noticed their reaction as she headed to the refrigerator. "Oh, Lawd," she muttered to herself, "trouble's come to town."

"What did you say, Clara?"

"Are y'all stayin' for lunch?"

***

It was late afternoon of the same day when Alice turned her car up the drive to her mother-in-law's home. She loved Merrebanks and the sense of belonging she always felt here. Merrebanks spoke of refinement and permanency. She always thought she and Everett would eventually live here. Not now, she knew. Life changed quickly but Alice was not one to dwell on misfortune. She was a naturally happy person, with a transparent clarity that often took others by surprise. To many she seemed flighty but she was grounded in ways that mattered. She was kind, considerate and thoughtful in her own unusual way.

She briefly chatted with Naomi Ruth and Robert when she

entered the kitchen then wandered down the hall in search of Ophelia.

"She had polish in her hand. You see it?" Robert asked his wife.

"Lord, yes. Poor Maize will be coming through the door any minute now."

Alice found Ophelia in the sunroom. She was concentrating on a piece of needle-point in her lap. Maize was asleep at her feet. They both looked up when Alice entered. "This is a belt I was needle-pointing for Everett for Christmas." Ophelia held up the unfinished belt. "Do you suppose Ev Jr. would like it?"

Alice politely assured Everett's mother that Ev Jr. would love it though she secretly doubted it. Everett would have worn it only to please his mother. She suspected his son would do the same.

Alice took a seat on the stool in front of Ophelia. "May I paint your nails this afternoon, Phe? I've found a new color."

"Of course, dear." Ophelia put away her needle work and held out her hands. This odd ritual had gone on between these two women for years. For some unexplainable reason Alice chose this scenario when she was in a quandary. Many a problem had been solved over a bottle of polish. But though it was soothing to Alice it was not so to Maize. With the first whiff of polish Maize got up and left the room, making little sneezing snorts as she went.

"I've spent the last two mornings at Minnie and Carter's," Alice began. "After Hobart said what he did I thought I should check on her...we go back such a long way." Alice started painting Ophelia's nails and Ophelia settled back to listen. There was no need for comment.

Alice proceeded to tell her mother-in-law of the constant traffic snooping down the Harris' street now that the word was out. She told her mother-in-law how relieved Minnie and Carter were now that everything was out in the open and they no longer had to live make-believe lives. They were making plans to create new lives for themselves.

"But, Alice," Ophelia interrupted. "Whatever will poor Minnie do?"

"Everyone worries about Minnie, Phe, but Minnie is fine. Minnie can let Carter go because there is a new man in her life. Minnie has a beau." Alice stopped painting and looked up at Ophelia. "I think you should know."

"What do you mean, Alice?"

"Phe, he's here in town. He came today when he heard what happened. He came to be with Minnie."

"And? Why do you need to tell me this?" Ophelia looked puzzled.

"You know him, Phe. He's a ghost for the Garretts."

Ophelia continued to stare at Alice.

"Her beau is Grant Whitworth."

***

Ophelia came into the kitchen shortly after Alice left. She had remained for a while in the sunroom to let her nails dry and to think. She stood beside the stove where Naomi Ruth was stirring something that she supposed would be their supper. She really had no appetite.

Robert was at the breakfast table shelling peas.

"Let's see your nails, Phe," he said. "What color you got this time?" He smiled. Naomi Ruth laughed. Ophelia held up her hands.

"What color would you call it?" she asked while waving her hands around. "It's really a most peculiar shade of green."

"Looks like pond scum to me," Robert observed.

"Think you are about right," Ophelia agreed. She looked down at her hands and sighed. "Oh, well."

She joined Robert at the table. "You can't shell peas, Miss O," he said. "You'll mess up those nails." He grinned.

"Well, what did Alice talk about?" Naomi Ruth knew what nail polish meant. Ophelia looked at her nails. "She wanted me to know that Minnie has a suitor."

"Oh?" Naomi Ruth said, looking closely at her. "And...?"

"It's Grant Whitworth," Ophelia said.

Naomi Ruth quit stirring. Robert quit shelling. They both stared at her with their mouths half opened.

"Grant Whitworth? Did you say Grant Whitworth? Back here?" Robert asked.

"Lord have mercy, don't let Julianna hear that," Naomi Ruth shook her head.

As Ophelia opened her mouth to reply she was distracted by a noise. It was the sound of a car door slamming. The back porch screen door banged shut. Footsteps crossed the floor. The kitchen door opened. Maize growled. Julianna walked in.

"Speak of the devil," whispered Naomi Ruth.

Chapter Eight

Julianna left Merrebanks and returned to her home in Raleigh Sunday afternoon. She was deeply disappointed that the Garrett Trust would remain available to Alice. She had not planned on that. At least when Linus died, Sarah was gone. Julianna saw no need for anyone who was not a Garrett to receive a penny of her family's money. Her mother's thinking was totally irrational. If only she still had her father to talk to. He would have listened to her. He would have agreed, she was sure. She was also furious with Hobart. She was glad to be home. Time spent at Merrebanks was becoming more and more tiresome. Besides, she had an appointment Monday afternoon for Botox.

That evening her phone rang. It was Pansy Perdue, a woman with whom Julianna occasionally played tennis. "Can you play tennis in the morning? Jane Elliott has a friend who has just moved to town and joined the club. She wants to get up a game and maybe have lunch afterwards."

"Sure," Julianna replied. "I could use some exercise."

"Meet at the courts at ten. I'll call Jane back." Pansy Perdue hung up.

Julianna arrived at the country club for tennis promptly at ten Monday morning. She thought the friend of Jane Elliott's a passable player but not quite in their league. After the game the ladies strolled into the grill room for a luncheon of salad and white wine. Jane's new friend gave them pause when she ordered a triple martini on the rocks. The conversation revolved around Raleigh gossip. Somewhere in the conversation Pansy asked Emma, for that was the new friend's name, why she and her husband had moved to Raleigh.

"Oh my dears," Emma replied, taking a sip of her martini, "my Benji got an offer he positively could not refuse." She rolled her eyes. "I'm sure you have heard of Whitworth Technologies. Well, they are building a new data center here in the Park and Benjamin will be its CFO." She beamed at the three faces watching her.

If she noticed Julianna's face blanch she did not acknowledge it.

"Grant Whitworth depends so on my Benji," Emma continued. "In fact Grant was supposed to be here today for a meeting with Benji but he called and canceled. Said an emergency had come up and he had to drive to some little podunk town east of here I've never heard of...Hope Springs? Something like that. I honestly don't know why he has never married. He is so good-looking...and so rich!"

She enjoyed another sip of her martini.

The conversation continued but Julianna sat in shocked silence.

Several hours later she was on the road back to Hope Springs and Merrebanks. She had forgotten completely about her Botox appointment.

"Why, Julianna, what an unexpected surprise." Ophelia was the first to recover when Julianna appeared in the kitchen door. "Is anything wrong?"

"For heaven's sake Mother, of course not. I was having lunch at the club today with my tennis group and a wave of sadness just poured over me." She dropped her eyes. "I thought of you here all alone coping with such sadness and decided to come be with you."

A look passed between Robert and Naomi Ruth.

"Well, that's very thoughtful of you, dear, but you know I'm hardly alone. I have Naomi Ruth, Robert and, of course, Maize. Eggie's over here every day. There's lots of coming and going. You just missed Alice, in fact."

"What did Alice want? Robert, get my bag out of the car for me." Julianna sat down at the table. "Anything going on in town?" she asked as Robert put down his peas and stood. Six eyes looked at Julianna. She was up to something.

***

While Julianna was surprising those at Merebanks, in Hope Springs Mildred was phoning her sisters. "You'll never guess who's back in town."

"Pour the wine. I'm on my way," each sister replied.

"We're here. What's up?" Athie and Mary Hester walked through the back door.

"Sit down. Julianna's back." They sat.

"Oh, dear!" Mary Hester took the full wine glass from her sister. "Are you sure? She just left yesterday. How do you know she's here?" Athie asked.

"I just got back from the Pig and I saw her getting gas at the Shell station across the street. That car of hers is hard to miss," Mildred replied. "Plus I went around the block to be sure!"

"But how in the world does she know anything this fast? We just found out?" The phone rang. They ignored it.

"Maybe she doesn't know. Maybe she is just back to check on her mother," said Athie.

"Julianna?" Mildred looked at her sister. "The only thing Julianna checks on is her makeup," she added.

"There is no way she could know about Grant Whitworth and Minnie or she would have said something at the funeral."

The sisters looked up as the door to the dining room swung open. "Why didn't y'all answer the phone?" Mother Bessie stood there with arms akimbo. "It was Julianna. She wanted to know where y'all were. She's coming over. Answer the phone next time."

Bessie turned and the door swung shut behind her.

"Do you have enough wine, Sister?" Mary Hester turned to Mildred.

***

A perfectly coiffed and stylishly dressed Julianna arrived at Bessie's back door twenty minutes later. Greetings were exchanged. Wine was poured. Seats were taken. The sisters were unnaturally quiet, watching Julianna. They waited, vibrating with anticipation.

"How is Miss Phe, Julianna?" Mildred prompted. "I'm sure you returned so soon because you are worried about her." Sister eyes watched.

"Honestly," Julianna answered glancing at her beautifully manicured hand holding the wine glass, "I am really worried about Mother. I am beginning to notice little lapses...she forgets things... and wanders."

"Well, I doubt if I could think at all if I had been through what she has these last few years!" Athie said. She sipped her wine.

"It's heartbreaking...losing two sons...and within such a short space of time. And now I hear Sam Jenkins is thinking about retiring. Ophelia has a lot of pain and stress heaped on her right now." Mary Hester contributed to the conversation and also finished with a sip of wine.

"And I have lost my two older brothers after losing poor John such a short while ago." Julianna paused with the look of a stricken martyr. "And now I also have to deal with Hobart."

She sipped her wine and continued. "I know you've discussed the announcement he made at the dinner table the night of the funeral...you were there, Mildred. Mother does not seem to grasp that Hobart has embarrassed our family. She's not even going to do anything about him."

She took a sip of wine and so did the sisters.

The sisters nodded their heads and looked expectantly at Julianna.

"And Carter Harris...well really! We all grew up together. What's that all about? Why now? And poor Minnie Mouse...oh, excuse me, that just slipped out. She's such a pathetic, timid little thing. She'll probably take to her bed or something equally dramatic." Julianna drank more wine.

The sisters glanced at each other over the rims of their glasses, mirroring the simultaneous thought that Julianna had not a clue about Minnie and Grant Whitworth. Mildred rose, went to the refrigerator, got another bottle of wine, opened it and filled their glasses. She left the wine bottle on the table.

"But, actually, what poor little Minnie does or doesn't do is of little concern to me. I need to ask you about something else." The sisters leaned in. "It's difficult..." Julianna paused...sipped more wine. "Something happened today that was so upsetting...really unsettling. I need an answer and I know you'll help me." She stopped and looked at the three sisters. They looked back at her, nodding in sympathetic syncopation. Julianna took another sip of wine. The sisters did, too.

"I had lunch at the club today as I usually do on Monday's after my tennis game. There was a new girl playing with us...Emma something. Not a particularly good tennis player and a total snob actually...a real social wannabe...talked incessantly about her husband climbing the corporate ladder...while she polished off a triple martini, please!" She paused and drank her wine.

"Anyway," she resumed, "it seems her husband is the new CFO for a corporation opening in the Research Triangle Park." She paused again and drank more wine.

The sisters glanced at each other. Then they, too, sipped their wine. Mildred poured more wine into the glasses.

Julianna continued. "And...the corporation is Grant Whitworth's! Can you believe it?" Julianna's voice rose. She drank more wine. Mildred poured what was left in the bottle into Julianna's glass and once again headed to the refrigerator.

"Oh, dear," said Athie. She finished her wine. Mary Hester finished hers.

Mildred returned with another bottle of wine and proceeded to refill the glasses. She once again placed the bottle on the table and sat down. The sisters remained quiet. Julianna had their complete attention. They bubbled like a shaken seltzer bottle. This was explosive!

"Apparently Grant was to join triple-martini-Emma's precious husband today in Raleigh for a corporate meeting. But he called and canceled because of an emergency." She swallowed more wine. "And...get this...the emergency was in Hope Springs! Right here!" Julianna's voice was shrill. The sisters gulped their wine. "Where's the emergency? Where is he? Why is he here?" Julianna wailed and burst into tears.

The sisters emptied their glasses. Then they told her.

***

"For someone so concerned about your welfare she certainly didn't stay with you long," Naomi Ruth observed as she cut out biscuits and placed them on the baking sheet.

Ophelia sat at the kitchen table with her evening gin and tonic, Maize asleep at her feet.

This was the time of day the old friends gathered in the kitchen.

"Very insightful, 'Omi," Phe said and laughed. Robert and Naomi Ruth both grinned. "We know that was bogus. She must have heard something in Raleigh...something, but not enough...and she knows if anybody knows what is going on in this town it is the sisters Hatcher."

"Even they might be scared to get involved in this one," Naomi Ruth said as she slid her biscuits into the oven.

Maize raised her head and looked at the back door. It opened and Ev Jr. walked in. "Do I smell biscuits, 'Omi?" he asked as he crossed the floor and kissed his grandmother on the cheek. He hugged Naomi Ruth and Robert then bent down to peer through the oven glass. "Can I stay for supper? Charlotte is playing bridge somewhere or other."

"We would love it. Naomi Ruth always fixes enough food for a boy scout troop. Plus we still have pies and cakes from the funeral. I expect y'all do too." Miss Phe looked at her grandson. "I must warn you, though, that your Aunt Julianna arrived back here today…just a while ago, but she didn't tarry long. She's gone over to the Hatchers."

"What's she up to? Not like her to forego the country club scene in Raleigh for dull little Chinquapin County. Though, I must admit Uncle Hobart's announcement has certainly livened the scene." Ev moved over to the cabinet holding the liquor. He was a bourbon man. He fixed his drink and came to sit by his grandmother at the table.

Ophelia, Naomi Ruth and Robert glanced at each other. "Actually we think she has heard a name from her past," Ophelia said.

"It seems that Hobart's declaration at the dinner table the other night has opened the door of a closet full of skeletons," Robert spoke.

Ev looked puzzled. He glanced towards his grandmother.

"It turns out that Minnie and Carter have been very open in their marriage. He has told her about his situation and she has told him about hers." Ophelia paused and looked at Ev.

"Hers?" he asked, eyebrows raised.

"Yes, Minnie has a suitor," his grandmother said.

"Lovely old fashioned term, Gran. She has a boyfriend? Lover? Girlfriend? What?" Ev sipped his bourbon.

"Quite definitely a man, my dear. And in the far distant past he was almost your uncle. Grant Whitworth."

"Grant Whitworth!" Ev sputtered, strangling on a sip of whiskey. "Are you kidding me? The brave man who left Aunt Julianna at the altar and went on to make gazillions of dollars in technology?"

"Yes, and somehow he knows Minnie and is here...over at the Harris'," Naomi Ruth added as she removed her perfect biscuits from the oven. "Though, of course he's staying out at the Holiday Inn," Naomi Ruth primly added.

Robert stood up. "Poor Minnie and Carter. I expect it's all over town by now. They are two nice people. The boys are grown. What in heaven's name is the big deal?" He went into the pantry to get Maize's dog food.

"I agree with Robert," Ev said, "except Julianna is in town. She's not exactly one who lets sleeping dogs lie. Sorry Maize."

"No. Julianna has never played by the rules," Ophelia said quietly. "She makes her own."

***

About eight-thirty Robert went out to take the trash. Ev Jr. had headed back home after dinner. Julianna had never returned from the Hatcher's. Naomi Ruth and Ophelia had gone upstairs. Robert had cleaned up the kitchen. It was a peaceful starlit night. He could hear the eight-forty-three freight train in the distance. Car lights turned up the lane to the house. He guessed it was Julianna finally returning home. Typical he thought. She's late, not a word from her, but he would bet good money she would expect Naomi Ruth to fix her dinner.

He stood in the drive as the car approached. He was surprised to see it was not Julianna's little red BMW. It was Bessie Hatcher's big old Lincoln. When the car rolled up beside him Hector grinned through the driver's window. In the backseat Robert could see the slumped form of Julianna. She appeared to be sleeping.

"'Fraid Miss Julianna has been over-served," Hector said as he opened the car door.

Chapter Nine

The following afternoon Ophelia sat in her favorite chair in the library at Merrebanks. It was leather, as was its twin on the other side of the fireplace. This was her Linus' room. She was always acutely aware of his presence when she was here. The paneled walls came from trees on Garrett land. They had mellowed with age to a rich patina. Linus' desk stood before the bookshelves that lined the east wall. The desk was very much as he left it fifteen years ago.

The curtains were pulled against the heat of the afternoon. In the room it was dim and cool. She and Maize were alone. After lunch Robert and Naomi Ruth had gone into town.

Julianna had yet to make an appearance. It was blessedly quiet. She needed to think.

Her thoughts drifted to Julianna. She had never been an easy child and she certainly had not been an easy adult. Very few people still living knew Julianna's true story. Naomi Ruth and Robert knew, of course, and Eggie.

She sighed and leaned back in the chair. Motes of dust danced on a sun beam coming through a slit in the curtains.

How well she remembered her first sight of Julianna. She was just an unwanted bundle of pink shoved into her arms by a mother ready to be shed of her. No softness of maternal love there. Linus took the mother aside. They talked; the mother signed the papers; he paid her.

Ophelia just sat and rocked the little girl who was now their child. The mother walked away without a backwards glance.

She and Linus had buried their stillborn son two days earlier in the churchyard of the Church of the Messiah. She named him William Gregory after her father. It was a quiet graveside service, just the two of them and the young priest. She still sent money to the church for the care of her son's tiny grave. She quietly celebrated his birthday each year.

They were living in Santa Ana, California, waiting for Linus to complete war time intelligence duties assigned him by the Navy. She and the two boys had ridden the train from North Carolina to California to join Linus. Everyone back home knew she was pregnant and then they received the announcement of the arrival of a baby girl.

Julianna was spoiled from the start. Her brothers adored her and Linus did, too. She was a beautiful baby who grew into a beautiful teenager and then a beautiful young woman. She was still beautiful, though Ophelia suspected she had help these days. Julianna very early on realized the value of her looks. It was a gift she had been given and she used that gift to get whatever her heart was set on at the time. Unfortunately she had never outgrown this habit. The only two people who ever told her "no" were Ophelia and Grant Whitworth.

Chapter Ten

It was late afternoon when Julianna finally emerged from her bedroom looking the worse for wear. She had thrown on old gym shorts, a t-shirt and flip-flops. Very large sunglasses covered most of her face. She found an old baseball cap of Everett's which she pulled low over her hair.

Most would not recognize her as the elegant Julianna Garrett Stafford.

She went through the kitchen past a startled Naomi Ruth and Robert. She ignored Naomi Ruth's question about something to eat and mumbled something about a trip to the Pig. She was gone about two minutes when she returned and asked for the keys to her mother's car. "I seem to have left my car at the Hatcher's," she said, and was gone again.

Naomi Ruth just looked at Robert and shrugged.

The Piggly Wiggly grocery store, affectionately known as the Pig, was a mainstay in most small southern towns. Hope Springs was no exception. It took Julianna fifteen minutes to get there. She parked her mother's Cadillac and entered the store. She took a cart and made her way to the drink aisle. All she wanted was a six-pack of Pepsi, Hershey bars and Alka-Seltzer. She was reaching for the Pepsi when she heard a familiar voice.

"Julianna, is that you?" She froze.

***

As Mary Hester turned her car into the Piggly Wiggly parking lot she saw Grant Whitworth entering the grocery store. She hastily parked and trotted into the store. She saw him by the onions in the produce section and pushed her cart in that direction, trying to appear nonchalant and absorbed. She picked up bananas and a cantaloupe as she watched him out of the corner of her eye. She was reasonably sure he would not remember her. It had been many years.

She was innocently selecting lettuce when she felt a presence beside her. She looked up.

Grant Whitworth stood beside her. “Mary Hester, isn’t it?” he asked. “How are you and your sisters? And your remarkable Mother?”

Mary Hester was nonplussed but quickly regained her composure and exclaimed, “Why Grant Whitworth…whatever are you doing in the Piggly Wiggly in Hope Springs? What a nice surprise.”

“Oh, come now Mary Hester, there is no doubt in my mind that you know exactly what I am doing in Hope Springs. Why, I’ll bet you, and just about every female in town, knows I’m here…and why.” Grant smiled a wicked smile.

Mary Hester felt heat creeping up her neck and flushing her face. Handling honesty was uncomfortable. She was much more adept at innuendo and evasion.

“Well, now that you mention it, I did hear you were over at the Harris’,” Mary Hester was trying to recover her poise. “Everyone is so worried about poor Minnie,” she added.

“No need to worry about Minnie, Mary Hester. She’s fine. Couldn’t be better. Minnie will be well looked after, I can assure you. Please reassure everyone…everyone…of that.”

Grant Whitworth smiled another interesting smile. “It’s nice to see you again, Mary Hester. Give my regards to your charming mother.” Grant Whitworth nodded and strode off towards the meat counter.

Mary Hester felt deflated. Regaining her wits she decided to keep an eye on Grant Whitworth and just ignore his rudeness. After all, news was news. She moved slowly towards the meat counter keeping a discreet distance from her quarry. She picked up chicken, bacon, liverwurst, pig's ears and all manner of foods she would never eat. She saw him turn down the drink aisle. She hurried over to the end of the aisle. When she peered down the aisle she could see him talking with some woman in shorts and a baseball cap. Big sunglasses hid most of her face. She wondered who in the world she was. Mary Hester knew she could not go directly down that aisle so she decided to go one aisle over to the dog food and paper products aisle.

She heard the screaming before she had gone two feet.

"You son of a bitch! How could you do this to me? How could you embarrass me this way? Minnie? You've got to be kidding! You are choosing Minnie Mouse when you could have had me! Are you demented?"

Mary Hester nearly fainted! That was Julianna's voice! Was that Julianna in shorts, t-shirt and flip flops? She heard a bottle break! She heard another scream and racing to the end of the aisle Mary Hester saw Julianna flying from the Pig…flip-flops flapping!

Grant Whitworth walked up beside her. His pants were splattered with liquid.

"Guess I'd best tell the manager there is broken glass on aisle five," he reported to wide-eyed and unusually silent Mary Hester.

***

While Mary Hester was submerged in the drama taking place at the Piggly Wiggly, her sister Mildred was visiting with Minnie. Mildred had gotten Clara to bake her famous sweet potato pie. Mildred walked it down to Minnie's when she saw the Harris' driveway devoid of cars. How could a body ask questions if hoards of people were circulating and constantly interrupting?

Minnie seemed genuinely glad to see her. She was delighted

with the pie for everyone in town loved that treat. Minnie took the pie to the kitchen and the two of them sat down at the kitchen counter with a glass of iced tea.

"How are you doing, Minnie?" Mildred began.

"Quite well, actually, Mildred. It is such a blessed release to have everything out in the open. Now we can get on with our lives… whichever way they lead. The boys are grown. They have been very understanding. It has been so sad, such a struggle for Carter. You know I love Carter, and always will…after all he is the father…a wonderful one, I might add…of my two precious sons. He has given me a good life. I want him to be happy."

Mildred sipped her tea while Minnie talked. She was listening intently. "What are Carter's plans? I do hope I'm not being too nosy by asking."

"Oh, no. I have lived with secrets for so long it's a relief to finally be able to answer these questions." Minnie paused and smiled. "Carter is going to pack up what he thinks he will need for the short term and drive down to Florida to meet Hobart. He thinks that talk here in Hope Springs will calm down sooner if he is out of the picture." Minnie took a sip of her tea.

"What will Carter do when he gets to Palm Beach?" Mildred wanted to be clear on everything.

"Now that I don't know, Mildred. Carter and I have not talked about that. Mostly we have just talked about settling things here."

"Will you sell your house, Minnie? You might want to move to Raleigh to be near your sister…or move to be near your boys." Mildred cast the bait.

A very coy expression played across Minnie's face. It made her look years younger and actually quite pretty. Mildred watched and waited, sipping her tea.

Minnie used her fingernail to make circles in the condensation on her glass. She looked up at Mildred. "I will be fine. I have plans."

Minnie paused.

Something in Mildred's look must have given her away, or either Minnie was not as naïve as she pretended.

"I expect you know who my plans revolve around, Mildred," Minnie continued. "There are very few secrets in this small town. Grant insists everyone knows we have been seeing each other."

"Grant Whitworth," Mildred stated, deciding on honesty. "Yes, I expect you are right. Everyone must know by now because it was the talk of *Kut & Kurl*."

"Good. Another thing out in the open," Minnie laughed. "He'll probably come strolling in here any minute. He has gone to the Pig to get a few things for supper."

"Minnie, do you know Julianna is back in town?"

Minnie's delicate face blanched. She set her tea glass down on the counter. "No, I didn't know that. Why? She has always disliked the slow life down here. What has she heard? I wonder if Grant knows?"

"I do now," Grant Whitworth said from the door. "I just ran into her at the Pig."

***

Sister Athie decided she would visit Ophelia this afternoon. Being practical she decided that what Ophelia needed most at this time was gin. After a quick trip to the ABC store she drove out to Merrebanks. She noticed that the big Cadillac was gone when she arrived but Eggie's car was parked in the drive. Athie entered the back door and greeted Naomi Ruth who was in the kitchen by herself. Athie gave Naomi Ruth the fifth of Tanqueray for Miss Phe then Naomi Ruth led her to the library.

"Here's Miss Athie to entertain y'all," Naomi announced and left.

"Oh, goodie," said Eggie, "a young person!"

"Now Miss Eggie," Athie was smiling as she took a seat on the sofa opposite them. "You and Miss Ophelia and Miss Mae Rose have much more of a youthful spirit than my staid old group. Y'all are always up to something fun. In fact, I can't wait to hear about your trip to Hilton Head."

Both Eggie and Ophelia started laughing. They were seated opposite each other in chairs on either side of the fireplace. "Yes, indeed, that was fun." The two elderly ladies looked at each other, nodded and laughed. "In fact, we are going to share a secret. You must promise not to tell a soul." Eggie leaned forward in a conspiratorial manner.

Athie sat on the edge of her cushion.

"Mae Rose met a gentleman there. They are courting!" Eggie announced.

"Miss Mae Rose has a beau?" Athie exclaimed.

"Yes, and he is coming to visit." Eggie sat back in her chair.

"Wonderful! When is he coming?" Athie asked.

Before an answer could be given footsteps could be heard coming down the hall and Mae Rose entered the room. "Naomi Ruth said y'all were in here. She's bringing us some iced tea. Isn't this heat horrible?" She sat down on the other end of the sofa. "What mayhem have y'all been plotting?"

"Actually, Mae Rose, your ears must be burning," Ophelia said.

"We have been talking about you," Eggie added.

"We just told Athie all about your Casanova," Ophelia continued.

Mae Rose sat up quite straight with a big smile crinkling her wrinkled face. "Isn't that a hoot, Athie? Who would think such a thing could happen at our age but really Hank has been quite attentive. He calls almost every afternoon. I must admit it has put a spring in my step! Attention is a marvelous tonic!"

"When is he coming for a visit?" Athie asked again.

Once again before an answer could be given footsteps could be heard coming down the hall but this time they were running. They all looked up to see a disheveled Julianna fly past the door and run up the stairs. A string of profanity trailed in her wake. Upstairs a door opened then slammed shut. Something was thrown against a wall. It broke.

Naomi Ruth appeared in the door. "I think something must have happened to Julianna at the Pig."

Chapter Eleven

Early the next morning Minnie waved good-bye to Grant as he backed out of the drive. He waved and was gone.

Grant had come by from the Holiday Inn to tell her good-bye before heading back to Raleigh. They would not see each other again until Carter left Hope Springs. She slowly walked back into the house. She could hear Carter upstairs when she entered. As usual he had the television on and the volume turned up. She headed for the silence of the kitchen. She poured another cup of coffee and sat down at the counter with her calendar. What would it feel like to see him back out the drive?

She had known Carter all her life. She had always depended on him. They grew up next door to each other and were inseparable as children and then as teens until they married the summer after she finished St Mary's College. He was the only man she had ever known or cared about until she met Grant last year. Carter chose her clothes, her jewelry and decided on the style of her hair. His personality was her personality. With Grant she realized what she had missed, what she had sacrificed.

Minnie thought back to the first time she met him. It was at the engagement party for Julianna and Grant hosted by Julianna's parents. Minnie and Carter were already married.

Julianna introduced them to Grant as a "couple from the cradle." Minnie had been impressed by his cordial response. She had also thought him quite handsome. She smiled to herself. He still was.

***

Over at Merrebanks that morning Sam Jenkins sat with Ophelia at the kitchen table. Naomi Ruth was at the sink washing the breakfast dishes. Sam and Ophelia were enjoying another cup of coffee. They had enjoyed a comfortable relationship since Big Linus' death, when Ophelia took over the management of the farms. They often had breakfast together to discuss farm issues. As none of Linus' and Ophelia's children showed any aptitude or interest in farming Ophelia relied heavily on Sam. But Sam wanted to retire and Ophelia understood, though she was worried about Garrett Farms without his guidance.

"I know we discussed my retirement next month, Phe, but that was before Everett's death. You have enough on you right now. Let me stay on a while longer till things settle down. Besides I still haven't found anyone I consider qualified to run your farming operation. I want just the right person for you."

"Oh, Sam, thank you," Ophelia replied. "You know how panicked I am about the farms without you. Have you had any replies at all to the ads?"

"Actually, I have. I even interviewed one or two. Hope you don't mind that I did that without you there. I just want to cull the applicants before I waste your time."

"I'm going to rely completely on your choice. I don't even have to be there."

"Well, I want you there for the final decision," Sam responded. "They're your farms and you need to be able to work closely and respect the decisions of whomever you choose to run them."

Ophelia nodded.

"Actually," Sam continued, "I've had an inquiry from a young man who graduated from N. C. State and then finished an advanced agricultural program. He is coming to interview with me next week. He has good credentials...summer farm work...family farming background...top of his class. I'll call you if he seems promising and you can see what you think." Sam took a sip of his coffee and placed his cup on the table. "Well, you don't pay me to drink coffee. I'd best get back out there. One of the combines is acting up." He stood.

Ophelia stood also and walked with him out to the backyard. "Thank you, Sam, for everything you've done and continue to do."

The aging overseer placed his dusty, well-worn cap on his balding head, smiled, and walked towards his truck.

***

Meanwhile back in Hope Springs Athie entered Mary Hester's kitchen just as she and Erwin were finishing breakfast. Erwin took one look at Athie and excused himself. "I know you two are going to blister somebody so I'm leaving," he said and headed toward the den.

"I just ran into Minnie at the cleaners. She was picking up Carter's clothes. He's leaving in the morning. You could tell she was a little shaken. She said Grant left this morning. She'll be alone after tomorrow." Athie frowned at her sister and sat down in the chair Erwin had just vacated.

Mary Hester piled the dirty dishes into the sink. "She might as well get used to it. You have to wait a year after a separation in North Carolina before you can get a divorce."

"It's Julianna I'm worried about," Athie said. "She's in a snit about Minnie and Grant...and Minnie is just so naïve."

"Well, honestly, Sister, what do you think Julianna's going to do?"

Athie stood to go. "I'm probably over-reacting but I'm nervous. We grew up with Julianna. She's like a hornet when she's riled."

Mary Hester looked at her sister. "I well know."

Athie turned toward the back door but stopped when Mary Hester asked, "Any chance you can take me to the beauty parlor this morning and come back and pick me up? I'm supposed to get my hair done at ten but my car is in the shop."

"I can take you but I've got a church meeting at ten thirty. Why not call Julianna and get her to pick you up. She's got to come into town to get her car. It's still in front of Mother's. That way we can keep an eye on her."

***

A little after ten o'clock Julianna strolled into the kitchen at Merrebanks. "Where's Robert?" she asked. "I need him to take me to get my car."

Naomi Ruth was ironing. She put the iron down and turned to Julianna. "Would you like me to fix you some breakfast, Julianna? You haven't eaten anything in a while. You must be hungry."

Both Ophelia and Naomi Ruth had tried to get Julianna to come down for dinner the night before. Julianna had just answered through the door that she wasn't hungry. They could both tell she had been crying by the tone of her voice. This morning she appeared composed, though her eyes were puffy. She was dressed immaculately and had a determined air about her. Her beautiful face had a hard look. Naomi had seen that look before. It usually boded ill will.

"No, I'll get something later," Julianna answered. "I've got to get to town to pick up Mary Hester from the beauty parlor. Her car is in the shop."

"What happened yesterday, Julianna, that upset you so much?" Naomi Ruth asked.

"'Omi, that is my business, but if you must know…and I'm sure you would find out anyway because of this damn little gossiping town…I ran into Grant Whitworth in the Pig."

"Did you know he was in town? Is that why you returned?"

"I had heard he was here but I certainly didn't expect him to be in the Pig! I looked awful!"

"You know why he's here?" Naomi Ruth asked.

"The Hatcher sisters told me but I find it very hard to believe. Grant and Minnie Mouse? Absurd!"

"It's been thirty years since we last saw Grant Whitworth, Julianna. A lot of water has flowed under that bridge. What Grant Whitworth does or doesn't do is no longer a concern of yours."

A cunning look played over Julianna's face. She looked directly at Naomi Ruth and answered, "We'll see."

***

Robert dropped Julianna off at Bessie Hatcher's house a little before eleven then headed back home. Julianna drove around the block and past the Harris' home. Carter was still here. His car was in the garage. Julianna drove on to pick up Mary Hester at the beauty parlor.

As she drove she reflected on her two phone calls of the morning. She had called the Holiday Inn posing as Grant Whitworth's secretary. He had checked out. She was sure he would return to Raleigh for his meeting with Emma-of-the-triple-martini's dear Benji. She suspected he wouldn't return to Hope Springs until Carter left town.

She also called Rico. He surprised and angered her when he refused to help this time. He told her to do it herself, actually laughed when he said it, and had the nerve to hang up on her.

She was still angry when she parked and walked into the beauty parlor. Norma Sue was taking the curlers out of Mary Hester's hair so Julianna sat down at the empty manicure table. She began to idly pick up the bottles of nail polish. She sat there quietly until Mary Hester was ready to leave.

***

Julianna was surprised to see Alice's car parked in the drive when she returned to Merrebanks for lunch. What did Alice want now? Julianna had never cared much for Alice. She thought her a bit of a ninny. How could someone be always smiling and running around doing good for everyone? It was just too, too much! And Alice's choice in clothing had always made Julianna shudder. She always wore jeans. Julianna wondered who had found the black dress Alice wore to Everett's funeral. As far as Julianna knew Alice didn't own a dress. Nor did she seem to own any make-up. Julianna would never understand how Alice was chosen May Queen at St. Mary's with all that curly blonde hair and freckles.

When Julianna entered the kitchen Ophelia, Alice and Robert were at the table talking and shucking early corn from his garden. Naomi Ruth was emptying the dishwasher.

"Hello, Julianna," Ophelia looked up. "Did you get your car?"

"Yes," Julianna replied, pulling out a chair at the table and sitting down. She made no attempt to help shuck corn. That chore would ruin her nails.

"Alice is joining us for lunch," Ophelia continued.

"How are you getting along, Alice?" Julianna turned to her newly widowed sister-in-law.

"As well as I can,I suppose," Alice answered while brushing silk from an ear of corn. "I cry a lot," and her eyes filled with tears, "but I guess that's normal. I miss him so much."

"You'll get over it," Julianna replied, looking closely at one of her nails. "You're not the first person to lose a spouse."

The slight jolted Alice but she bit her lip. Ophelia, Robert and Naomi Ruth looked at each other. Ophelia reached over and took Alice's hand. She squeezed it gently and smiled at Alice. Julianna didn't miss this demonstration of affection. It maddened her.

Robert rose from the table and gathered up the corn. "Don't you fret, Alice. You know we are here for you. If you feel like crying just come over here and we'll all cry together." He carried the corn to the counter next to the stove.

Lunch was a stilted affair. Afterwards, as Alice was preparing to leave, Ophelia hugged her and said. "I'm sure the beach will be difficult for you but you will have Ev and Charlotte with you."

"Yes, I'm thankful for that," Alice said. "I'm going by Minnie's on the way home. Carter is leaving tomorrow morning. I think I'll ask her if she wants to come with us. Her life is as topsy-turvy as mine right now."

Julianna looked up at the mention of Minnie. Naomi Ruth noticed the expression on her face. "Carter is leaving tomorrow?" Julianna asked.

"Yes," Alice nodded. "Minnie will be on her own."

Immediately after Alice walked out the back door, Julianna turned to her mother "When is Alice going to the beach?

"She's going Friday, Julianna," Ophelia answered. Naomi Ruth looked up. "Ev Jr. and Charlotte are going with her. It's just a short trip...just the weekend...baby steps, you know. It would be nice if Minnie went, too. Distractions help."

"Minnie Mouse certainly is popular these days," Julianna snipped as she left the room. Naomi Ruth's eyes followed her.

***

Alice pulled into the Harris' driveway right behind Carter. He parked in the rear and came forward to welcome her with a quick hug.

"Are you packed, Carter?" Alice asked as they walked inside.

"Pretty much," he replied. "All this seems so strange, I must admit, like I'm watching a movie of someone else's life."

Minnie greeted them from upstairs. "I'll be right down. I was folding your shirts, Carter."

Alice and Carter walked to the back sunporch and sat down. They began to discuss Carter's travel plans and his hopes for a job in Palm Beach.

Minnie entered the room with a tray of frosted glasses filled with iced tea and mint. She passed to Alice, to Carter and then placed the tray on the table and sat down with her own glass. "Where have you been today, Alice?" she asked.

"I had lunch with Ophelia." Alice thought it best not to mention Julianna. "I went over to tell her that I was going to the beach Friday. I've got to face that hurdle. Ev and Charlotte are coming with me and I wanted to ask you to come, too." Alice looked at Minnie. "I think a little change of scenery would be good for both of us."

Minnie looked at Carter, then quickly away. Her decisions now were her own. It would take getting used to.

Carter, however, spoke right up. "Why, Minnie, that's a great idea. You can stretch your wings."

Chapter Twelve

At five-fifteen the Hatcher sisters were taking their first sips of wine and settling in for a tart taste of gossip. Before they could utter the first word Frances breezed through the door.

"I'm back," she announced.

"Obviously," muttered Athie.

"Did you get Sallie Bett settled at camp?" Mary Hester asked politely.

"Yes. As long as that child is within sight of a horse, she's happy," Frances answered. "Have I missed anything? What's the news?"

Mildred stood and removed another wine glass from the cabinet. She filled it and set it before Frances on the table. They then filled her with the news. Frances was more intoxicated by the gossip than the grape.

The four of them were deep into spicy speculation when Mildred rose to get another bottle of wine. Looking out the kitchen window she saw Julianna's red BMW coming down the street.

"Lordy, here comes Julianna again," Mildred exclaimed. She looked at her sisters.

"Oh, goodie," said Frances.

The Hatcher sisters were well aware what Julianna was up to with her visits. Julianna was fishing…and they were casting the bait. Frances, on the other hand, was just plain nosey.

Julianna swept into the kitchen and took a seat at the kitchen table. Mildred once again rose and removed another wine glass from the cabinet. She filled it and placed it before Julianna, silently congratulating herself on having the foresight to go to the wine shop that morning.

Frances, in her forthright manner said, "Julianna, I thought you had returned to Raleigh."

"I did," Julianna replied.

"What brought you back so soon?" Frances pried.

"Things…that are really not your concern, Frances," Julianna said.

Frances' lips pressed tightly together.

Ignoring her completely, Julianna continued, "Alice had lunch with us at Merrebanks today."

"And how is sweet Alice? This is a hard time for her," Mary Hester asked.

"As dull as ever…Alice never changes." Julianna dismissed Alice with a shrug.

"Alice is a good person," Mildred said. "She's a might whimsical and seems flighty at times but her heart is in the right place."

"It seems she is returning to the cottage for the week-end. Ev and Charlotte are going with her. She also said she was going to ask Minnie to come with them."

A quick glance flew between the sisters. Frances listened, sitting with arms crossed.

"I don't know if Minnie will leave with the Bishop coming Sunday," Athie said. "She's on the food team…Heavenly Hosts. In fact, we're meeting in the church kitchen tomorrow morning at nine to start preparing the luncheon."

Julianna smiled into her wine glass. She could always count on the Hatchers.

***

That evening Julianna waited until she heard Robert take Maize out after he finished the dinner dishes. Her mother and Naomi Ruth were in her mother's room having their devotionals. She crept down the stairs and made her way to the kitchen pantry where she knew Robert kept his toolbox. She removed the hammer and a jar of nails. Then she quickly made her way back upstairs to her room.

Chapter Thirteen

Carter left his drive and his past life early the next morning. He and Minnie had an emotional farewell. Minnie stayed in the house as he backed from the drive. She couldn't watch. After crying for a spell her thoughts turned to Grant. She dried her eyes and fixed her breakfast. She was due at the church to prepare the upcoming luncheon for the Bishop. She best hurry or she would be late.

***

Julianna had packed her bags the night before. She was ready. She ate breakfast with her mother then asked Robert to take her bags to her car. No one noticed or commented on her appearance. She was in jeans and a tee shirt, very casual attire for Julianna. She said good-bye to everyone and shortly after nine headed down the drive. It would take her twenty minutes to get to the church.

Julianna parked way down the street and around the corner from the church. Her red BMW was conspicuous so she parked on a little used side street. She had seen Minnie's car when she passed. It too was on a side street, for which she was thankful. She put on the wig of long black hair, then a large floppy hat. She picked up her grocery bag, put on the large sunglasses and set out. Five minutes later she was standing by Minnie's car. She glanced up and down the street and, seeing no one, took the hammer and jar of nails out of the bag.

***

Minnie finished making fruit kabobs about noon. She explained to the women that she would not be there to help serve on Sunday as she was going to Nags Head with Alice. Everyone understood for everyone knew everything.

The heat and the humidity were stifling as Minnie walked back to her car. She started her car and immediately turned the air-conditioning on high. She dreaded returning to her empty house. She decided to drive over to the neighboring town of Newtons Fork and pick up a few grocery items. The Pig would be full of friends thinking, "Poor Minnie." She didn't want to deal with that today.

She had an uneventful afternoon in Newtons Fork and headed home about four o'clock. Minnie was a fast driver. She considered the speed limit only for other drivers. She turned off the major highway and ignored the fact that she was speeding on a country road through a farming community. She rounded a curve and a combine appeared directly on the road in front of her.

She slammed on her brakes and as she did she heard a muffled pop and felt her car veer. Her car twisted and turned and eventually came to rest in the ditch paralleling the road.

The farmer driving the combine witnessed her accident. He pulled the huge piece of farm machinery off the road as best he could and rushed back to check on her. She was dazed but fine. A motorist arrived, followed by an old farmer in an equally old pickup truck. Between the three of them they managed to get her out of the car. The driver's side door was pressed against the ditch bank so Minnie had to be pulled up and out the passenger door. The motorist called the Highway Patrol. The combine driver helped her get her purse and its contents from her car. The old farmer got into his pickup truck and continued down the country road.

Minnie finally arrived home just after six that evening. She was exhausted. Her first day alone was a disaster. The Highway Patrol officer was convinced she was speeding. He said her tire was defective and burst because of the heat. AAA sent a tow truck. She rode home in the cab with the driver. He was very nice but said air-conditioning gave you arthritis. She was hot. She had a headache. She poured a stiff bourbon.

Her doorbell rang. When she opened the door there stood Frances.

"Did I just see you get out of a tow truck?" Frances asked before Minnie could say a word. "And was that your car being towed?"

"Yes, Frances," Minnie said, "you did and it was. I had a slight wreck coming home from Newtons Fork this afternoon."

"That's like saying you are slightly pregnant," replied Frances as she stood on the threshold of Minnie's front door. "Are you all right?"

"Yes. I'm fine. I'm just tired, Frances. It has been a long unsettling day." Minnie was beyond being polite.

Frances looked at her carefully. "Of course, but please feel free to call me tonight if you need anything."

Minnie assured her she would, not meaning a hint of it. Frances turned away and Minnie watched her hurry down the walk. Minnie wasn't a bit surprised when Frances turned left at the sidewalk toward the Hatcher's house instead of right, toward her house.

***

Eggie and Ophelia were sitting on the side porch. They gazed down the lawn at the muddy waters of the Chowan. "Always something peaceful about gazing at the river," Eggie said. The two old friends were enjoying an afternoon gin and tonic, languidly fanning with old funeral home fans.

"What are we going to do about Mae Rose's beau?" Eggie asked. "I think he's coming next week. You know, I could have sworn you were the one he was interested in. He latched right on to you at first."

"We just did the 'do you know' thing...polite nothingness," Ophelia fanned. "I think a small dinner party would be appropriate. We'll have it here. What do you think?"

"You don't think people will talk about you entertaining so soon after Everett's death, do you?"

Ophelia laughed. "Now you know me better than that, Eggie. Life goes on."

Eggie smiled. "That's you, my maverick friend. I'll call Mae Rose tonight and ask whom she wants to invite."

The two old friends continued to rock in their chairs and sip their drinks. Their gazes were both directed down the lawn towards the river.

"Julianna left this morning," Ophelia broke the silence. "She spent most of her time while here with the Hatcher sisters."

"Did she say anything about Grant Whitworth?" Eggie asked. "I'm assuming that's why she turned up so unexpectedly…heard he was here. I imagine his return to Hope Springs was certainly quite a shock for her. For everyone, actually," she added.

"She told me she heard he was in Hope Springs from one of the girls in her tennis group. She did not know why until she got here and asked the Hatcher sisters. They told her about Minnie." Ophelia sipped her drink and gazed down the lawn.

Eggie nodded. "Yes, that is certainly the surprise. Can't quite see sweet Minnie in the role of *femme fatale*."

"No one can. She's always stood in Carter's shadow…a quiet, proper young woman. After Hobart's announcement all anyone could say was 'Poor Minnie.'

"Well, they're not going to be saying '*Poor* Minnie' any longer."

***

The Hatcher sisters were once again seated at their mother's kitchen table. Since the day had been so abysmally hot the sisters decided a vodka and tonic would be more refreshing than their usual white wine.

"Where is Frances?" Mildred asked.

"I'm sure she'll turn up," Athie answered, "right when we are in the middle of a discussion and she'll make us repeat everything we've discussed."

"Probably," Mary Hester agreed. "By the way, I saw Carter pull out of the driveway this morning when I went out to get the paper."

"Convenient," Athie eyed her sister. Mary Hester grinned.

"Anyway, he's gone. Minnie did not come out of the house," Mary Hester added.

"She was fine at church today. Cool as a cucumber." Athie said. "We were prepping the food for the Bishop's visit Sunday. Minnie told everyone that Carter left this morning. I think that was a very smart move. By telling all those slicing and dicing women she cut off any gossip. She also said she was going with Alice to Nags Head."

"It'll do them both a world of good to get away," Mary Hester said.

"Did I tell you that Miss Mae Rose has a suitor?" Athie asked.

The sisters were discussing Mae Rose's beau when Frances rushed through the door. "Minnie had a wreck!" she exclaimed.

"What?" Athie said. "Is she okay?"

"Yes, a wreck and yes, she's okay. Is that a vodka tonic? Could I have one? I moved way too fast in this heat to get here with the news." Frances sat down, snatched up the evening paper and started fanning herself.

"Oh, Lord, think we all need a drink with that news," said Mildred and the sisters rose to get more ice, more vodka, more tonic, more limes. Fortified Frances launched into her tale.

"I was taking a slow stroll around the neighborhood, trying to see who has flowers or foliage to use for the Garden Club tea. You know that's next week. Anyway, a tow truck passed. It stopped in front of the Harris'. Minnie got out, looking quite bedraggled, I might add. She went around to the driver's side, said something to the driver and passed him something. Money, I guess. Then he drove away and she went into her house.

"So I just went right over and rang the bell," Frances added. She took a righteous drink of her vodka tonic.

"Minnie answered the door but she was quite abrupt. It was obvious she was worn out, poor dear. Of course, I didn't want to pry so I just asked if she was all right." Frances nodded at her recollection.

"Is that all?" Athie asked, clearly disappointed with the lack of information.

"Well, it was obvious she wanted me to leave…so that's all I know."

"Was her car totaled? How bad was the wreck?"

"Her car didn't look totaled but cars are so cheaply made these days who knows. The wreck must not have been bad. She didn't have any blood on her that I could see."

The sisters looked at each other and rolled their eyes.

"I went by to check on her this afternoon," Mildred said. "I wanted to make sure she was okay, this being her first day alone and all. I guess she wanted to escape this town because of the gossip."

They sat quietly. Frances was the only one drinking. The sisters were oddly silent. Finally Athie broke the silence, "I don't like this."

"An odd coincidence," Mildred said.

Mary Hester just nodded.

***

Julianna arrived home. She unpacked her car. She collected her newspapers from the front stoop. She read her mail. She checked her messages. She made a quick trip to the Harris Teeter up the street. She watered her plants. She started the washing machine. Then she poured a glass of white wine and sat in her den. She wondered if anything had happened to Minnie this afternoon. She wondered how she could find out. She decided to call Mary Hester later in the week with some pretext or other. She sipped her wine.

She rose from her chair and called Pansy Perdue. She told Pansy she needed exercise. How about a tennis game and lunch tomorrow? Pansy Perdue was agreeable for Pansy Perdue lived, breathed and ate tennis. Julianna asked Pansy to call the two ladies they had played with on Monday because she enjoyed them so much and they had a good game. Pansy Perdue agreed.

They hung up and Julianna waited for the return call.

The phone rang. It was Pansy Perdue calling back. The game was on for tomorrow at the club, same time and lunch afterwards. Julianna smiled.

Chapter Fourteen

Ophelia was in the kitchen with Maize and Naomi Ruth the next morning when Eggie called. "I talked with Mae Rose last night," Eggie reported. "She is thrilled we are going to help entertain Hank. I think she is a little nervous about his visit. She doesn't want us to go to a lot of trouble. Of course everybody always says that. She said she thought she would take him to the club one night but had no earthly idea what to do the other night. We were an answer to prayer."

"So what does she pray we will do?" Ophelia asked her friend.

"For someone who said not to go to any trouble she is asking a lot," Eggie answered. "She thinks it would be nice to have an early cocktail party so Hank can meet all her 'lovely friends.' Her words. Then maybe after the cocktail party our age group could sit down to a light dinner."

"That is so typical of Mae Rose. Robert will come pick you up this afternoon about the usual time. Naomi Ruth can help us with decisions about the food and 'lovely friends.'"

Ophelia looked over at Naomi Ruth and made a check in the air. Naomi Ruth laughed.

***

Julianna was the first of the tennis group to arrive at the Carolina Country Club. Pansy Purdue arrived shortly after and Jane Elliott and Emma arrived together minutes later. These were serious tennis players so play began and continued for almost two hours with a minimum of chatter. The heat finally drove them into the grill room for lunch.

The waiter appeared for their drink orders. Once again three white wines were ordered and one triple martini on the rocks. After the drinks arrived and the salads were ordered the girls began their conversation.

"Can you believe this heat?"

"No end in sight."

"Have you gotten settled in your new house, Emma?"

"I don't think I'll ever be settled again. I cannot find a thing. And Benji is absolutely no help. He is so involved with his new job I hardly see him. Of course, I cannot complain because that new job has bought us a fabulous house inside the belt line." Emma sipped her triple martini and glowed.

"And what was the new job?" Julianna asked. "I believe you mentioned it Monday but, I declare, I just can't remember a thing." Julianna waited.

"My Benji is the CFO of the new Whitworth Technologies operation in Research Triangle Park. I am so proud of him. He is Grant Whitworth's, the founder, you know, right-hand man."

Julianna watched Emma take another sip of her martini. She knew none of these women had a clue about her past connection with Grant Whitworth. It had been thirty years ago. Jane Elliot and Emma Hendricks were too young and Pansy Perdue was too old and not from the area.

"Didn't Benji's new boss leave him up in the air this week? Canceled on him. Do I remember that correctly?" Julianna took a sip of her wine.

Emma quickly turned to her. "That was not Benji's fault. Grant Whitworth had some family crisis in some hick town east of here and he had to go take care of it. He did and he's back. He and Benji have been in meetings for two days. They are practically joined at the hip."

"I read an article in Time last year about Grant Whitworth," Pansy Perdue said. "He has certainly done well. Your husband has hitched his wagon to a star."

The comment annoyed Julianna but she bit her lip and asked, "Where do these wealthy corporate types stay when they come to Raleigh?"

"Anywhere they want, I guess," Jane Eliott said and laughed.

"I don't know about anyone else," said Emma, "but Grant Whitworth is staying at the Washington Duke Inn."

***

Ev Jr, Charlotte, Alice and Minnie set off that afternoon for Nags Head and arrived at the beach around cocktail time. The ocean was as slick as glass. It was a beautiful summer afternoon.

They unpacked the car. Ev Jr. made a quick trip to the seafood market for fish, shrimp, and scallops. Charlotte made a trip to the grocery store for breakfast supplies and salad ingredients. Minnie and Alice prowled around the cottage commenting on pictures and raking up memories.

When Ev returned he announced that what they all needed was one of his famous margaritas. After all, tequila was medicinal and well known for soothing the spirit. Drinks in hand they settled on the porch. Pelicans were diving for fish. The sun was hovering on the horizon before its drop into the sea. Peace reigned.

"This was Everett's favorite time of the day," Alice said softly.

"Now, Mama, don't get maudlin on us," Ev Jr. said. "It was Dad's favorite time of day because it was the cocktail hour and he usually had everyone up and down the beach here drinking with him."

Alice laughed. "I guess you're right. Your father loved a party." They sipped their drinks.

"Alice, can I ask you and Minnie something?" Charlotte turned to her mother-in-law.

Alice turned in surprise. "Of course, Charlotte. What do you want to know?"

"It's about Julianna," Charlotte said.

Alice and Minnie laughed out loud. "Mercy, Charlotte, we could write a book about Julianna. It would be X-rated, though! Ask Minnie. They grew up together. I met her later."

"What do you want to know, Charlotte?" Minnie asked.

"Well," Charlotte began, "while I was playing bridge last week Celeste Redborne...who, I have noticed, likes the sound of her own voice...said her mother was a suite mate of Julianna's at St. Mary's... the high school, of course. She said Julianna sneaked out all the time with some guy she dated at home...somebody her family did not approve of. Apparently her father sent her to St. Mary's to get her away from this boy. Her mother told Celeste he was really good-looking... quarterback of the high school football team...all that kind of stuff. I was just wondering if any of that were true. Julianna seems too aloof...too proper...to do something like that." Charlotte looked at Minnie.

"Oh, yes," Minnie replied, "it's true all right. His name was Jake Denton. Not only was he the quarterback of the football team but he was its captain. He was also the star of the basketball team and baseball team. He was quite an athlete. He was also very, very good-looking. All the girls were in love with him but he was mad about Julianna. She was quite a beauty...cheerleader, homecoming queen, all that. If there was an honor to be bestowed that had to do with looks Julianna won it.

"Anyway, she and Jake were inseparable. I think her father started getting nervous about their relationship. Jake's father was the mill manager for the cotton plant. The Dentons were a nice, respectable family but not on a social par with the Garrett's, by any means. When their junior year rolled around Julianna was enrolled at St Mary's High School.

"So she went to St Mary's but obviously that did not stop them from seeing each other," Charlotte said.

"Oh, no," Minnie continued. "Jake would just drive up to Raleigh every weekend. I'm not sure the Garretts knew what was going on. Then one weekend at the very beginning of her senior year she got caught. She was expelled from St Mary's and came back to finish her senior year at the high school...which was exactly to her liking. Her parents, of course, were horrified...and embarrassed. There was the usual gossip. I remember my parents talking about it. They were so relieved I was dating a nice young man like Carter." Minnie grinned.

"Anyway, Jake and Julianna ran off to South Carolina right after graduation and got married. They returned to Hope Springs and moved into a trailer on one of the Garrett farms."

"I can't see Julianna in a trailer," Charlotte interrupted.

"Neither could anyone else," Minnie continued. "Anyway they were married a couple of months when somehow or another Big Linus had the marriage annulled and poor Jake found himself drafted. He was eventually sent to Vietnam and never came back. Linus was on the draft board. It wasn't hard to figure out what happened. Jake's poor family was devastated."

Minnie gazed at the horizon and sighed. Slowly she sipped her margarita. "It was all handled quietly but there was a lot of whispering going on.

"In truth, our age group was always in awe of Julianna. She was a year ahead of us and we thought she was like a movie star. She was so beautiful; so elegant, and she had Jake Denton following her around. I never knew what happened till years later. That's when I learned she was pregnant. She found some hokey doctor to abort her baby. Her parents didn't even know. I tell you who did know... Mary Hester Hatcher. She and Julianna were best friends back then. I think Mary Hester went with her to the doctor. Now you know the Hatcher sisters have never been known to keep a secret so eventually the truth leaked out. Mary Hester told someone that she tried her best to talk Julianna out of having an abortion but Julianna was vehement. She told Mary Hester she was too young to be a mother; she didn't even like babies and besides it would ruin her figure."

The sun slid into the ocean. The light grew dim. They all sat quietly thinking of what Minnie had just told them. Finally Ev Jr. said, "I didn't know all that about Aunt Julianna."

Alice looked at her son, "It happened so long ago...before I met your dad even. Certainly way before you were born. And, actually, there's more. There always is with Julianna."

***

Ophelia sent Robert to pick up Eggie a little after five o'clock. Eggie would stay for dinner and then Robert would drive her home. The old friends no longer drove at night.

A little before six they were seated at the kitchen table with paper and pencil and gin and tonics. Naomi Ruth was moving about the kitchen. Robert and Maize left to water his garden.

"Let's do the cocktail party first," Eggie said. "Food, then guest list."

Ophelia took up her pencil and after much discussion a menu was created that all three women agreed on. They then began to list the friends and family who should be in attendance. Ophelia's pencil paused when Eggie asked if Minnie would bring Grant Whitworth. Phe tapped the eraser against her teeth as she thought.

"I'm going to tell her to bring Grant, if she wishes. He'll probably feel uncomfortable about coming to Merrebanks. But, if he does come we can certainly all act like civilized adults. What happened was a long time ago and Julianna won't be here."

Several other couples were added to the list.

"Okay," Eggie said, "let's do the dinner menu and we are through."

"Can I make a suggestion?" Naomi Ruth asked. "Let me just fry up some chicken and make some deviled eggs and maybe a congealed salad. You will have asparagus left over from the cocktail party and probably ham biscuits, too. That will make a nice light supper. I'll also make a chocolate meringue pie."

"Oh, 'Omi, that sounds divine," Eggie exclaimed. "Can we start with dessert?"

***

That evening in Nags Head Ev fried the most delicious seafood dinner while Charlotte added a salad and corn bread. Minnie and Alice just rocked on the porch till they were called in to dine. Supper was quite jovial. Charlotte shared humorous incidents from an art class she was giving for five and six year olds. Minnie gave them a light-hearted, hilarious account of her ride home with the tow truck driver after her wreck. They were laughing out loud.

Finally, after clearing and cleaning the dishes the group returned to the porch with a night cap before retiring for bed. The sky was littered with stars. The ocean stretched into the night sky. It was peaceful and beautiful.

"I hate to break the spell," Charlotte said, "but could you continue the Julianna story? I am mesmerized."

"Julianna's hypnotic all right," Alice said. "Continue Minnie."

"Let's see. Where was I?" Minnie asked.

"Poor Jake was drafted and Julianna had gone to the witch doctor," Charlotte answered.

"Well, after Jake left town for Fort Benning Julianna was oddly removed. She rarely left Merrebanks. Whenever I saw her at the club or church Jake's name was never mentioned. The problem for her parents was what to do about her...where to send her to college. Julianna desperately wanted to go to Chapel Hill but back then girls had to go to another college and transfer to Carolina their junior year... unless you were real, real smart...which Julianna wasn't."

Minnie looked around at the group sitting with her. Alice nodded agreement.

She continued. "Saint Mary's college would not take her back, of course. No telling what Big Linus offered them but they held firm. St. Mary's was every girl's choice around eastern North Carolina back then...for high school and college. So Big Linus had to look elsewhere. He had some maiden aunt who had gone to a girl's college in South Carolina and some way or another he got Julianna in that school. Surprisingly Julianna liked the school. Her parents were thrilled. She discovered an avocation, you might say. Julianna found the stage. This particular college had a very strong drama department. An unknown Julianna emerged. Or maybe the old Julianna just came out in a different way. When she came home at Christmas she was wafer thin and had long, straight blond hair...and the clothes she wore...mercy! Her actions, movement, language, everything, was very theatrical. She even used a cigarette holder. She was still beautiful, though, in a distracted, ethereal way.

"Julianna didn't come home often from that college. During the summer she went to New York for an internship with a theater company. We just knew she was destined for the bright lights. But then, in the spring of her sophomore year, the old Julianna reappeared and in another tragic way. Julianna and several college kids left a fraternity party that was held at a cabin outside town. She was driving. They had all been drinking. They wrecked. One of the young men was killed and several were hospitalized. Julianna didn't have a scratch. She was speeding.

"Somehow or another she was not expelled. No telling what Big Linus paid for that one. And somehow or another the accident wasn't recorded. Big Linus had powerful friends. Once again, Julianna escaped without consequences. She was like the old 'rubber and glue' saying...everything bounced off her...nothing stuck."

Minnie grew quiet. She looked out over the dark ocean.

"Basically that's the end of the Julianna's story for me," Minnie said. "Julianna did transfer to Chapel Hill. That's where I introduced her to Alice...while we were at St Mary's College...and in turn, Julianna introduced Alice to Everett. Alice can take up the story here."

"Let's do it tomorrow," Alice said. "Let's sit in the quiet of the evening. We've had enough of Julianna for one day. The one good thing she did was introduce your father to me. For that I am eternally grateful." Alice smiled at her son.

***

While the group at the beach was enjoying a peaceful evening the object of their conversation was anything but serene. She was slowly sipping a martini while sitting on a stool at the far end of the bar of the Washington Duke Inn. She appeared an elegant, composed woman, long legs crossed, skirt just above the knee. She had been here for little over an hour. She had caught the bartender glancing at her several times, but she was used to men looking at her.

Suddenly, out of the corner of her eye she saw Grant enter the room. He glanced around. His eyes fell on her. A look of surprise played across his features but was quickly replaced by a look of speculation. Julianna did not notice this. She acted as if she did not see him. He knew otherwise.

Grant walked directly through the crowd towards Julianna. He took the seat next to her at the bar. When the bartender asked what he would like he requested a Scotch and water. He then turned to Julianna.

"What are you doing here, Julianna?"

"Hello, Grant. What a surprise. Actually I'm staying here for the evening. I have an early appointment in Durham so I decided it would be easier to just spend the night in town. Are you staying here, too?"

"You know damn well I'm staying here. How you know is beyond me but you know. What do you want? I'm not interested in your games, Julianna."

Julianna smiled...a coy, flirtatious invitation. "You never were. You were always direct, honest, blunt." She trailed her fingernail around her cocktail glass. "I always admired that in you. I still do."

She looked up at him through long lashes.

"What do you want?" He repeated.

"You. I want you back. See? I can be honest and direct, too."

Grant stared at her. Then he burst out laughing. Heads turned in their direction.

"After thirty years you can sit there and say that. Amazing." He shook his head and took a sip of his Scotch. "I walked out on you, Julianna. Do you have any idea why?"

"No, but I can forgive you…though it was probably the most humiliating moment of my life. I always thought you must have gotten cold feet. Maybe you weren't ready. Maybe marriage is an anathema to you…after all, you've never married."

"Marriage is not an anathema to me, Julianna…you are."

Julianna's eyes widened. Her face stiffened.

"I said 'no' to you thirty years ago, Julianna. I'm saying 'no' to you again…now. I want nothing to do with you. Do you understand me?" He took a long look at Julianna. Her face was hard.

She smiled a slow, enigmatic smile. "Oh, I understand…but do you?" She slowly slid from the bar stool and walked from the room.

The bartender appeared before him. "Sorry, Sir."

"Don't be." Grant got out his wallet. "She's poison."

"No, I mean, she didn't pay."

Grant laughed. He placed several bills on the bar. "Don't worry. I got off light."

Chapter Fifteen

Saturday morning Julianna had another tennis match scheduled. The previous night she had driven home from the Washington Duke in a state of agitation and near intoxication. She was furious with Grant Whitworth. Hatred, that dubious twin of love, crept into her emotions. He had refused her again. Memories from thirty years ago had filtered through her brain…her parents stricken faces when she turned from the altar, the way Grant's coat stretched across his back, Sarah's gasp beside her. She felt the debilitating pain of thirty years ago slowly spreading through her. She did not sleep.

Consequently, Julianna's tennis game that morning was not its best. She was distracted.

After play and over lunch Julianna was oddly quiet until Emma mentioned that Grant Whitworth's lady friend was arriving for a few days. Emma gushed about meeting the woman who might actually snare Grant Whitworth.

Anger bubbled within Julianna, stiffening her pride and her determination. She drove home and called Mary Hester Hatcher to find out if anything had happened to Minnie. Julianna was growing impatient.

***

A little after four o'clock the Hatcher doorbell rang. Mildred went to the door. A nice looking young man in khakis and a golf shirt was standing on the stoop. Behind him parked in the street was a man in a late model Mercedes.

"Ms. Hatcher? Mildred Hatcher?" he inquired of her.

"Yes," Mildred hesitantly answered.

"I was asked by Mr. Grant Whitworth to give you these." The attractive young man handed her a set of car keys. "Mr. Whitworth has purchased a car for a friend of his, a Mrs. Harris. She is not at home. He didn't know where to leave the keys. He thought of you as you are her friend and live just down the street. Will you keep them and give them to her when she returns?"

Mildred looked down at the set of car keys. "Yes, of course. Where exactly is the car?"

"It is in her driveway. Thank you so much. I'm sure Mr. Whitworth will be in touch."

The young man turned, walked down the walk to the waiting Mercedes, got into the passenger seat and rode away.

Mildred stood on the stoop, keys in hand, and watched, but not for long. She slammed her front door and ran down her walk to the sidewalk where she could look down the street to the end of the block. The Harris' house was right on the corner. She saw no sign of a car. They must have parked it in the rear. She headed that way at a brisk pace. She came to the end of the block, crossed the street, and walked up the Harris' driveway to the back. There it was. Mildred didn't know one make of car from another but she did recognize a big, beautiful, expensive sedan when she saw it.

Oh, my, she thought. *Minnie, you have done well!*

***

Alice and Minnie ate a late breakfast. They made it clear to Ev and Charlotte that they were not going to stray far today. Ev and Charlotte could do whatever they wanted but Alice and Minnie would be reading on the porch. As the day progressed friends popped in at regular intervals to commiserate and reminisce. Finally about five o'clock they all decided to hide.

Ev Jr. made a big batch of his margaritas and put them in a cooler with cups and ice. They grabbed beach chairs and went down on the beach. It was a golden afternoon.

Eventually Charlotte brought the conversation back to Julianna.

Ev looked at his wife. "Charlotte, you aren't getting obsessed with Aunt Julianna are you?"

"No," Charlotte said. "I just don't like an unfinished story."

"Julianna's story is far from finished," Alice said. "And that might prove worrisome." Alice gazed at the horizon slowly sipping her margarita. Then she turned to her daughter-in-law. "I'll continue the story of Julianna if Minnie says so." Alice looked at Minnie. "You know this is where Grant comes in. Are you okay with that?"

"I am," Minnie said. "He has told me almost everything about their time together. It'll be interesting to hear it from your perspective." She smiled at Alice.

"All right. Let's see. Minnie and I were at St. Mary's...the college...but we often went to fraternity parties at Chapel Hill. They had good bands. Minnie was dating Carter and he would find me a date and off we would go. Minnie and Carter introduced me to Julianna at one of those fraternity parties. I thought she was so beautiful." Alice laughed. "Later that evening I was looking for my date. I think he passed out somewhere in a bush. I never did find him. Julianna saw me and when she found I was alone she called this handsome man over and said, "Everett you have to be this pretty young girl's knight in shining armor. Her date has disappeared and she is alone." Alice smiled at the recollection. "And the rest is history. It was my Everett."

"So I've watched Julianna from the angle of an insider...the family angle. Everett and I were dating when Grant asked Julianna to marry him. Grant was at Wharton then. It was Julianna's last year at the University. I was at Merrebanks during Christmas holidays when Grant gave her the engagement ring. It was a beautiful ring in an exquisite antique setting. I think it was his grandmother's. Julianna obviously expected it to be much larger. The ring was probably his first inkling that Julianna might not be what she seemed…or what he thought she was.

"Then in February, on Valentine's Day, Ophelia and Linus hosted a huge engagement party for Julianna and Grant. It was something else. I think everyone in the county was invited. It was black tie. Julianna wore a red satin dress. When I told my mother about the dress she nearly fainted…not exactly virginal…even if it was Valentine's Day…but Julianna looked absolutely beautiful…and Grant in a tuxedo was not a bad sight either. You remember, Minnie? You and Carter were there. Y'all were married by then.

"The wedding was scheduled for June. Grant went back to Philadelphia. Julianna went back to Chapel Hill. Miss Phe and Naomi Ruth went to work. They were in charge of the wedding and it was going to be a large affair. You know how eastern North Carolina loves a wedding…and a funeral," she added.

"There is a saying, 'Absence makes the heart grow fonder.' My crazy Aunt Eloise used to always add 'for somebody else' at the end. Maybe Aunt Eloise wasn't so crazy after all because I suspect that is what happened with Julianna. She had to have an adoring male at her beck and call. Grant was far away so she needed a substitute. Whenever I saw her in Chapel Hill she never had on her engagement ring and some handsome, well-dressed male was hovering. "Julianna graduated in May. She came home to enjoy all the attention and all the parties of a bride-to-be. Miss Phe and 'Omi had everything organized. There was one hitch Everett told me about, though. Julianna wanted to wear Miss Phe's wedding dress but Ophelia said 'no.' I guess it was because it was white and Ophelia knew Julianna didn't belong in a white dress…remember poor Jake. Anyway, Julianna pouted and plead but Ophelia held firm.

"The wedding was to be held at St. Andrews at high noon with the reception following at Merrebanks. The wedding party was movie star good-looking, all of them. Everyone was not only gorgeous but also fun loving, especially Grant's roommate from Wharton. I even remember his name…Smythe Hughes. He had rugged good looks and a devil may care attitude that was irresistible. All the bridesmaids were chasing him and if Everett hadn't been in my life I might have been right there with them. His personality charmed everyone. No one was immune, even Ophelia. He was a mess." Alice laughed, recalling.

"The day of the wedding was glorious. Not a cloud in the sky and not the usual stifling hot June day. My family came but Everett wanted me to sit with his family. Therefore, when Grant came out with the minister and his father, who was his best man, I had a very good view of him. I thought he looked very pale, odd really. He looked like his face was chiseled from alabaster. It wasn't the look of a man about to marry but I just thought he was hungover. The rehearsal party was a huge affair the night before that lasted well into the night.

"Then the wedding march began and Julianna glided down the aisle on Big Linus' arm…in an ecru dress, I might add. I have never seen a more beautiful bride. The service followed its normal course until the priest asked Grant if he took this woman to be his lawfully wedded wife. There was a long pause…a very long pause. People started rustling in their seats. I saw Ophelia and Linus look at each other. Finally, Grant said, 'no.' It was said quietly, distinctly and firmly. He turned from Julianna and walked out of the church."

***

Back in Hope Springs about the same time Charlotte, Ev Jr., Alice and Minnie were settling on the beach at Nags Head, Mildred was greeting her sisters. "Do not sit down," she said. "We are going on a field trip."

"But I have news," Mary Hester said.

"It can wait. Come on." Mildred was out the door.

They followed her to the end of the block, then across the street to the Harris'. They followed her up the driveway to the rear. Then they stopped. There was the car.

"Mercy," Mary Hester said.

"Lordy pie," Athie said.

They moved closer and just stared. Then they looked at Mildred. "Where did this come from?" Mary Hester asked.

"Grant Whitworth," Mildred answered.

"Oh, my," Athie was circling the car, looking in the windows.

"About an hour ago this nice young man rang the doorbell," Mildred explained. "He said Grant Whitworth had purchased a car for his friend who was out of town and would I give her the keys when she returned. Then he gave me the keys and left."

"Too bad we can't take it for a spin."

"Wait till Julianna hears about this!"

"Speaking of Julianna," Mary Hester chimed in. "She called me today."

Chapter Sixteen

Sunday morning dawned as another beautiful beach day. After a leisurely breakfast on the porch Alice and Minnie decided to take a walk on the beach. They strolled at a leisurely pace, walking barefoot and enjoying the cool salt water washing over their feet.

"I hope to goodness Charlotte's curiosity about Julianna hasn't driven you crazy," Alice said to Minnie. "I'm beginning to think Ev is right. She's obsessed!" Alice laughed.

"It doesn't bother me. I hate it for Grant and what he went through. I don't believe you and I have ever talked about that wedding," Minnie said. "It was a long time ago but I remember it well. Who could forget? What I remember most is the absolute quiet as Grant walked out of the church. He did not look to the right or left. He stared straight ahead, icy calm and remote."

They walked in silence, remembering.

"Then Julianna screamed and collapsed. The minister just stood there looking down at her. No one moved. It was as if we had all turned to stone. Everyone just stood in shocked silence. I think Naomi Ruth was the first to move toward Julianna. The wedding guests just turned and filed slowly out of the church. It's awful to say," Minnie looked at Alice, "but I always wondered what happened to all that food back at the house? And all those flowers? Did you go back to the house with Everett?"

"Yes," Alice answered. "I tried to stay out of the way, though.

Everett kept saying, 'Damn, damn, damn.' They brought Julianna back to the house and up to her room. They had to give her something to calm her down. The rest of the wedding party just roamed around eating the food and drinking the liquor and whispering in corners. I don't remember if anyone from town had the nerve to show up. I found Sarah and we found a bottle of champagne...or two. We sat together and drank and wondered out loud what in the world had happened. It was awful and thrilling at the same time, I hate to admit.

"It's funny how it all went away. It was so horrible and so embarrassing people didn't want to talk about it. They sent Julianna off for a 'rest cure,' as Eggie called it. Everyone looked the other way when they were around a Garrett. Julianna wasn't mentioned.

"I have always wanted to know what happened," Alice said. "Don't you?"

"No, not anymore," Minnie answered.

"You don't?" Alice looked at Minnie with surprise in her voice. "Why not?"

"Because I know."

***

Naomi Ruth, Robert and Ophelia attended the Weeping Mary Church that Sunday. Ophelia did not want to endure the expressions of concern everyone felt compelled to heap on her at St. Andrew's. Nor could she abide the undercurrent of curiosity about Julianna, Minnie and Grant Whitworth. The Weeping Mary Church was so much more peaceful, even if the service was considerably longer. They visited with church members after the service, finally making their way back to Ophelia's big black Cadillac.

On the way home to Merrebanks Ophelia, seated on the backseat, announced, "When it is my turn to journey to the great beyond I want to be sent off from the Weeping Mary Church."

"Hope you're not planning on leaving any time soon," Robert said over his shoulder as he drove slowly along.

"No time soon. I'm tired of funerals. But you know what they say, 'What happens twice, happens thrice.'"

"Hush, Ophelia," Naomi Ruth said. "Don't even think it."

***

"What's the latest with the Garretts?" Erwin asked, fork piled high with mashed potatoes. The Hatchers, with the exception of Athie who was at the church feeding the bishop, were at their regular table at the country club for the Sunday buffet. "I saw Julianna riding around in that sporty red BMW of hers last week. I was measuring a house over by the church and she drove by."

Mary Hester looked up from her plate. There was a speculative look on her face. "What day was that, Erwin?"

"Let's see," Erwin paused in thought, his fork again hovering over the mashed potatoes, "must have been last Thursday. Yep, that's right. I was hurrying because of Rotary. We met that day." Erwin nodded, quite pleased with his ability to recall. He returned to the business at hand...his lunch.

Mary Hester continued to stare at Erwin.

"What about that new friend of Minnie's? The one that almost married Julianna about thirty years ago. If that don't beat all, him turning up like this." Joe Allen pulled his pecan pie toward him. "Buster at the Shell station told me he was here for a while, staying at The Holiday Inn but spending most of his time at the Harris'. Buster liked his car. He must have made a ton of money since walking out on Julianna."

"He's gone home." Mary Hester hoped that ended it. The less men knew the better. Just give them a television remote control and tell them to hush was Mary Hester's theory of male participation.

"I would imagine Julianna isn't pleased a bit with his

reappearance," Bessie looked at her daughters. "I wish I knew what happened thirty years ago. That's a long time to keep a secret in this town." Bessie finished her second piece of coconut cream pie.

***

Alice stopped. She turned to Minnie, who had taken a few more steps. "You do?" Alice asked, then added, "Grant told you?"

"Yes," Minnie answered. "Grant told me." She resumed walking.

Alice caught up with her. Minnie quietly began to explain. "When Grant and I first met it was the oddest experience. Of course I knew who he was. He laughed out loud when I told him where I was from. We just started talking and talking to each other. You know I'm not a 'talker'...and neither is Grant...but for some reason...some comfortable reason...we could share. It drove Martha Jane crazy. When Grant and I sat or stood together talking for long periods of time she was a nervous Nellie. She kept reminding me I was a married woman."

Minnie laughed at the memory then continued in her soft voice, "I met Grant about a year ago when I went up to Grandfather Golf and Country Club to visit Martha Jane and Brad. The member-member golf tournament was scheduled the first weekend I was there. Brad was playing so we went to all the social events. Friday night there was a picnic on the beach by the lake. Brad and Grant were in the same foursome that day so Brad introduced us. That's when we started talking, and kept on talking until Martha Jane came and got me. The same thing happened the next night at the dinner dance. We were all seated together but as far as Grant and I were concerned we were the only ones at the table. Martha Jane about had a hissy fit.

"That was the beginning. Martha Jane never knew we were dating till she came to Hope Springs when I called her about Carter. She was floored...about both things."

"So...in all this talking Grant told you why he walked out on his wedding day?" Alice had to ask.

"I told him about Carter and he told me about Julianna," Minnie replied.

"And are you going to tell me?" Alice stopped walking and looked at Minnie.

"Yes," Minnie laughed. "I know you. You're dying of curiosity. I also know you won't tell anyone else. You are the most trustworthy friend I have ever had."

"I cannot believe you have not told me before now," Alice muttered.

"It's not a long story. It basically confirms what you told last night. Grant began getting nervous about Julianna after her reaction to his grandmother's ring. Then he started getting reports from his fraternity brothers of her dating. He had gotten an anonymous letter about the speeding incident in college where the young man was killed but Grant just thought that was youthful bad luck. Oddly enough he knew nothing of Jake Denton. I told him about that.

"But Grant loved Julianna, or thought he did. He told me he was totally infatuated with her. He could not accept that she was not who he thought she was.

"The wedding weekend arrived. He and his family stayed with Eggie out at Mayfield. Everything was going smoothly; everyone was having a great time. Ophelia and Naomi planned it beautifully. The rehearsal dinner at Merrebanks was elegant. The tent was like a fairyland with it's tulle and white lights and elegant arrangements of orchids, lilies, hydrangea. Remember? The band set up and started playing and the dancing began. Of course, the drinking had been going on for quite a while. There was a lot more drinking that night apparently."

Alice nodded her head. "Yes, there certainly was." She laughed at the memory.

Minnie smiled and continued. "Julianna was beautiful. She had on a silver chiffon gown. I remember it well. It was exquisite. She looked like a Greek goddess. Carter and I stayed for a while but went home early since I was pregnant. So I don't remember much about the party. You know lots more about it than I do. I heard it went on into the wee hours."

Alice nodded.

"Well, about midnight Grant said Julianna came to him and said she was going to bed. She didn't want circles under her eyes on her wedding day. He kissed her good night and she went back to the house.

"He stayed a while longer and then decided he had best go back to Eggie's. He didn't want to have a hangover on his wedding day. Before he went he decided to sneak into the house and use Linus' and Everett's bathroom. He was washing his hands when he glanced out the window and saw Julianna walking through the boxwood hedges towards the back gate.

"He was surprised. He went back downstairs with the intention of following her. A group of friends was standing in the hall and he was unable to break away. When he finally did he went through the library and out the French doors but standing on the patio looking towards the boxwoods he could see no sign of Julianna. He went down the walk to the gate and looked right and left. About fifty feet to the left was Miss Phe's art shed. He could see a dim light through the side window. Curious he moved to the window and looked in. There were Julianna and Smythe Hughes. You can guess what they were doing."

"What?" Alice exclaimed. She stopped walking. Her hands flew to her cheeks. "Are you telling me Julianna and Smythe were doing the dirty deed when she was going to marry Grant the next day?"

"Yes, they were screwing on the floor of Miss Phe's art shed."

"Oh, my goodness! Oh, my goodness!" Alice repeated in shock. "What did Grant do?"

"Grant said he felt like the world stopped. He turned away. They never saw him. He can't remember much about getting home. One of those black funeral home cars Big Linus hired to drive everyone back and forth took him back to Eggie's. He went up to his room, locked the door and sat in the dark till dawn trying to decide what to do. He finally figured the best thing to do was go through with the wedding and then get a divorce. Everyone had gone to so much trouble and he did not want to embarrass Julianna's family or his."

"What changed his mind? Since that is definitely not what happened." Alice asked.

"Grant said that when the priest asked that question and he looked into Julianna's eyes he just knew he could not marry her. He said it was like standing on a precipice staring into a big black hole. He turned toward the light of the open doors and walked out."

***

The Hatcher sisters had no idea what time Minnie would return home from Nags Head so they took no chance they would miss her. They situated themselves at their mother's and kept a watchful eye down the block. About four-thirty they saw Ev Jr's Tahoe pass the house. They ran out the door and stopped at the sidewalk. They saw Ev turn into Minnie's drive and stop.

Normally he would drive to the back so Minnie could go in through her kitchen door. The sisters knew they had seen the Mercedes. The sisters set out with all speed for the Harris'.

Ev Jr. abruptly stopped the Tahoe. "Wow! Minnie, look what's parked in your driveway."

The girls had been talking. They stopped and stared. "Is that a Mercedes?" Charlotte asked.

"That is the biggest, most beautiful car I have ever seen," Alice said.

"What is it doing in my driveway?" Minnie asked.

As the four climbed from the Tahoe the Hatcher sisters came flying up the drive. "Yoo-hoo! Yoo-hoo! Minnie, can you believe it?"

Minnie turned. "Believe what, Athie? Do y'all know where this car came from?"

"Grant sent it. It's yours! Here are the keys." Mildred waved the keys in the air.

***

After the excitement at Minnie's and getting Alice home Ev and Charlotte unlocked the door to their house a little before six o'clock. "We have a message from Gran," Ev announced. "She would like us to come for supper tonight. I think she wants to know about the weekend."

"Happy days for me," Charlotte answered. "Naomi Ruth's food is manna from heaven! Hope she has biscuits!"

"Thought you were going on a diet," Ev needled.

"Tomorrow."

***

Ophelia did indeed want to know how the weekend had gone. Ev and Charlotte related the events of the weekend while they enjoyed supper. Ophelia was relieved to hear they had enjoyed a relaxing time without any emotional lapses. All the visitors Saturday had been upbeat and supportive. Alice and Ev had cleaned out some of Everett's things without completely falling apart so Charlotte thought the weekend was a success.

"And Gran, I've got to tell you," Ev turned to his grandmother, "a lot of our conversation was about Aunt Julianna. Charlotte thought that by talking about Aunt Julianna she could get Alice and Minnie distracted from their problems. It seemed to work."

"I'm sure you had plenty to talk about if Julianna was the topic," Naomi Ruth said.

"Probably more than you bargained for," Robert agreed.

"I must admit I was surprised by some things I learned," Ev admitted.

"And I was totally amazed," Charlotte said, "because I knew nothing."

"What surprised you the most, Charlotte, if I might ask?" Ophelia glanced at her granddaughter-in-law.

"I hope I don't get myself into trouble here." Charlotte looked at Ev then Ophelia and Naomi Ruth. "I learned Aunt Julianna is not the person I thought she was."

Ophelia and Naomi Ruth looked at eachs other in surprise.

Charlotte continued. "I have always thought Aunt Julianna was different. She's not like the rest of the Garretts. She doesn't have that down to earth quality that is so endearing. She's what my grandmother used to call 'high fallutin'.' She's aloof…like she's better than anyone else. She seems so sure of herself but she has made some wretched choices in her life…hurtful choices…for others." She paused, looking around at everyone, "I hope I haven't over spoken."

"Not a bit, child," Ophelia assured her. "You are quite perceptive." She smiled at Charlotte.

"And quite right," Naomi Ruth added.

"Charlotte, I would very much like to continue this conversation, just not tonight. It's been a long day and I'm a little tired." Ophelia glanced at Charlotte. "I also need your help with a painting I'm doing. The perspective is off."

"Of course, Phe," Charlotte answered. "Would tomorrow suit? I could come about two-thirty? I have an art class right after lunch."

"Perfect," agreed Ophelia. "Also pencil in Thursday night for cocktails here and perhaps dinner. Mae Rose's beau is coming to town and we are entertaining him."

"So we heard. We can't wait to meet him," Ev said. "Think they are a little old for courting but whatever."

Ev and Charlotte rose to leave. "Oh, by the way Gran, when we got to Minnie's house today there was a big Mercedes parked in her drive. Grant bought it for her. What do you think Aunt Julianna will do when she sees that?"

"I shudder to think," Ophelia laughed.

Chapter Seventeen

Minnie called Alice early the next morning to thank her for the beach weekend and to let her know she was joining Grant that afternoon in Durham. She would not stay long because she had so much to do here in Hope Springs. She needed to get her life in some kind of order. Minnie would call Alice when she returned. They would have lunch and talk.

***

Sam Jenkins joined Ophelia for breakfast. He had an applicant for the farm manager position he wanted her to meet. Could he bring him by tomorrow morning at nine? Sam told Ophelia he was quite impressed with the young man but wanted to be sure she liked him and thought she could work with him. His name was Ward Covington.

***

Mary Hester, Athie and Mildred met for lunch at Slater's Drugstore. It was a Hope Springs landmark and luncheon tradition. You could get a fountain drink, a grilled cheese or pimento cheese sandwich, a hot dog all-the-way or a chicken or egg salad sandwich. You always saw half the town while you were there. As it was past one o'clock the sisters were able to get one of the three booths available. While Mary Hester ate her chicken salad sandwich, and Athie ate her grilled pimento cheese sandwich, and Mildred ate her hot dog, all accompanied by potato chips and a pickle, they discussed the problem Athie brought up. Athie thought Minnie's accident was no accident.

"I am convinced Julianna is behind this." Athie ate a potato chip. "Erwin saw her near the church Thursday. While Minnie was cooking for the Bishop Julianna could have fiddled with her car some way." Mary Hester had told her sister what Erwin said at the Sunday buffet.

"The telephone call pretty much seals it, as far as I'm concerned," Mary Hester agreed. "Why else would she call out of the blue and ask about Minnie?"

"Well, how are we going to find out for certain?" Mildred took a bite of her hot dog. Chili ran down her chin.

"As much as I hate it I think we are going to have to ask a husband for help," Mary Hester said after a bite of her chicken salad sandwich. "They were mighty skimpy on the mayonnaise today," she observed while inspecting the halves of her sandwich. "Men know more about cars," she added.

"You're probably right, Mary Hester," Mildred agreed putting down her hot dog and taking a sip of Pepsi.

"Let's ask Joe Allen. He's in the insurance business so he ought to know about wrecks," Athie said.

Quickly finishing with lunch the sisters trotted down Main Street to Joe Allen's insurance office. They waved at the secretary and blew into Joe Allen's office.

Surprised, he looked up. "To what in the world do I owe this delightful visit from the three of you?"

"Joe Allen, you know what I told you," Athie said. "We all think Julianna is behind Minnie's accident."

"And you know what I told you, Athie. You girls have too much time on your hands," Joe Allen responded.

Mildred sighed. "Joe Allen, for your peace of mind...and ours... will you help us find out whether you are right or we are right?"

Joe Allen was not a dumb man. He had been married to Athie for thirty years and he knew her bulldog nature. She was not going to let this go. Compound her nagging with her sisters' and he knew he was a beaten man.

"What do you want me to do?" He sighed.

Immediately the sisters sat down in the chairs around his desk, hemming him in. "Find the tow truck," Mary Hester said.

"Find the lot where the car is," Athie said.

"Check out the car," said Mildred.

***

Charlotte arrived at Merrebanks promptly at two-thirty that afternoon. She came through the back door into an empty kitchen. She walked towards the sunroom. She found Ophelia there needle-pointing.

"I didn't hear you come in," Ophelia said. "I guess my ears are getting as bad as my eyes," she laughed. "I'm surprised Maize didn't hear you." She looked down at the Labrador at her feet.

Charlotte took the seat across from her. "Where are Naomi Ruth and Robert?" she asked.

"They've gone over to Ahoskie to visit Robert's sister. They will probably be back before you leave."

Charlotte nodded.

"I'm glad we can resume our conversation," Ophelia said. "One forgets that young members of the family might not know everything they need to know about the older members. That includes Ev though I have found that men are not as naturally curious about things as we women." She smiled at Charlotte.

"I hope you don't think I'm being a busybody, Phe. There was talk about Aunt Julianna and her past at bridge the other night. I was playing with Celeste Redborne. You might not have met her. She and her husband just moved here from Birmingham, Alabama. Her family is originally from here but I've forgotten the connection.

"Yes, dear, I know exactly who she is. She's Arthur Taylor's sister's grandchild."

"Well, then you probably remember that her mother was a suite mate of Aunt Julianna's at St. Mary's High School in the early sixties."

Ophelia nodded.

"Celeste mentioned Aunt Julianna sneaking out all the time to meet some boy from her hometown. I asked Minnie and Alice about that because I just could not picture Aunt Julianna doing something like that. Minnie then told us all about Jake Denton and how he and Aunt Julianna eloped after graduation but Big Linus had the marriage annulled. Then he had Jake drafted. Jake was killed in Vietnam and Aunt Julianna had his baby aborted."

Ophelia nodded again. The pain of the past was reflected in her eyes.

"Then Aunt Julianna went to a college in South Carolina for two years. Minnie told us that Julianna had an accident her sophomore year that killed a young man. Big Linus hushed everything up and Julianna went on to Chapel Hill. That's where she met Grant Whitworth."

Charlotte paused. "It seems that a lot of bad things have happened to, or around, Aunt Julianna. I knew nothing about Aunt Julianna and Jake Denton. Basically, what I know about her I have learned while married to Ev. Ev knows very little, himself. Honestly, though, everybody has a past but usually it stays past. What's so surprising is the return of Grant Whitworth…back to Hope Springs… and the 'past' is the 'present.' It's strange and disturbing, I'm sure, for those who remember what happened when he was here last time."

Charlotte paused to look at Ophelia. "That must have been a difficult time for the family…and you."

Ophelia nodded.

Charlotte continued. "I know things *about* Aunt Julianna but I really don't know her. I never met her first husband, Gilbert Thomas…actually second husband, I guess. I know he was the father of Meggie and Bingo and that he was killed in a car accident. Then, of course, I know about poor John and the financial ruckus that caused him to take his own life. Julianna and John were married when Ev and I started dating. We had been married about a year, I think, when he killed himself.

"Minnie and Alice didn't talk much about Aunt Julianna's husbands. They talked primarily about Jake and then, of course, Grant Whitworth. He was the biggest surprise. He's so rich and famous."

Charlotte cocked her head in thought then looked at Ophelia. "Phe, do you know why Grant Whitworth walked out on Aunt Julianna on their wedding day?"

"No, dear, I don't." Ophelia was watching Charlotte.

"Aunt Julianna always talks about herself but never about her past. She has a rather superior sense of self-worth and entitlement because she is a Garrett but I have always gotten along with her. I just agree with everything she says and never criticize her about anything."

Ophelia laughed. "That, my dear, is a very good way to deal with Julianna."

The two women sat in silence for a few minutes until Charlotte asked, "Do you think Aunt Julianna can handle Grant's return?"

Ophelia looked steadily at her grandson's wife then turned her head and looked out the window. She was quiet for a few seconds then turned back to Charlotte. "No, I do not.

"Life around Julianna has often been unsettling. As a child she created problems that her brothers took the blame for…or covered for…they loved her so. She had an angelic way about her that made you think she could not possibly be the cause of any trouble. She would look at you with those big, innocent green eyes. Remember, too, she was the only girl, spoiled and catered to constantly by the Garrett men. She just sailed through any agitation unscathed. Linus saw no fault in her. He laughed at me and Naomi Ruth when we suggested he look more closely at her. I begged Linus not to interfere when she ran off with Jake Denton. I thought marriage to Jake...an introduction to the real world...would be good for her. And I truly hoped Julianna cared for Jake. Linus couldn't stand the thought of her living in a trailer on a farm. He wanted more for her." Ophelia paused and glanced down at Maize asleep on the floor.

"Linus removed Jake by having him drafted. I suspect Julianna asked Linus for help. I know she asked her father to buy them a house in town. To Jake Denton's credit he refused the offer. She was not at all thrilled with the life she realized was ahead of her married to Jake.

"Julianna likes the excitement of a situation...the *extraordinary*. Ordinary things bore her. Julianna also likes the finer things in life...as you said, 'high fallutin'.'" She paused again."Linus never knew Julianna was pregnant. I did. I asked her what she wanted to do about the baby. She knew I was bitterly opposed to abortion so she promised me she would have the baby then put it up for adoption. She had it aborted when Linus and I were out of town the next weekend.

"We were relieved when she showed an interest in drama while at the college in South Carolina. She was really quite good. We thought she had found herself. Wishful thinking, I guess." She sighed. "Then the accident happened. Linus paid a great deal of money to that young man's family to keep them from sending Julianna to jail. He always covered for her. A very bad mistake.

"At Chapel Hill she met Grant. She brought him home over Thanksgiving to meet us. We were charmed by him. He was from a nice family; he was very intelligent; he had goals in life; and he had a calming influence on Julianna. As parents we could not ask for anything more. When they became engaged we were very pleased.

"You know the rest. In fact, you know as much as I do as to why he walked out on her. I will tell you this, though...the next day Grant called Everett to ask if he might speak with Linus and me. Everett arranged it. We went over to Eggie's. Grant apologized to us for any harm he had done but something had happened...and he refused to tell us what...that made him realize more harm would be done by marrying Julianna than by not marrying her. Linus was furious.

"He actually threatened Grant. Grant turned to him...this I shall never forget...and said, 'Mr. Garrett, I loved your daughter, in some ways I still do. She's beautiful, tantalizing...like a flame to a moth. Julianna has a core of destruction that goes beyond mischief...a self-absorbed indifference born to hurt. You need to recognize this.' Then Grant turned and walked out of the room. We never saw or heard from him again. Until now."

Ophelia and Charlotte sat in silence.

"So nobody actually knows what happened," Charlotte said, "except Grant."

"I honestly have no idea," Ophelia said. "I just know I don't. On his deathbed Linus wondered about it."

"Maybe Grant will tell Minnie," Charlotte speculated.

"Well, if he does and you learn what it was please come and tell me. Now, speaking of Minnie and Grant, Ev said last night that Grant has given her a big new Mercedes. I know Minnie is thrilled with that."

"She had to have something after the wreck. A Mercedes is a nice replacement."

"Wreck?" Ophelia looked puzzled. "Minnie had a wreck?"

"Oh, I'm sorry. I thought you knew. Yes, last Thursday afternoon. That's why Grant sent her the Mercedes. Minnie was coming back from Newtons Fork and her tire blew. She's lucky no cars were coming in the other direction. She spun around a few times and ended up in the ditch on the other side of the road."

Suddenly, Maize raised her head. Then she rose and trotted out of the room.

"Naomi Ruth and Robert must be back," Ophelia said. She pushed up from her chair. "Come with me."

Charlotte followed her into the kitchen. Naomi Ruth and Robert were just entering. "Did y'all know Minnie Harris had a wreck last week?" Ophelia asked.

Both Robert and Naomi Ruth stopped and turned to her. "No," Naomi Ruth answered.

"Yes, her tire blew...Thursday...the day Julianna left," Ophelia added.

"And I couldn't find my hammer and jar of nails," Robert said.

The only sound in the kitchen was Maize lapping up water.

***

"All right," Joe Allen sighed. "Let's get this ball rolling so you girls will go away and I can get back to business. First, we, and I say 'we' because you three are not going to dump all this on me. It's your little red wagon, as far as I am concerned. Got it?"

The sisters Hatcher rolled their collective eyes. "Yes, Joe Allen, we 'got it'" Mary Hester said.

"Why, of course we want to help you, Joe Allen," said Mildred too sweetly.

"Oh, honestly, Joe Allen, just get on with it," said Athie.

"Just so we understand each other." Joe Allen looked at each of the sisters. "Now, first we must find the truck that towed Minnie's car back to Hope Springs. Then we must find the lot where he took the car and then we must go to that lot and inspect the car. That's the plan."

"First I am going to call the Highway Patrol and ask if the officer who answered the call knows which towing service it was. If that doesn't work we will call AAA." Joe Allen had his plan.

"Why don't you just look in the yellow pages," Athie asked. "There can't be that many towing services around here."

Joe Allen looked at his wife. "If you already know what to do why bother me?"

"Do it your way, Joe Allen," Mildred said. "Athie, you hush up."

Athie shrugged, got up and left the room.

Joe Allen dialed the Highway Patrol. The investigating officer was out on patrol. He then called AAA. After being put on hold for several minutes Joe Allen made his inquiries and began to write on his tablet.

As he finished thanking the lady Athie reappeared in the door of his office. She had a piece of paper in her hand. She looked at her husband and said, "Peck's Towing Service. He has a lovely advertisement in the yellow pages. His business is right outside of town. I have the address. I have talked with Mr. Peck and he is expecting us. Let's go!"

***

"You don't by any chance know where Minnie's wrecked car is, do you, Charlotte?" Naomi Ruth asked after brief glances between Robert, Ophelia and herself. Charlotte was observant and didn't miss the exchange.

"Actually I do," Charlotte answered her. "Minnie had us in hysterics at the beach with the story she told about her ride home in the tow truck. I never realized Minnie had such a sense of humor. Peck's Towing Service. "

"Isaiah Ipock Peck," Robert said. "He's a member of our church. We just talked with him Sunday, Phe. He's got a happy spirit."

"And a very unusual way with words," Naomi Ruth laughed.

"His business is just outside of town," Robert nodded and continued.

"Should we go see him and ask about the car?" Ophelia looked at Robert.

"Probably. At least it might put your minds at rest."

"No time like the present," Charlotte glanced at the three faces before her.

"I'll get the car." Robert headed out the back door.

***

Mary Hester, Athie and Mildred piled into Joe Allen's car and set off. They had gone only one block and were stopped at a red light when Athie, in the passenger side of the front seat, said, "I have an idea."

"Well, alert the press!" Joe Allen sarcastically exclaimed.

"No, seriously," Athie continued. "Drive by Mother's and pick up Hector. He's there this afternoon helping Clara move rugs. He knows all about cars."

"How does he know all about cars when he only rides a bicycle?" Joe Allen dripped sarcasm.

The light changed. Joe Allen stepped on the gas and headed in the direction of Bessie Hatcher's house. He might argue but he obeyed.

Athie ran into the house and emerged shortly thereafter followed by a bewildered Hector, hat in hand.

"You ride shotgun, Hector. I'll get back here with my sisters. We're on a mission."

"Oh, Lord," Hector said as he slid into the front seat. "Not again," he said as he looked back at the faces of the sisters. "I gotta guess this has somethin' to do with the Harris'. I told y'all I do not want any part of y'all's shenanigans."

"Too late," Joe Allen said and grinned. "Our goose is cooked." Off they sped.

"More like a wild goose chase. Where we going?"

"Peck's Towing Service. Outside of town."

"What y'all want with Brother Ipock?"

"You know him?"

"He's in my church...Weeping Mary."

"He towed Minnie's car after her wreck last Thursday."

"Minnie wrecked?" Hector shook his head. "That little lady has had a tough time lately. Except from the looks of things that's about to change. That new car of hers is definitely saying something."

"We're more interested in what happened to the old one."

"Stirring the pot. What I tell y'all about stirring up trouble?"

***

Joe Allen drove his car slowly up the dirt road toward a steel frame building surrounded by cars in various stages of decomposition. He stopped in front of the open garage doors. Strains of gospel music drifted through the air. The dust had barely settled when a very round man appeared in the door. He squinted their way and began to wipe grease from his hands with an oil soaked cloth. He made his way towards them with a swaying gait that reminded Joe Allen of a sea buoy.

"A lovely afternoon to you. You must be the Hatchers. I am Isaiah Ipock Peck." About that time Hector popped up from the passenger side of the car. "Yo, Brother Ipock."

"Well, truth to tell, if it ain't Brother Hector. Always a de-light!" Ipock beamed at Hector over the roof of the car.

"You might change your mind when these ladies finish pestering you with their questions," Hector said.

"I 'spec I know what they want. Little Miss Minnie's car is very popular. Y'all ain't the first asking questions about it."

The sisters had gotten out of the back seat and were standing beside Joe Allen listening to the exchange between Ipock and

Hector. Their ears pricked up.

"What kind of questions?" Athie asked.

"Same ones you gonna ask. You want to see Miss Minnie's car, too? She's a fine little lady. Knows her gospel music, too. I tell you Brother Hector, she's got a fine voice, fine voice." Ipock Peck started leading them toward a fenced in area.

They were at the gate when Hector pointed, "Who's that?"

Coming down the road was a big black car swirling up a cloud of dust as it approached. "Don't know," Ipock said as he too watched the approaching car. "Not expecting nobody else."

The car came to a stop beside Joe Allen's, dust enveloping it.

"Why, it's Miss Phe with Naomi Ruth, Robert and Charlotte. But, who is that other person?"

"Damn, Mary Hester, you need to get your eyes checked. That's Maize!" Athie answered her sister.

They watched as Robert helped Ophelia from the passenger seat. Charlotte put Maize on her leash and she, Maize and Naomi Ruth slid from the back of the car. They all walked toward the group by the gate.

Ipock welcomed Ophelia profusely, having just visited with her after the service Sunday at the Weeping Mary Church. He was totally surprised, however, when she too asked to view Minnie's car.

If the Garrett clan was surprised to find the Hatcher's on the same quest, they cordially ignored it. Hope Springs was a small town. Everyone, except Ipock Peck, knew why everyone was there.

Ipock Peck turned towards the gate. Hector stopped him. "Brother Ipock, best tell these folks what you told us about the popularity of Miss Minnie's car."

"Oh, yes. Of course, indeedy." He turned to Ophelia. "I had a telephone call Friday 'bout lunchtime from a Mr. Worth-somethin'. I'm not too good with names, no sir-ee! Wrote it down inside somewhere. This Mr. Worth told me he was a friend of Miss Minnie and he would like me to hold on to her car…all of it…tires, lose parts, every nut and bolt…until he could come look at it. But in the meantime he was sending somebody over on Saturday…the man did show up…to take pictures of the car. I told him that was okey-dokey. He sounded nice. He didn't tell me why he was doing this. I'm a might curious, I must say. All y'all showing up just makes me curiouser! Is that dog gonna sniff out something?" He looked at Maize who was patiently sitting and watching him.

The Hatcher group didn't know what to say. There stood Miss Phe and they were here because they suspected her daughter of doing something to Minnie's car. Apparently Grant suspected Julianna, too.

Ophelia broke the silence. "Mr. Peck, we are all here, I'm sure, because we don't think Minnie's accident was an accident." Hector and Ipock Peck looked at Ophelia in surprise. The sisters looked at the ground. Joe Allen looked at Athie. Naomi Ruth, Robert and Charlotte knew what Ophelia knew. Maize walked over and sniffed Ipock Peck.

"We would very much like to look at Minnie's car for clues as to what happened," Ophelia continued. "I don't know a thing about cars so I will rely on Robert and you…and I am so glad Hector is here, because I have always heard he is the best at finding a rattle." She smiled at Hector. "And obviously the Hatchers and Grant Whitworth are worried, too."

"So, lead on, Brother Ipock, lead on," Naomi Ruth said.

The car had definitely been in a wreck. The driver's side was badly dented and scratched. One of the headlights was cracked. The front windshield was shattered. One tire was shredded. Grass was still under the chassis. Everyone just circled the car. There wasn't much conversation. Eventually everyone but Ipock Peck, Robert and Hector went back to their cars. Joe Allen said he had to get back to work. Athie, Mary Hester and Mildred rode back with him. Charlotte drove Ophelia, Naomi Ruth and Maize home in the big black

Cadillac. She felt like she was driving a floating tank but she got them there. She could not wait to tell Ev about her afternoon.

After everyone drove away Ipock Peck walked over to a metal cabinet and took out what appeared to be a piece of rubber tire. "Want to show y'all this here. Didn't see no need to show it to everybody. What you think?" Robert and Hector looked at the strip of tire with nails hanging from it and then at each other.

"Maybe you best put that back in the cabinet. Save it for Mr. Grant Whitworth. Know what I mean?" Robert said.

The three men looked at each other. Ipock nodded and took the tire piece back to his cabinet. "We'll sit a spell then I'll drive y'all home," Ipock said. "What y'all gonna say we think? Hector, those sisters ain't gonna give you no rest…no, siree. Robert, what you gonna tell Miss Ophelia?"

"I'll tell her the truth. Always have. I think she suspects something or someone. Whether the actual accident was an accident seems immaterial. The intent was there. I know who it must have been 'cause a hammer and a jar of nails went missing from my tool kit. That's more than likely my nails…and they didn't line up nice and straight on the road by themselves. They were hammered into Miss Minnie's tire."

Hector looked at Robert. "I ain't about to tell my girls 'bout them nails" He shook his head. "This is fuel for the fire. They too busy stirring the pot, as it is."

"Yep," Ipock agreed. "We can hypostulate on if it was an accident. Can't know for sure. They're old tires. Could have just blown when Miss Minnie depressed the brakes…'cause of the heat…except for them five nails all in a pretty little row." He slowly shook his head from side to side. "Seems to me somebody wishes Miss Minnie ill will. Yes, indeedy."

He looked carefully at Robert and Hector.

"Who's this person you think done this to sweet Miss Minnie?" he asked.

"Miss Ophelia's daughter," Robert answered him. "Julianna."

Chapter Eighteen

In Raleigh that afternoon Julianna prepared for the night. She donned a well padded under garment that was a remnant of her acting days. She went into her bathroom and put in her mouth and teeth inserts. She carefully made up her face applying the gray eyebrows at the end. She placed the gray short-haired wig over her hair and styled it carefully. She then put on the suit she had purchased yesterday at Crabtree Mall. She donned her pearl earrings and necklace. She smiled. Her mother would be proud. She slipped into the low heels she had purchased to match the suit. She put on the stylish glasses. When she stepped before the full length mirror in her bedroom even she was surprised at the refined matronly lady looking back at her. She smiled. She would do. She picked up her matching purse and the elegant silver headed cane, turned off the lights and left the room.

Several minutes before seven she parked her rental car in a side parking lot of the Washington Duke. She walked slowly in the back side door near the golf course and took the elevator to the third floor. She passed no one. She walked carefully, leaning on her cane, to the central elevator bank and took the elevator down to the lobby. She entered the bar, which was crowded as usual at this time of day. She looked around. She saw Grant and Minnie at the far end of the bar, leaning together in conspiratorial conversation. She took a secluded seat near the exit. A waitress approached and Julianna asked for white wine. She knew Grant and Minnie were dining here tonight. She knew they had dinner reservations at eight o'clock. She knew because she had called.

Julianna watched Minnie and Grant with a jealous eye. They were completely oblivious to anyone and anything around them. They laughed together often, talked incessantly and seemed wrapped in a cocoon of pure mutual enjoyment. Their innocent touching, smiling, whispering made Julianna slightly nauseous.

Julianna noted that Minnie was drinking red wine while Grant sipped his Scotch.

A little before eight Grant signaled for the check. Julianna recognized her bartender from the night before bring him the bar tab. She would leave a few minutes after they did and follow them to the dining room. Grant signed the ticket, the bartender said something to him and they both laughed. Grant turned and helped Minnie from the barstool. A gentleman still, brooded Julianna. Minnie took his hand and smiled up at him. Grant continued to hold Minnie's hand as they walked from the room, moving right past Julianna without a glance. She watched them go, bitterness welling inside her. They walked across the lobby in the wrong direction. They were not going to the dining room. They were returning to their room. Julianna was angry, disgusted, resentful. They're in heat!

Love never entered her mind.

***

When Julianna arrived back home that night she was depressed and frustrated. She removed her theatrical clothing, scrubbed her face and put on her nightgown and robe. She made herself a bourbon and water and sat in the kitchen. All she could think about was Grant and Minnie. Their absorption with each other filled her with loathing. What on earth did he see in Minnie? Why would he prefer her? It was baffling.

She knew Minnie and Grant were going to the Angus Barn tomorrow night. Emma-of-the-triple-martinis had innocently revealed that information during their tennis luncheon. Then Emma bragged about joining them. Julianna would go, too, but they would never know it. She smiled to herself. She would be watching.

Chapter Nineteen

The next morning at Merrebanks, Ophelia made her way downstairs just before nine.

Sam Jenkins was always on time. She hoped this young man Sam was bringing for her to meet would be acceptable. It would be a big relief to have Garrett land remain in caring and capable hands. It would also be a relief for Sam. He could train the young man…Ward, his name was…with his retirement again within sight. She knew Sam would always be close by to help but he wanted to travel with Estelle. They had purchased a very nice RV just before Everett died. It was in one of the barns waiting.

Ophelia was nearing the kitchen door when she heard a loud crash. It was the brittle sound of china hitting the floor. That was odd. She could not ever remember a time when Naomi Ruth dropped a plate. She pushed through the door. A young man was kneeling with his back towards her picking up the broken shards of china. Sam Jenkins stood by the back door as if he and the young man had just entered. Naomi Ruth and Robert stood still as statues staring at the kneeling man who slowly rose and turned towards her, broken porcelain in his hands.

Ophelia's left hand flew to the pearls at her throat. Her right hand reached out and grasped Naomi Ruth's arm. Her wide eyes stared in disbelief. "Linus?"

***

Minnie drove mid-morning from Durham over to Raleigh to her sister Martha Jane's home. Martha Jane was enthralled with Minnie's new car. Minnie begged Martha Jane to drive the Mercedes. Driving in Raleigh terrified her, especially in this car that was new to her. Martha Jane happily agreed. They went for an early luncheon then Martha Jane took Minnie to have her hair styled by her own stylist. Martha Jane was all for a new look to go with a new life for her baby sister. Martha Jane offered her opinion with every snip of the scissors.

When finished Minnie admitted to her sister she was startled but happy with her appearance. Indeed the cut and color took years from her face enhancing her fine cheek bones and big brown eyes. Then the sisters went to Martha Jane's favorite dress shop where Minnie found a white linen sheath that revealed the fine body that had been hidden all these years.

Minnie was delighted with the woman who stared back at her in the mirror. Gone was the pretty little frump. In her place was a lovely, refined lady. Next Martha Jane and Minnie went to Main and Taylor where shoes with high heels were purchased that accentuated Minnie's long beautiful legs. Minnie was transformed!

***

Julianna prepared for her evening at the Angus Barn. She would go as a man. That was always a challenge. Julianna dressed with care. She wore the undergarment that bound her breasts and padded her shoulders. She removed her rings. She removed her nail polish and trimmed her nails. She put on the wig of auburn hair swept back in a fashion similar to Wild Bill Hickock. She carefully applied a mustache and beard. Her clothing was the traditional male attire of khaki pants, blue blazer and loafers. The white oxford cloth shirt had padding sewn into the neck and shoulders. She had a man's wallet and transferred cash and credit cards. She would pay in cash. She put on a man's watch. She found the horn rim glasses and put them on. She studied herself in the mirror. She looked like a professor or a similar academician. She would pass if she stayed in dim light. At seven o'clock she grabbed the keys to the rental car and set off. She wanted to be at the restaurant when they arrived, seated where she could watch. She had called earlier to learn their reservation time.

***

Ophelia and Naomi Ruth, shadowed by Maize, slowly made their way upstairs for the night. It had been an amazing day. As she prepared for bed Ophelia wondered aloud at the startling appearance of Ward Covington.

"I don't think I've ever had such a shock. When Ward stood and turned toward me it was as if I were nineteen again and my Linus stood before me. He has Linus' coal black hair and ice blue eyes that crinkle with humor in an instant. He might be a shade taller than Linus but he is broad shouldered and muscular, exactly like his grandfather was."

Naomi Ruth sat down on the chair beside the bed. "Yes, it was quite a surprise." She shook her head again at the memory and laughed.

"Poor Sam, he didn't know what was going on. When he took Jethro Murchison's job as farm manager Big Linus was older and with that premature head of white hair. There was no way Sam could have seen any similarity between grandfather and grandson. No one would think he was young Linus' son either. Linus III took after my side of the family....blond, tall but blocky...all that Scottish blood. And of course Ward uses his step-father's last name. I did pause when I heard his christened name. That was the name young Linus said he would name his first born son...James Howard Garrett... after that little best friend of his...Jimmy Howard.

"Remember how torn apart young Linus was when Jimmy died? They were playing together one day and Jimmy was dead the next. No one knew he was deathly allergic to bee stings. They were just eleven years old. A heart-breaking lesson for one so young."

"That was mighty strong of Sarah to name her son that," Naomi Ruth said. "No one would have blamed her for choosing any name she wanted. How would we know? We didn't even know she was pregnant."

"Talking with her today was special," Ophelia continued. Naomi Ruth nodded. "She sounded just the same, like she was at her home in town and we were talking and twenty-five years had not flown past. I can't wait to see her."

"Having her back here will be wonderful," Naomi Ruth said as she reached down to stroke Maize's head. "Maize herself was surprising. When Sam came through the door she got up to greet him. Then after I dropped the plate and Ward was standing looking at you good old Maize went right up to Ward and sat on his feet! Her supreme act of devotion! She knew!"

Ophelia looked at Maize. "Of course she knew. She knows her own."

"Yes, she does." Both women's thoughts were one.

"What do you think our Bible reading ought to be tonight? The return of the prodigal?"

"More likely Esau and Jacob and the birthright," Naomi Ruth answered.

Chapter Twenty

An unrecognizable Julianna watched from a dark corner as Emma Hendricks and her Benji arrived at the bar in the Angus Barn to await Grant and Minnie. True to form Emma ordered her martini. Julianna smiled to herself as she watched dear Benji frown at his wife and obviously offer an unheeded cautionary word. Maybe this evening will be more interesting than expected, thought Julianna as she sipped her bourbon.

Grant and Minnie arrived ten minutes later. Julianna was shocked by Minnie's appearance. Minnie looked beautiful. She had a new and quite becoming hairstyle and the white sheath she was wearing set off a body Julianna did not realize Minnie possessed. Julianna was not pleased with Minnie's transformation. She finished her bourbon and ordered another as she watched Grant introduce and seat Minnie.

Eventually their party moved to the dining room. Julianna requested a table that was near Grant and Minnie, out of their sightline but not out of hearing distance. She ordered another bourbon and placed her dinner order. Then she sat back to listen. The foursome placed their dinner orders. Minnie obviously preferred fish to steak. Grant ordered a bottle of red wine after consulting briefly with the sommelier. Emma chimed in, much to her husband's horror, and asked Minnie if she wouldn't prefer white wine with her fish. Minnie smiled and answered politely that she always drank red wine whether it was proper or not. They all laughed.

The foursome indulged in small talk, Emma asking Minnie about living in a small town.

Minnie related amusing stories most of which Julianna had heard before. She was surprised, however, to hear that her mother was having a party Thursday night. Ophelia did love to entertain. Grant was going with Minnie. That bothered Julianna. How could her mother allow him at Merrebanks?

Minnie asked Emma how she was adjusting to Raleigh. Emma began listing her favorite places to shop and eat, a list of the finest Raleigh had to offer. When she mentioned her tennis games at the Carolina Country Club Julianna's heart skipped a beat. She had not considered this.

Emma rattled on about the doubles games she enjoyed with friends of her dear friend Jane Elliot, president of the Junior League. She found the games and luncheon afterwards in the grill room delightful even though she found one of the women rather tiresome. This particular woman had a very high opinion of herself and continually blamed missed shots on her partner. She also drove a red BMW which ought to tell you something. Julianna saw Minnie and Grant look quickly at each other.

"That wouldn't be Julianna Stafford by any chance?" Grant asked.

Emma paused. She glanced at her husband who had been frowning at her for some time. "You know her?" she asked hesitantly, quite aware that her husband was fuming.

Grant looked at Minnie and laughed. "I knew her in another life. It was a long, long time ago." He squeezed Minnie's hand.

Julianna saw and heard it all.

Chapter Twenty-One

"Well, I guess Mae Rose is all aflutter with the beau arriving shortly," Naomi Ruth laughed as she fried eggs for breakfast. "Hate to say it but I keep thinking of that saying, 'no fool like an old fool.'"

Ophelia laughed as she got down two plates from the cabinet. "Are we all set for the party?"

"Pretty much. Robert will get what all else we need today. He's gone to the liquor store. I got the silver all polished, though it hasn't had much chance to tarnish since the funeral. Seems like eons ago."

"I know. So much is going on but it's good to be busy. Distractions. Distractions." Ophelia set the plates on the counter beside the stove. "I think we should ask Ward to the party. It will be an ideal time for him to meet everyone...but only as the new farms manager. I don't think we should tell anyone who he really is quite yet. I don't want to do that until Hobart is home...and Julianna here." She turned to Naomi Ruth. "What do you think?"

"Think that would be fine...and I definitely agree with keeping his identity secret 'til the children are here, which I hope is soon 'cause secrets are hard to keep in Hope Springs." Naomi Ruth spooned eggs on their plates. "Especially since Sarah is showing up, too."

"He's picking his mother up Friday morning from the Raleigh/Durham airport. Right now the plan is for her to stay at Eggie's since that's where he's staying, but I would rather she stayed here with us."

"I imagine Sarah will have a very odd feeling when she heads this way after so many years." Naomi Ruth placed toast on the plates. "I hope she will share why she left us."

"Yes, I've always wondered." Ophelia picked up her plate and moved to the table.

Naomi Ruth followed.

"How many people we expectin' tomorrow night?" Naomi Ruth changed the subject.

"No one has declined," Ophelia answered as she put jam on her toast.

The phone rang and Naomi Ruth rose to answer it. "Yes, she's right here." She handed the receiver to Ophelia. "Julianna," Naomi Ruth mouthed.

Ophelia frowned. "Good morning, Julianna. You're up mighty early. Yes, I'm fine, thank you." Silence. Ophelia turned to look up at Naomi Ruth who was still standing by her chair. Her eyebrows rose and an annoyed expression appeared on her face.

"Yes, tomorrow night. Of course you are welcome to come but I'm afraid you will find it rather dreary. It's just a few friends." Ophelia cradled her head in her free hand. She listened. "Fine. We'll see you this afternoon then." She nodded her head, said good-bye and handed the phone back to Naomi Ruth.

"Julianna is coming," Ophelia said. "She's heard about the party some way, probably from the Hatcher sisters."

"Now why in the world does Julianna want to come to Hope Springs for this party? That is so unlike her. She constantly talks about how boring it is here." Naomi Ruth sat back down.

"Well at least now we know why no one has declined," Ophelia said.

***

Julianna arrived just after four o'clock that afternoon. Naomi Ruth and Robert were in the kitchen folding napkins and placing silverware on the bamboo buffet trays. Julianna did not offer to help. She asked Robert to go get her bags and asked Naomi Ruth where Ophelia was. When she learned Ophelia was in her art shed she headed back out the door. Ophelia was not surprised when Julianna entered the art shed. Ophelia hated having her quiet interrupted when painting, and Julianna well knew this, but Julianna never considered the wants of others when something was on her mind.

"What are you painting, Mother?" Julianna asked as she came around the easel to look.

"I'm working on a landscape. I'm not making much progress, though," Ophelia answered. "What do you think?"

Julianna turned her head this way and that and finally said, "You'll get there, I guess. Tell me about this party."

"Everyone wants to meet Hank," Ophelia said.

"Hank?" questioned Julianna.

Ophelia looked at Julianna. "Mae Rose's beau. He's visiting from out-of-town."

"Aren't they a little old for that sort of thing?" Julianna asked.

Ophelia put her brush into the can of water and took off the smock she wore to protect her clothes. "Let's go help Naomi Ruth and Robert, shall we?"

When Julianna and Ophelia entered the kitchen Naomi Ruth and Robert were just finishing the trays. Robert carried them into the dining room and stacked them on the sideboard.

"I'll get your bags now Julianna." He went out the back door.

Julianna sat down at the kitchen table. "Well? Who is invited to this geriatric shindig?" Ophelia and Naomi Ruth glanced at each other.

Ophelia poured a glass of iced tea. "Tea, anyone? It's going to be a relatively small group...her closest friends. They're looking forward to meeting Mae Rose's special friend. He is a delightful man, I must admit. We all met him while in Hilton Head." Ophelia set

Julianna's iced tea in front of her and stood by the sink with Naomi Ruth. She started drying dishes.

"How many people you expecting?" Julianna asked.

"Around forty for the cocktail party and then perhaps sixteen or so will stay for a light supper."

Robert returned carrying Julianna's three suitcases and a hanging bag. "How long you planning on staying?" he asked her.

Julianna laughed. Robert shook his head and left the room with his burden. "So, who's coming?" Julianna refocused.

Ophelia walked over to the counter and picked up a piece of paper. "Here's the list." She handed it to Julianna and went back to drying dishes.

Julianna quickly glanced down the list.

"I must tell you, Julianna, that I told Minnie to bring Grant if she wishes. She is going to let me know this evening if he will be in town." Ophelia watched her daughter.

Julianna continued to study the list. "Whatever, Mother. I'm sure he will come." She put down the paper and stood. "Think I'll run into town and have a glass of wine with the Hatchers. I should be back before seven." She picked up her keys and departed.

Ophelia and Naomi Ruth looked at each other. "She was surprisingly calm," Ophelia said.

"She's up to something," Naomi Ruth said.

***

When Julianna called Mary Hester and asked if she might drop by for wine Mary Hester immediately called her sisters. "Julianna is in town. That means she'll be at the party. She's coming over for wine. Better hurry."

Athie and Mildred barely beat Julianna into Mary Hester's kitchen. Julianna trailed through the door just behind them. They settled around the table and began to discuss the party.

People were surprised that Ophelia was entertaining so soon after her son's death but they were not so concerned that they refused to attend the party. Discussion about the party continued for several minutes until the subject they were all skirting finally was broached. Mildred casually asked if Minnie was coming? Alice told them she was out-of-town.

"Oh, yes," Julianna answered. "Minnie will return home this afternoon. She's been in Durham with Grant. Mother said Minnie would let her know this evening whether Grant would be able to get here for the party but I'm sure he'll come." Her smile was odd.

The sisters sat quietly. They were all rather surprised that Julianna knew so much about Minnie's whereabouts and equally surprised by her calm demeanor. Where was the raging, wronged Julianna of a few days ago? Here sat a collected, serene woman. It was not like Julianna.

Julianna continued. "I'm quite surprised by the change in Minnie. She actually looks good. I think she's had some work done. I've never thought of her as being at all attractive or having such a good figure."

"Oh, that's because you were married to Gil and were living in Enfield. In the summers when we all took our children to swim at the club pool, the men would just accidentally-on-purpose happen to come by to check Minnie out in her swimsuit. She was so naïve she never realized what was going on. No, Minnie has always had a drop dead figure though Carter tried his best to muffle it." Athie sipped her wine, watching.

It was obvious these were not words Julianna wished to hear.

Mildred continued, "And Minnie has kept her figure some way or another. I go to Stretch & Tone every morning religiously. I exercise like crazy and still can't get into my clothes from ten years ago." She sipped her wine.

"Well, Minnie might need to be more careful about what she

wears. She has a white sheath that makes her look like a lady of the night, if you get my meaning." Julianna looked at the sisters and shrugged her shoulders. "Just my opinion," she added. "Maybe that's what Grant likes these days."

It was impossible to miss Julianna's insinuation. It was equally impossible for the sisters to envision Minnie looking like a prostitute. She was so sweet and pure and unaffected and always very properly dressed.

"Carter chose her clothes for so long. He dressed her well but a tad on the frumpy side." Mary Hester rose to get the wine from the refrigerator. She refilled Julianna's glass. "I hope to goodness she does something about her hair. She is too cute to have that beehive Betty hairdo."

"Oh, she has," Julianna mentioned.

Julianna noticed the sisters looking at her. She realized her mistake. "I play tennis with the wife of Grant's new CFO in his Raleigh venture. They had dinner with Minnie and Grant. She told me." Julianna improvised.

The sisters nodded and took another sip of wine. Interesting.

***

Julianna arrived back at Merrebanks just before seven. Everyone sat down to supper.

After saying grace Ophelia made small talk asking about the Hatcher sisters and their children. Julianna reported that the children were scattered all over but doing well. Ophelia mentioned that Harriet was coming to the party with her parents.

After a period of silence, when everyone was concentrating on their dinner, Ophelia announced, "Julianna, I have hired a new manager for the farms."

"Really, Mother? Well, that's a relief for you, I'm sure…and Sam."

"Yes, it is. I am going to ask him to come to the party tomorrow night. It seems a good way for him to meet people. Hope it doesn't make Mae Rose mad...stealing thunder from her suitor...but maybe Hank will be more comfortable not being the sole center of attention."

"Do you think it necessary to invite the help to a Garrett social gathering, Mother?"

Ophelia caught Naomi Ruth's eye. She winked.

"This young man is quite presentable. He comes from a very good family. He has also just completed the advanced agriculture and environmental studies degree at State. I think we are extremely lucky to have him."

Naomi Ruth added, "We'll be very interested in your opinion of him, Julianna."

***

Shortly after eight o'clock Minnie called Ophelia and told her Grant would love to come to the party at Merrebanks. He was looking forward to seeing Ophelia again and returning to her lovely home. Ophelia did not mention that Julianna would also be there.

Chapter Twenty-Two

Athie was on her way home from the cleaners shortly before noon the next day when she spotted a very big car turning into Minnie's driveway. She promptly circled the block. She saw Grant get out of the car and Minnie come out of the house to greet him. Athie raced home to call her sisters. Julianna was right, Grant would indeed be with Minnie at the party.

***

While Athie was circling the block in town, out at Merrebanks Julianna was making her way downstairs to the kitchen. She grabbed a leftover piece of toast from breakfast, told Naomi Ruth that she had to pick up something from the Pig and departed. She drove into town, past the Pig, down Main Street and turned off at the street that took her past the Harris' home. She saw Grant's big Mercedes sedan parked in the back. She then continued her journey.

She drove downtown and made a stop at Jeffrey's Hardware Store. She then drove to Walgreen's and made a purchase in the nail care aisle. She drove home by way of the Pig and stopped in and bought a six pack of Diet Pepsi. She had to return to Merrebanks with something from the Pig. 'Omi didn't miss much.

***

Eggie called Ophelia in the early afternoon.

"Ward is back," Eggie reported. "He hesitantly agreed to come to the party tonight. I told him you wanted to introduce him to folks as your new farms manager. So tell Robert he does not have to come get me. Ward will bring me and take me home. I now have a handsome, young chauffeur!"

***

The cocktail party formally began at five thirty. Alice, Ev and Charlotte arrived at four thirty to help Robert with the bar and Naomi Ruth in the kitchen. As Hank was the guest of honor Mae Rose and Hank arrived early. Eggie and Ward arrived shortly after them. Eggie, Ophelia and Hank renewed their acquaintance from their time in Hilton Head. Ophelia then introduced Hank to Ward. Ward was dressed in a khaki suit with a white shirt and pink tie and Gucci loafers. He looked handsome. When Hank shook Ward's hand there was a long look, then Hank turned to Ophelia and said, "I know you are very proud of him." Ophelia was taken aback but decided she must have misunderstood him. She agreed that she was indeed proud to have Ward as their new farms manager. Then other guests began to arrive so their conversation went no farther. The meeting, greeting, mingling and introducing of Hank and Ward were the main concerns.

The party was in full swing when Julianna descended the stairs and made her way to the bar for a drink. Julianna had taken special care with her appearance and looked particularly good. She had on a form fitting green knit dress that matched her eyes. Shoulder-length blond hair framed her beautiful face.

The bar was set up on the side porch. Several couples stood beside it talking. Julianna spoke casually to them then asked Robert for a gin and tonic. She wandered back into the house, walking through rooms or peering inside them. She was looking for someone. She walked into the sunroom and saw Harriet Pearson, Mary Hester's and Erwin's youngest daughter, talking with quite a handsome young man. He was certainly worth investigating. She made her way forward.

"Hello, Harriet," she greeted the young woman. "Are you still at Meredith?"

"Oh, hello, Mrs. Stafford. How are you? Yes, I'm still at Meredith. I have one more year. How are Meggie and Bingo?"

"Please call me Julianna. They are fine…and who is this?" Julianna cast her eyes on Ward.

"Mrs. Stafford, I mean Julianna, this is Ward Covington, the new farm manager your mother just hired."

Julianna extended her hand. "Hello, Ward Covington. I knew Mother and Sam had found the perfect manager but I didn't realize just how perfect."

Harriet looked uncomfortable but Ward just extended his hand and shook Julianna's. "It's a pleasure to meet you, Mrs. Stafford," he said. "You are a Garrett?" he asked with the most innocent expression.

"Yes, I am the daughter. I expect we will be seeing more of each other."

"I look forward to learning more about your family as well as your land."

Julianna smiled at him. She did not acknowledge the presence of Harriet as she turned and walked from the room.

Entering the hall she saw Minnie and Grant coming in the front door. Minnie had on the white sheath she had worn to the Angus Barn. She looked stunning, which certainly did not please Julianna. Julianna watched as Ophelia greeted them and introduced them to the gentleman standing with Mae Rose whom Julianna assumed was the new beau. They stood and talked, laughing together at some witticism. Then Grant and Minnie turned to make their way into the parlor. Grant glanced up and saw Julianna. He frowned. Unbidden, Julianna took a step toward him. He turned away, took Minnie's elbow and steered her into the living room. Julianna stopped and stood, cold as stone, staring after them.

Athie nudged Mary Hester when she saw Minnie and Grant enter the living room.

Mildred, across the hall, also noticed their arrival. She also saw Julianna at the far end of the hall. Her reaction was easy to read. Mildred swiftly walked into the living room to join her sisters.

"Minnie looks fabulous! That must be the dress Julianna was talking about. And, let me tell you, Julianna is not happy."

The sisters slowly angled their way towards Minnie and Grant, acknowledging friends as they moved. Minnie and Grant went through the French doors out to the porch where Robert and Ev were serving drinks. That is where the sisters Hatcher finally caught up with them.

"Minnie, look at you. I absolutely love your new hairdo." Mary Hester was the first to speak.

"Hello, Grant," the sisters said together. Grant acknowledged the sisters then excused himself to go to the bar. Charlotte approached with an empty tray and he stopped her.

"Thank you, Mary Hester. I like it, too." Minnie fluffed her hair with her hand. "Martha Jane talked me into it. She's determined to modernize me. She also talked me into this dress. It's only the second time I've worn it. Seems a tad snug to me but Grant likes it."

"Minnie, you look fabulous in it," Mildred gushed.

"So it's new?" Athie asked.

"Yes, I purchased it when I was in Raleigh shopping with Martha Jane this week…Tuesday. I wore it that night for Grant when we went out for dinner. I have new shoes, new hair and a new dress. I am a new person!" Minnie smiled her delightful smile.

"Well, it becomes you. Here's Grant."

"Minnie, Charlotte has gone to get you a glass of red wine. Let's go speak with everyone. Ladies, always good to see you." Grant nodded to the sisters and steered Minnie toward the sunroom.

"Minnie looks damn good," Mildred said. Mary Hester agreed. Athie was quiet.

"Help me here," Athie finally said. "If Minnie wore the dress for the first time Tuesday night, how come Julianna knew all about it Wednesday afternoon?"

***

Charlotte entered the kitchen and asked Naomi Ruth if there was any red wine. Minnie would like a glass. Naomi Ruth looked up from arranging deviled eggs on a silver tray. "Don't have much call for it in this heat. Julianna must drink it, though, because she brought a bottle with her. It's over on the counter. Go ask her if she'll share. Just don't tell her who it's for."

A few minutes later Julianna entered the kitchen. Charlotte was right behind her. "Let me uncork it," Julianna said. She got down two glasses and poured the red wine. "I'll have a glass, too. Go to the bar and get two cocktail napkins, Charlotte."

Charlotte went out to the bar and returned with the napkins. "Here, take this one to Minnie." Julianna took a napkin and handed Charlotte the glass. Charlotte left.

Naomi Ruth's hand paused over the tray. *How did Julianna know who the wine was for?*

She looked up to see Julianna smiling into her glass. Naomi Ruth recognized that look. She rushed from the kitchen.

Charlotte was coming back down the hall. "Did you tell Julianna the wine was for Minnie?" Naomi Ruth asked her.

"Of course not," Charlotte replied.

"Where is Minnie?" Naomi Ruth grabbed Charlotte's arm. "Go take it from her. She best not drink that wine!"

Charlotte turned and walked quickly toward the sunroom. Minnie stood talking with Hank and Mae Rose. Minnie still held her glass of red wine in her hand. As Charlotte moved toward her, Minnie raised the glass to her lips. Time slowed, the glass slowly rising, Charlotte slowly moving, her arms outstretched. Charlotte arrived as the glass touched Minnie's lips. She knocked the glass away. It fell with a thud and a crash onto the rug, splashing red wine all down the front of Minnie's white dress. Mae Rose and Hank somehow managed to stay clear. Only Charlotte and Minnie were splattered.

Minnie looked at Charlotte with wide eyes. Naomi Ruth hurried in. "Come with me Minnie," she said. "Charlotte take care of things." Charlotte nodded and bent down to pick up the pieces of wine glass. Mae Rose and Hank stood in bewildered silence.

Ophelia intercepted Naomi Ruth and Minnie in the hall. Naomi Ruth whispered something in Ophelia's ear then went back to the kitchen. Ophelia took Minnie's hand and led her toward the staircase. "Don't worry Minnie. Naomi Ruth has some magic potion she concocts that gets stains out of everything. It even gets lipstick stains out of my linen napkins after my book club is here. Think it has something to do with orange peels."

"Really, Ophelia, there is no problem. It just seemed as if Charlotte came out of nowhere. It was the surprise of it all and I'm just such a klutz." Minnie was explaining as she and Ophelia stood in the guest room upstairs. Ophelia was frowning as she used a damp cloth from the bathroom to dab at the stains.

"Will you promise to bring the dress back here tomorrow so Naomi Ruth can work on the stains?"

"I promise." Minnie smiled.

There was a knock on the door. "Come in," Ophelia said. Grant entered. "Everything okay?" he asked.

"Oh, yes," Minnie answered. "Just an accident. Maybe I'd best find something less staining to drink." She laughed.

Grant glanced at Ophelia. It was a telling look. "Probably a good idea, but right now I think maybe we should say our goodbyes and thank you's and head home. You look like you've been in a paintball fight." Grant smiled at Minnie.

The three walked down the stairs together into the hall towards the front door. No one was in the front hall except Charlotte. She stood by the door with a paper bag in her hand. When Grant and Minnie approached she handed the bag to Grant. "Thank you, Charlotte…in many ways."

He took the bag and turned toward Ophelia. "Old sins cast long shadows." There was a long look between them. Then he nodded and walked out the door with Minnie.

The rest of the evening passed peacefully. Very few people knew of the wine debacle. Mae Rose and Hank were the only witnesses and they were wise enough to make no comment. Ophelia noticed Hank talking at length with Ward and later with Julianna. His cryptic comment still puzzled her. And what must he think about the wine incident?

Supper was also an uneventful affair. The older crowd dined together at the table in the dining room. The younger crowd spread themselves between the sunroom and library. Ophelia, who was the last to take her seat, noticed that Ward and Harriet Pearson were sitting together in the sunroom. She did not see Julianna join them but Charlotte did. Consequently, she steered Ev with his tray into the sunroom to join them. The Hatcher sisters and spouses, along with Alice, were in the library.

Charlotte put on one of Naomi Ruth's aprons to cover the wine splatters on her dress. She chose not to eat but instead help Naomi Ruth in the kitchen. Only she and Naomi Ruth knew of Grant's request for the wine glass fragments. He was in the kitchen when Charlotte brought them in after cleaning up in the sunroom. He and Naomi Ruth were talking. Grant asked them to bag the pieces but tell no one, except Ophelia, of course.

When the evening was over and the last of the guest had departed, Naomi Ruth and Ophelia sat talking in the kitchen. Robert was at the sink washing glassware. Dirty plates were piled high on the counter top. Maize, released from Ophelia's room, was lying on the floor.

Julianna had long gone to bed. She took one look at the dirty plates and glasses and headed up the stairs. She made no comment about the red wine. The wine bottle disappeared.

"Do you think Julianna put something into Minnie's wine?" Ophelia asked.

"We'll know the answer to that soon enough," Naomi Ruth answered.

"Julianna knew who the wine was intended for. I looked up in surprise when she said Minnie's name. She was standing there, looking into her glass with that self-satisfied smile she has always worn when she has done something she shouldn't but is full of pride for doing it."

Chapter Twenty-Three

Frances waited until she saw Joe Allen leave for work the next morning then she hustled over to Athie's house. "Well," she asked, "any fireworks after I left?" She poured herself a cup of coffee and sat down at the table.

Athie was at the sink washing breakfast dishes. "No. It was an amazingly calm evening. I think everyone was dreadfully disappointed."

Frances laughed.

The back door opened and Mary Hester walked in. "Good morning, all. Are y'all discussing the party?"

"Now all we need is Mildred," Athie said.

"She's gone to exercise. I just talked with her," Mary Hester answered. "She said she over-indulged last night and needs to work out. Thank goodness I do not have that gene!" She picked up a piece of toast from a platter on the counter and sat down at her sister's table. "It was a very nice party. Mae Rose's beau was delightful...the embodiment of a Southern gentleman."

"There was just something comfortable and folksy about him," Frances agreed.

Mary Hester rose from her chair to get another piece of toast. "Ophelia's new farms manager wasn't bad either. I think all the girls... of all ages...will suddenly be developing an interest in agriculture."

They all laughed. "Your Harriet might have the edge," Frances observed. "They seemed to have a lot to talk about."

"She could certainly do worse. Harriet told me she and Ward were talking in the sunroom when Julianna...Harriet called her Mrs. Stafford, of course, as well she should...anyway, when Julianna slinked in...Harriet's words...and started flirting with Ward. Harriet said she was mortified but Ward handled it beautifully."

"Julianna did look good last evening...and so did Minnie." Frances added.

"Was that the dress Julianna was telling us about?" Mary Hester asked. "It's a shame she spilled red wine all down the front. Red wine is almost impossible to get out."

Athie turned from the sink. "When did that happen?" she asked her sister.

"Law, I don't know. I was coming across the back hall toward the sunroom. I could see Ophelia at the door with Minnie and Grant. Charlotte was there, too. She gave Grant a doggie bag. The front of Minnie's dress was splattered with what I assumed was red wine. I figured that was why they were leaving early because they hadn't been there very long. Minnie loves her red wine but she is a tad clumsy, you know."

Athie turned back to the sink. She put her hands back into the sudsy water and resumed washing the dishes. Her mind had taken a dirty turn.

Chapter Twenty-Four

Eggie called Ophelia a little after nine o'clock. After thanking Ophelia for a lovely time the previous evening she reported that Ward left early to pick up his mother. They should be back around four o'clock. Ophelia told Eggie she wanted Sarah to stay at Merrebanks if Sarah felt comfortable doing so. Hopefully Julianna was leaving. It would depend on that, of course.

Eggie agreed.

Julianna came down for breakfast about nine-thirty. If she noticed that Naomi Ruth hardly spoke to her she made no mention of it. Robert left the room. Ophelia was just hanging up the phone with Eggie. She too found it hard to be civil to Julianna if what they suspected were true. She chastised herself for prejudging but with Julianna there was usually no benefit of the doubt.

"Your party was lovely, Mother," Julianna nonchalantly announced, seating herself at the breakfast table. "May I have a cup of coffee, 'Omi?" she asked Naomi Ruth over her shoulder. She turned back to her mother. "I must admit though that I wasn't too keen on Mae Rose's beau. He seemed rather nosey…asked me some questions that were really none of his business." She paused as Naomi Ruth placed a cup of coffee in front of her. "Is sugar and cream in it, 'Omi?" she asked.

"It's on the table in front of you, Julianna. I think you can handle that yourself," Naomi Ruth replied and turned her back.

Julianna shrugged and reached for the Sweet and Low. "I must say the new farms manager you've hired was certainly a surprise. He's drop dead gorgeous. I couldn't believe he had on Gucci shoes. He's a far cry from old Sam."

"Clothes don't make the man, Julianna," Ophelia replied.

"Whatever, Mother." She stirred her coffee then took a sip. "I will be going back home this morning as soon as I can get my things packed."

"Whatever, Julianna," Ophelia answered and rose and left the room.

***

Ophelia called Eggie back and told her to send Sarah over to Merrebanks when she arrived. Julianna was going back to Raleigh.

However, Julianna did not go directly home when she left her mother's house. She had an appointment at *Kut & Kurl* for a manicure. If she noticed that everyone seemed surprised when she walked in and sat down at the manicure table, she did not acknowledge it. If she noticed that Ramona had very little to say to her as she did her nails, Julianna showed no concern. She spoke when spoken to, did what she came to do, paid and departed. Needless to say, there was plenty of talk in the beauty parlor when she went out the door.

Chapter Twenty-Five

Ophelia was painting in her art shed when Naomi Ruth rapped on the sill and entered. Maize was asleep at the foot of the easel and woke with a look of surprise at an intrusion. Ophelia also was surprised. Naomi Ruth never interrupted her here.

"Ophelia, you have a caller. It's Mr. Hank. He is on his way home. He wants to say 'good-bye.'"

"Good-bye? How odd," Ophelia said. "He said 'good-bye' last evening and thanked me profusely." She took off her paint smock and walked back to the house with Naomi Ruth and Maize.

Hank was sitting in the bright morning light of the sunroom. He rose when Ophelia entered. "Forgive me Ophelia, I just couldn't leave without thanking you again for your hospitality." They sat down in chairs opposite each other.

"It was wonderful having you here in Hope Springs, Hank. We all hope, now that you know the way, you will return soon. Would you like a Pepsi or perhaps iced tea?"

"No, thank you, Ophelia." He paused then looked steadily at her and said. "Actually there is something else I wished to tell you before I left. I fear I have not been entirely truthful with you."

He could see the surprise on Ophelia's face. "Oh?" was all she said. He noticed her hand stray to the pearls at her neck.

He continued. "When you, Mae Rose and Eggie walked into

the cocktail party at our friend's home on Hilton Head I recognized you immediately. You have not really changed. A few wrinkles here and there but you are still a fine looking woman...and quite recognizable to me. I, on the other hand, am quite different." He patted his girth and laughed.

"We met many, many years ago and not under happy circumstances. I use the nickname Hank now that I am retired. My given name is Henry. My last name is not MacAllister. That's actually my middle name. I used it when I introduced myself because I did not wish to bring you pain. My surname is Bloom."

"Father Henry Bloom?" Shock registered on Ophelia's face. "Father Bloom? My goodness, after all these years?" Amazement registered on her face and then uncontrollable tears welled up in her eyes and rolled down her cheeks.

"Yes, Father Bloom." He looked down and sighed. He reached for her hand. "The burial of your infant son that day so long ago was my first burial of a child. I never forgot it. I never forgot you or your husband either. Your grandson looks just like him."

Ophelia smiled through her tears. Of course, he had recognized her Linus in Ward. Father Bloom handed Ophelia his handkerchief.

"But I understand he has just arrived at Merrebanks and no one seems to know his true connection to you." Hank cocked his head and looked inquisitively at her.

"Yes, that is true. Thank you for not giving him away. It's all rather complicated." Ophelia looked down at the handkerchief then back up at him. "You have totally surprised me! Don't leave now... there is so much to talk about."

"My staying will not make it easier. Life has marched on."

"Indeed it has," Ophelia agreed.

"I suspect your life has been very difficult at times," Father Bloom continued, settling back in his chair. "You've recently lost two sons in as many years. That is tragic. I'm so sorry."

He looked carefully at her. "And I suspect Julianna has always been a trial for you. I would guess that she is whom you are referring to when you say 'It's all rather complicated.'" He tilted his head and gazed steadily at her.

Ophelia nodded slowly. She remained silent.

"A very long time ago I felt the strength of the young mother who stood by the grave of her stillborn son. Much more so than her husband. You are born of strong substance. You have fortitude and a finely tuned sense of grace. You will overcome, of that I am certain." He smiled his gentle smile.

She sat quietly, dabbing her eyes. She looked at Father Bloom, remembering that young priest who was so kind and concerned when she and Linus buried William Gregory. "Thank you, Hank… Henry….Father Bloom." She gave a short laugh then looked down at her hands tightly clenching his handkerchief in her lap. She looked back up, steadily holding his eyes. "May I ask why you just said that about Julianna? What did you mean?"

"Obviously she is adopted for she told me her birth date. I asked, by the way…and it was three days after the burial of your baby." Hank paused, a look that questioned on his face.

Ophelia hesitated, then looked into his soft eyes. "Yes. Her mother brought her to us shortly after…" she hesitated again, looking down at her clenched fists. "It was odd. Linus said it was Fate. She was such a beautiful baby…so…unwanted."

"Not even by you?" Hank asked.

"Not even by me." She reached up and touched her pearls. "I did it for Linus." Hank sat quietly studying her. Finally he spoke.

"Well, she is certainly a beautiful woman though she doesn't have an ounce of your nobility…nor your dignity. She is self-centered, if you'll pardon me for saying so, and conflicted. She has obviously been raised in the lap of luxury, adored and admired as the Garrett daughter…yet I would say she is very insecure. She talks of herself and wants what she cannot have…or…*more* of what she does have.

"As a man of the cloth I felt uncomfortable around her...but, as an ordinary man I found her deadly attractive. She knows this. She uses it to get what she wants. I would imagine that she had her father wrapped around her little finger and probably her brothers as well. Feminine wiles, I think it's called. You, however, were not fooled. I think that because you loved your husband so much you probably let Julianna get by with things she should not have. Unfortunately you have paid for it."

He stopped and looked at her. "I'm being brutally honest here," he apologized, "but I know you can handle it and maybe you need to hear it."

Ophelia sat silently listening to his words. They were unsettling because they were true. Here was Father Bloom, the priest who asked God's blessing on her small son days before Linus asked her blessing on a little unwanted girl. Her blessing was hesitant and inadequate. Her blessing became a burden. She was not good enough. This she had known for a very long time. This she accepted in herself. What she had never acknowledged to herself was her resentment of Linus for asking it of her.

Father Bloom was watching her closely. "You are wise, Ophelia, do not berate yourself. You acted from love. You have done your best...more than most, I would guess, in similar circumstances."

"I've lived with my choices as best I could." She looked at Father Bloom and smiled.

"You will be fine. However, the day will come, and probably soon, when you will have to confront Julianna...and the ghost of your promise to Linus."

He patted her hand. "I must get going," he said as he stood. "I have a long drive ahead of me. We will stay in touch. Here is my telephone number should you need to talk. I apologize for appearing today and speaking so frankly. I hope you will forgive me. I did it out of concern...in respect for that young mother I knew so long ago and the older mother I know now."

She watched his old car creep down the drive. When it disappeared from view she went to find Naomi Ruth.

Chapter Twenty-Six

Ward and Sarah arrived at Merrebanks as the old grandfather clock in the hall was striking five. Ophelia, Naomi Ruth and Robert flew out the door to welcome Sarah. It was a grand reunion with hugs, exclamations and rejoicing for Sarah had been a great favorite of the three of them. Maize also joined in, though Sarah was new to her, barking and circling till she got a clear shot at Ward's feet. Then she sat on them.

Ward watched his mother engulfed by these people he was learning to love. It made him happy just to see his mother so happy, and indeed she was. Tears were pouring down her cheeks as she hugged Ophelia, Naomi Ruth and Robert in turn.

Ward picked up his mother's bag and they all walked into the house, talking, laughing, crying. He now understood the look on his mother's face when she told him stories as a child of this faraway place and his father's family. It had always seemed like a fairy tale, too good to be true. And for him, it wasn't, until now.

Robert took Sarah's bag from Ward and carried it up the stairs to the guest room. Sarah followed him to take her purse and freshen up. Impulsively, as if they were afraid she might disappear, Ophelia and Naomi Ruth followed along, as did Maize. It was a parade of talkative women full of the excitement of rediscovery.

Ward wandered into the library. He sat in his grandfather's leather desk chair and waited, marveling at the strange turn his life had taken since he announced to his mother he was going to North Carolina State and learn about farming.

Ward began his life in his grandparent's home just outside Chicago. His mother fled there when she left his father and Hope Springs. At the time she had not realized she was pregnant and was quite surprised, and very happy, when she discovered it. Ward was born eight months later. With a sense of guilt for not letting him know, Sarah named her son the name Linus had always wanted his first born son to bear, James Howard Garrett. They called him Ward.

Ward's maternal grandparents doted on him for they lost their only son, Sarah's brother, in the Vietnam war. His mother's younger sister, Isabelle, also adored him. Sarah's parents had Isabelle late in life and she was born with Down's Syndrome. To her Ward was a marvelous bundle of energy whom she worshipped. She rarely let him out of her sight. Sarah realized shortly after his birth that she would stay with her family because of the trauma and heartbreak it would cause if she and Ward moved away. Her parents hired an attorney to handle her divorce stipulating that their daughter's whereabouts remain unknown. She found a job with an advertising firm and left the day-to-day raising of Ward to her parents and Isabelle. He was surrounded by love.

When Ward was ten Isabelle died. The next year Sarah met a man from Texas while she was doing an ad campaign for a cattle company. Within the year she married him and they moved to his Texas cattle ranch. Ward had no fault with his mother's new husband. His name was Jackson Allman Covington and he was extremely kind to Ward. Jack had no children of his own. Ward always thought it funny that Allman was Jack's middle name for Jack was certainly all man. He was a big, strong, boisterous man with a heart of gold. He taught Ward how to hunt with not only a rifle but also a bow and arrow. He taught him how to fish, how to ride a horse, how to respect the animals he was responsible for. He taught him how to exist off the land and to always leave it better than he found it. Ward thrived under his tutelage and didn't rebel when Jack asked to adopt him. Jack was the only father he knew. He was well aware his biological father existed in some far away town in eastern North Carolina but Jack was here. Jack was real. Jack was also extremely wealthy.

Unfortunately, Jack was thrown from a wild horse he was trying to break when Ward was a junior in high school. He broke his neck. Jack was buried on his ranch and Sarah began the awesome task of trying to run the ranch. In his will Jack left everything to her for her lifetime. At her death it would all pass to Ward. It was a considerable fortune.

During his senior year in high school Ward announced to his mother that he wanted to go to North Carolina State University. Sarah was surprised but agreed. She would manage the ranch until he graduated. Then it would be his.

This plan of action worked well for two years. During Ward's junior year at State he began to ride through the farm lands of eastern North Carolina on weekends. He began to sense a certain affinity for fields of cotton, corn, peanuts, soybeans. The area felt like home. He debated getting in touch with his father's family but decided against it. He often drove through the family's farmlands admiring how the farms were tended. Whomever was in charge knew what he was doing.

That summer he told his mother to sell the ranch. Ward knew in his heart any farming he did would be done in eastern North Carolina. This time his mother was not surprised. It was in his blood. Selling the ranch was not a problem. It was quickly purchased by a neighboring rancher for a ridiculous amount of money. Sarah returned to Chicago and Ward returned to N.C. State University for his senior year. He began quietly buying farmland in eastern North Carolina. Weeks before graduation he happened upon his father's obituary in the *News & Observer.* It was a shock to him. He attended the funeral and watched the family he did not know. The next year he enrolled in an advanced environmental program at N.C. State and returned to Raleigh. Two weeks before the completion of this degree he happened to see the advertisement for a manager for the

Garrett Farms in Chinquapin County. He blinked. He called his mother and told her he was going to apply without revealing who he was. She hesitated then wished him well. Blood will tell, she said before she hung up.

Chapter Twenty-Seven

The sisters sat at their mother's kitchen table. It was late afternoon and Athie had something on her mind. It had needled her since that morning. She needed to talk.

"I was not about to say anything in front of Frances this morning but I want to know more about that red wine on Minnie's dress."

"What are you talking about?" Mildred asked, puzzled.

"You were at Stretch & Tone, Mildred. We were talking about Miss Phe's party last night. Mary Hester saw Grant and Minnie leaving early and Minnie had splatters all over the front of her dress."

"Yes, that's right," Mary Hester agreed. "What else could it have been but red wine?"

"That's about all Minnie drinks," Mildred said, "so I expect you're right. What a shame if that dress is ruined. It looked so good on her."

"So what are you worried about, Athie? We all know Minnie is a klutz." Mary Hester looked at her sister.

"Too much is happening to Minnie. And let me just ask again how Julianna knew about Minnie's white dress and her new hair-do the very next day?" Athie stared at both her sisters.

"Well, Julianna did say she got her information about Minnie from some tennis friend," Mildred said.

"She said Minnie looked like a lady of the night," Athie continued.

"That sounds to me like she actually saw her."

"Well, how are we going to find out about either one? Where did this tennis friend see Minnie? Did they play tennis Wednesday morning before Julianna drove to Hope Springs?" Mary Hester asked.

"And how could Julianna have seen Minnie?" Mildred added.

There was a pause while the sisters thought. Their need-to-know was in high gear. "I guess we could call the Carolina Country Club and ask if they played tennis Wednesday morning," Mildred suggested.

"Or we could ask Grant about his new CFO and his wife. That's who Julianna said the tennis friend was." Athie looked at her sisters.

"We could go right over to Minnie's and tell Grant that we think Julianna is up to something. He obviously thinks so too if he's looking into Minnie's car accident." Mary Hester looked at her sisters.

"I say we join forces with Grant," Athie agreed. "He'll probably dismiss us as meddling, middle-aged busy bodies but it might be worth a try. We might learn something from him, too. Who knows. Let's go. There's no time to loose. It's time for action."

The three sisters paraded down the street towards the Harris home. They were a determined group moving at a fast pace. No one in their right mind would have tried to slow them down.

They went around to the back of the house. Grant's car was there, parked next to Minnie's in the garage. "Surely is a lot of money parked under that roof," Mary Hester said, looking at the two very large Mercedes parked side by side.

"Yoo-hoo, Minnie," Athie cried out for she had spied Minnie and Grant sitting on the back patio. Athie opened the gate and the sisters marched in. They were not shy. Minnie and Grant both looked startled but stood and welcomed their surprise guests. The sisters noticed that Minnie's welcome was a shade warmer than Grant's. Undeterred the sisters took a seat.

"Minnie and I are having a glass of wine. Could I interest you ladies in one or perhaps a cocktail?" Grant had manners, at least.

"We'll have a glass of white wine, please, if you have it." Athie spoke for all.

The girls made small talk until Grant returned. Settling down with their wine glasses in their hands Mary Hester spoke. "We hope it is not too forward of us...or too rude...and you don't think us a bunch of nosy Parkers...but we are worried about Minnie." She looked at Grant.

Grant looked at the sisters in surprise. This was certainly not what he expected to hear.

Minnie also looked startled.

"And we suspect you are too or you would never have asked Ipock Peck to keep all the parts from Minnie's car after her wreck," Athie added.

Minnie looked at Grant in surprise. This was obviously news to her.

Grant met Minnie's gaze and shrugged. He then looked back at the sisters. "You have my full attention. What is on your mind?"

***

While the Hatcher sisters were speculating with Grant and Minnie, Alice was sitting on the back porch of Ev and Charlotte's home enjoying the gathering coolness of what had been a very warm June day. Ev had fixed a batch of his margaritas. The steaks were marinating in the kitchen. The potatoes were in the oven. A salad was in the refrigerator. All Ev had to do was light the grill. They were in no hurry as they had much to discuss. Last evening's party at Merrebanks was their topic, as it was in most households in Hope Springs that night.

After discussing Mae Rose's suitor and the pros and cons of a seersucker suit the conversation shifted to the new farms manager.

"He's really good-looking," Charlotte said. "Did you see Aunt Julianna make a beeline for him?"

"He looked so familiar to me," Alice added, "but I can't imagine where I could have seen him. I think he's from Texas."

"Speaking of Aunt Julianna, she didn't look half bad herself. She was a mite poured into that dress but she's got the figure for it."

"Minnie looked better," Alice said. "She looked absolutely stunning in that white sheath. I only saw them for a minute when they arrived. I don't know why they left so early."

"Because Charlotte spilled a glass of red wine all down the front of that white dress." Ev looked at his wife. Charlotte winced.

"You did, Charlotte? I didn't hear about that." Alice looked at her. "Did you do it on purpose?"

Charlotte looked at her mother-in-law. "Now why did you say that?" Charlotte asked, cocking her head to one side. Sometimes Alice surprised her. For all her artless ways Alice missed very little.

She laughed. "You are quite right."

Ev looked at the two women like they were speaking Greek. "What are y'all talking about?"

Charlotte looked at her husband. "This stays right here on the porch." Charlotte then recounted to her husband and mother-in-law the wine incident of the previous evening.

"But how do you know Grant also thinks Julianna doctored the wine?" Alice didn't miss anything.

"He asked me to bag the glass fragments. He's having them analyzed."

"You mean, Aunt Julianna tried to poison Minnie?" Ev was shocked.

"Surely looks that way," his mother replied.

***

At the Harris' Athie began to explain. "Julianna is on our minds. Your reappearance, Grant, in Hope Springs has rattled her…

unhinged her...angered her...reminded her...insulted her, whatever...and your preference for Minnie is an affront to her.

"We all grew up with Julianna. We know she's capable of some underhanded shenanigans but she seems to have taken it to a new level. We suspect Minnie's wreck wasn't an accident or if it was... as Ipock Peck thinks...those five nails in the tire didn't help any. And, yes, Hector told us about the nails." The sisters smiled at the recollection of poor Hector finally throwing his hands in the air and telling all.

"Someone hammered those nails into Minnie's tire. Our money is on Julianna. Mary Hester's husband Erwin saw her in the vicinity of the church that morning. Why was she there? She was supposed to be heading back to Raleigh.

"What is really bothering us now though is the dress."

"The dress?" Minnie asked. "What dress?"

"That beautiful white linen sheath you wore Thursday night," Mary Hester answered. "I do hope you can get the wine stains out."

"Minnie laughed. "Naomi Ruth has it...working her magic."

"What in the world does her dress have to do with this?" Grant interrupted and leaned forward.

"I'm coming to that," Athie answered. "Whenever Julianna comes to town she comes over to have wine with us and, of course we do gossip a little, I must admit." Athie grinned. "It's a mutual thing. Who can get the most out of whom, you know."

Grant nodded at the honesty. Maybe he had underestimated this trio of sister snoops.

"Julianna arrived about five last Wednesday evening. The conversation turned to you and Minnie, as it usually does these days. Julianna made a reference to Minnie in a white dress. Julianna was totally unaware that Minnie had such a good figure." She turned toward Minnie.

"We of course knew you did from so many summers together

at the club pool with the children and the golfers coming by to ogle you." Minnie turned red. Grant laughed out loud.

Athie continued. "Then Mary Hester, I think...well, one of us... said, and I hope this doesn't hurt your feelings," she nodded towards Minnie. "We hoped you got a new hairstyle because your hair-do was so dated. And Julianna said you had a new hairstyle. About this time Julianna noticed us looking at her because all of a sudden we began to wonder how Julianna knew all this and it must have shown on our faces. She said she knew it all because she played tennis with the wife of your new CFO and she told her." Athie stopped, took a breath and looked at Grant.

"That's true," Minnie said. "Remember, Grant? At dinner Tuesday night with the Hendricks at the Angus Barn Emma was talking about playing tennis with Julianna."

"Yes, Minnie, I remember." Grant had not taken his eyes from Athie. "However, you purchased the dress and had your hair styled with Martha Jane that day...Tuesday. Julianna did not play tennis with Emma the next morning...Wednesday...because Emma and Ben left early for Greensboro. It was her mother's birthday and they were taking her to lunch. Emma therefore could not have told Julianna anything Wednesday morning about how you looked Tuesday night." He paused to let what he said sink in.

"So one must ask how Julianna knew about your new hairstyle and your new dress Wednesday afternoon...unless she saw you Tuesday night."

"But I didn't see her at the Angus Barn. Did you, Grant?" Minnie asked.

"No, I did not see her," Grant replied quietly.

***

When Julianna arrived back at her home in Raleigh that afternoon she fixed a drink and sat down. She thought back to the previous evening. Mae Rose's nosy Hank had been quite soulful when he described the accident to her. Poor Charlotte had accidentally tripped on the rug fringe just as she handed Minnie the glass. Wine had splattered everywhere. Alas, Minnie's elegant dress was ruined. What a shame, he added, with an uncomfortably piercing look.

Julianna was annoyed. The party had been the perfect opportunity to doctor Minnie's red wine. It was so simple but once again the plan failed. Mousy little Minnie was proving difficult. But she had another plan.

Julianna took a sip of her drink. She sat quietly. In the stillness her mind began to wander. Ramona looked old. There had been no reason to talk with her. They had never gotten along. She smiled to herself as Jake's handsome face floated across her memory. What a good-looking couple they had been, the envy of everyone. It had been so thrilling...eloping and surprising them all. She hadn't even minded the tiny trailer, at first. Jake called it their "love nest"...corny but true. It was exciting. She didn't know how to cook but she solved that problem by taking the pots and pans to Naomi Ruth and her mother and filling them with whatever they were cooking. She didn't know how to do laundry either so she just took all their dirty clothes over to Merrebanks. Naomi Ruth and her mother washed and ironed them for her. Jake never knew.

The novelty wore off after about three weeks, she remembered. A frown creased her lovely face. Jake actually sat her down and talked about a budget. She knew her mother never was told about a budget by her father. Jake even told her to take a dress she bought back to the store. They could not afford it. Thank goodness her father had purchased it for her.

Then her bubble completely burst the day she returned to the trailer and found him home early from the cotton plant. He sat there in his underwear drinking a beer, watching some sports event on television. He didn't even look up when she came in. Her future flashed before her. It was not to her liking.

Two weeks later when she was sitting in the library at Merrebanks her father entered the room and sat down at his desk. He silently regarded her for a few minutes.

"Are you happy, Julianna?" he asked.

"No, Daddy, I'm not," she truthfully replied.

"Don't worry. I'll fix it." And he did. Her daddy always fixed everything for her.

How she wished he were here now. She was unhappy again.

Julianna looked up from her reverie. She sighed and put her glass down on the table. She held up both hands. She would call her regular manicurist tomorrow and have her nails redone.

***

When Ophelia, Naomi Ruth and Maize retired to Phe's bedroom that evening they were joined by Sarah. Maize placed herself between Ophelia and Sarah. Sarah slowly rubbed Maize's ears. The dog had found a new friend.

"I'm sorry about Linus and Everett, Phe. You have had more than your share of heartbreak. Losing two sons so quickly must be devastating. I don't know what I would do if something happened to Ward." Sarah looked at her mother-in-law.

"It's difficult," Ophelia answered, "but with the bad comes the good. I have found a grandson…and you are here." She smiled at Sarah.

"Tell me about everything I've missed in twenty-five years," Sarah laughingly said and the three women talked into the night of past events and family and friends.

Finally Sarah said she must go to her bed before she fell asleep in the chair. It had been a long and emotional day. She stood and hugged both Ophelia and Naomi Ruth. "I have missed you so. I am very proud of Ward for taking the necessary steps to meet his family and so very thankful that he recognizes how special his father's family is. He will be happy here."

As she reached the door she turned, "I know you have noticed that I have avoided mention of Julianna but to be honest, I just don't care what she has been doing all these years."

Ophelia and Naomi Ruth looked at each other in obvious surprise. That statement was so unlike Sarah. Sarah never said an unkind word about anyone.

"Forgive me. I shouldn't have said that," Sarah sighed.

"But why did you? There must be a reason," Ophelia asked her daughter-in-law.

"Did Julianna have something to do with your leaving?" Naomi Ruth spoke slowly.

Sarah looked at Naomi Ruth. "Yes, she did." Sarah turned and left the room.

***

As the Hatcher sisters sat with Minnie and Grant in the growing dusk trying to make sense of peculiar details, Grant's cell phone rang. He glanced at the number, excused himself and went onto the house to take the call.

"I really just can't believe all this," Minnie said. "I have always gotten along quite well with Julianna."

"That's because you weren't a threat to her," Athie answered. "Now you are. You have something…or someone…Julianna wanted, but couldn't have…and probably would like to have again."

"Well, it's her fault she doesn't have him," Minnie stated.

The sisters stopped. "Minnie, you know!" Mildred squealed.

Minnie just looked at the sisters. She didn't answer.

She was saved from further prodding when Grant came out of the house and sat back down. He looked at Minnie and then at the sisters.

"I think I owe you ladies an explanation. You've given me some very helpful information so I would like to reciprocate. At the party Thursday evening I was looking for Minnie. We had both gone our separate ways but I wanted to be sure Charlotte had brought her red wine.

"Someone mentioned they had seen Minnie going up the stairs with Ophelia. They thought she had spilled her wine. I looked into the sunroom and saw Charlotte cleaning up broken glass. Then I saw Julianna walking into the library. She looked smug. I know that look, unfortunately. I went into the kitchen to talk with Naomi Ruth, whose opinion I have always valued, by the way. She is a very astute woman. What she told me made me very nervous. Had Julianna put something into Minnie's wine? I asked Charlotte to put the glass chards into a bag for me. I was going to have them analyzed."

Minnie looked at Grant in surprise. The sisters looked at Grant in respect.

"I called my friend at the SBI last evening. I asked him to run the glass through his labs. My secretary came early this morning and picked up the bag. That was my friend calling back with the results. The wine was laced with strychnine."

"Strychnine?" whispered Minnie.

"Oh, my goodness!" exclaimed Mary Hester.

"You know not," said Mildred.

"How strong?" asked Athie.

Grant looked at her. "Strong enough."

Chapter Twenty-Eight

Ophelia and Sarah were sitting at the breakfast table having their second cup of coffee the next morning. Robert had gone into town to the Pig with a lengthy list handed him by Naomi Ruth. Naomi Ruth was pouring herself another cup of coffee when the phone rang. She answered it. Words were exchanged and she hung up. Ophelia and Sarah paid no mind. They had so much catching up to do.

"That was Grant Whitworth," Naomi Ruth interrupted as she sat back down with her coffee. Ophelia and Sarah paused in their conversation and looked at her.

"Grant Whitworth?" Sarah asked in dismay. "Surely not the same Grant Whitworth who left Julianna at the altar."

"Yes, the same," Ophelia answered. "He has returned to Hope Springs. We will explain later."

"He's on his way over here," Naomi Ruth continued. "He said he must talk with us. It's very important."

"That doesn't sound good," Ophelia said as she replaced her cup in its saucer.

"Oh, dear, I guess I'd best skedaddle," Sarah stood to go.

"No," Ophelia looked up at her, "I think you should stay. Naomi Ruth and I might need you. Please."

Naomi Ruth nodded. Sarah sat back down.

***

Athie walked over to Mary Hester's house after breakfast. She found her sister sitting in her robe at the kitchen table with a cup of coffee and her crossword puzzle. Mary Hester looked up when Athie came through the back door.

"Thought you might come over this morning. Last night was truly a revelation. Now that you've slept on it, what do you think?"

Athie poured herself a cup of coffee and joined her sister at the table. "I'll answer in a sec." She sipped her coffee. "I know Mildred is going to come through the door any minute. Her antennae are probably tingling as we speak. This beats out Stretch & Tone."

The words were barely out of her mouth when Mildred walked in. "Saw you out of the kitchen window," she said to Athie. "Decided to skip Stretch & Tone."

Mary Hester and Athie looked at each other and laughed out loud.

"What?" Mildred looked from one sister to the other then poured herself a cup of coffee and joined them at the table. "I barely slept a wink last night. We could be mourning Minnie right now." Mildred shook her head. "What in the world has gotten into Julianna? I mean, really! This is just scary crazy!"

"Does Julianna honestly think she can just poison poor Minnie and get away with it?" Athie was upset. "Is she so far gone that she thinks she can go around poisoning people and puncturing their tires without anyone noticing?"

"We grew up with her. We know what she's capable of. Remember Samantha Barnes and the cheerleading episode? And poor Margaret Hughes." The sisters sat remembering.

"She's always managed to get what she wants without paying the piper," Mildred added.

"Maybe she has paid and we just don't know it," Mary Hester looked at her sisters. "Do you think she's happy?"

"Hell, no, she's not happy, Sister. She doesn't have Grant Whitworth." Athie stared at Mary Hester.

"It's odd you saying that, Mary Hester," Mildred said. "At the party the other night I was in the hall when Grant and Minnie arrived. Julianna was at the far end of the hall watching. Grant looked up and saw her. She took a step toward him…like she anticipated something…but he looked away and led Minnie into the living room. The look on Julianna's face when he ignored her has bothered me. She looked so…vulnerable…that's the only word for it. I've never seen that in Julianna."

"The only thing Julianna's vulnerable to is the flu," Athie said. "She tried to poison Minnie, for Pete's sake. Don't be getting soft about Julianna."

"I think she needs help," Mildred continued. "Psychiatric help…again."

"Yes, she probably does," Mary Hester agreed. "I tell you, though, I'm just nervous about what to do if she shows back up in Hope Springs…and you know she will. She'll call us and what should we do?"

"Well, I personally hope she does. Somebody's got to keep an eye on her. Might as well be us. Has been so far," Athie said.

"Maybe Ophelia can do something about her daughter…or Grant…or the two of them together. He said he was going to talk with Phe and 'Omi this morning."

"Poor Miss Phe. She's lost two sons and now she has to deal with her lunatic daughter…again. I wish Hobart were here."

"Well, at least Phe has a nice new farms manager. She doesn't have to worry about that anymore," Mary Hester added.

"I hope to goodness he doesn't pack up and leave when he gets a closer look at the family," Athie said.

***

Grant parked his car in the rear and came through the back door. This was the way he entered the house at Merrebanks back in the days when he and Julianna were dating. He did it today from past habit.

When he entered the kitchen he saw the women at the table, Ophelia and Naomi Ruth and, with surprise, he recognized Sarah. He stopped and stared. She looked back at him and smiled.

"Hello, Grant," she said.

"Sarah, is that you? What a wonderful surprise."

She rose and greeted him with a brief hug. "It's been a while. I'm surprised you even recognized me."

"Oh, I'd recognize you anywhere," Grant continued. "You have changed very little." He turned to Ophelia and Naomi Ruth who had been quietly taking in this exchange. "Forgive me for not speaking. I was shocked, and, of course, happy, to see Sarah sitting here. Time seemed to roll back."

"Sarah is visiting for a few days," Ophelia answered. "You're right, it has been quite a while since she sat here. It has also been a while since you sat here. Please...," she gestured toward the chair beside her.

"Would you like a cup of coffee or a glass of iced tea, Grant?" Naomi Ruth asked.

"Tea, please, Naomi Ruth."

Grant turned to Sarah. "I was long gone when you and Linus separated. I was sorry when I learned of it. I have always tried to keep up with you Garrett's." He smiled at Ophelia.

The four made small talk for several minutes until Grant said, looking at Ophelia, "I'm not happy about what I've come to talk about this morning."

"I'm an old woman, Grant, but I am not a stupid old woman.

I don't think I will be surprised by what you have come to tell me unless you tell me there was nothing in the wine glass." She smiled ruefully. "Naomi Ruth and I have discussed this." She looked across the table at her old friend.

"There was strychnine in Minnie's wine. Red wine masks the bitter taste so it's a good liquid to put it in," Grant explained.

"Do you know how much was present?" Ophelia asked. "Was it enough to just make Minnie sick? Or was it enough to do more harm?"

"Probably enough to make her very, very sick. It's hard to say for sure."

Ophelia nodded. Then she looked at Naomi Ruth. Their eyes mirrored twin thoughts. Ophelia glanced at Sarah and saw astonishment reflected on her face.

Ophelia sighed. "I know of the nails in Minnie's tire. Robert told me. I hoped that was just a prank to scare Minnie. I think with tires these days the air just oozes out when they get nails in them. When the tire went flat Minnie would have gone to the filling station for air. When the mechanic told her she had five nails in a neat little row alarms would have gone off in Minnie's head. That is how Julianna usually operates. She attacks from the rear...or the sides. Innuendo produces fear. I must admit I originally thought the blowout was just an accident. I looked at Minnie's tires when I went out to Ipock Peck's. They were very old."

Ophelia paused, looked down at Maize peacefully sleeping at her feet, then continued. "Julianna has spent a lot of time in Hope Springs lately. I don't believe for one minute that it is because of concern for me. She relies on the Hatcher sisters...uses them...for information about Minnie...and you." Ophelia looked at Grant.

"Julianna is envious of Minnie. Minnie has succeeded where she failed...and failure is not an option for Julianna. She refuses to accept it. Julianna in her paranoid conceit thinks she deserves you...is entitled to you. She's used to getting what she wants. She's conniving.

If she doesn't get what she wants she gets very, very angry. My Linus unfortunately set her on that path. I think he realized it but was too stubborn or too full of pride to acknowledge his mistake."

Naomi Ruth nodded then spoke. "Julianna thinks Minnie is beneath her...not worthy of you...or your money...which is a part of this, have no doubt. If Minnie is gone then she can have you. We all know that's not true but we are rational, Julianna is not. She cannot fathom what you see in Minnie. To her there is no comparison between Julianna Garrett and Minnie Harris. When Minnie appeared Thursday night in that white sheath, we suspect Julianna was startled. Here was a worthy opponent. Julianna didn't say anything about Minnie, though, which surprised us. She's usually so critical when she feels threatened. And we can't figure out how she knew Minnie drank red wine or how she had strychnine on hand."

"This was planned," Grant looked at Naomi Ruth, then Ophelia. "Julianna had already seen Minnie in the dress."

"Oh, when was that? Minnie said the dress was new." Ophelia turned towards Grant.

"We think Julianna has been spying on us....following us."

There was shocked silence.

"I'd best tell you what I know." Grant recounted his conversation with the Hatcher sisters. "We never realized anyone was following us...certainly not Julianna."

Everyone sat in silence for several minutes, digesting Grant's words. Eventually Ophelia quietly addressed Grant, "Do you know anything about Julianna's years at the college in South Carolina, before she came to the University and met you?"

"No, not really. When I met her she was very much into the social scene at Chapel Hill."

"Yes, Julianna can be quite charming and she can adapt easily to different environments...much like a chameleon...or an actor... actress in her case."

Grant looked inquisitive. Sarah and Naomi Ruth nodded.

"Julianna discovered a bit of herself while in South Carolina. The school had a marvelous drama department and Julianna immersed herself in the stage. She was quite talented. There is your answer to her stalking. You never knew she was there because she was disguised as someone else."

Grant's eyebrows rose.

"I'll bet even if you went back to the places you and Minnie went together and asked for their surveillance tapes you would have difficulty identifying her. She is that good. She would have been a marvelous actress."

Grant looked at her steadily. "What do you want me to do, Ophelia? I'm worried about Minnie. I won't let anything happen to her."

He stood to go. "You have a wonderful family, Ophelia. I always enjoyed being with the Garretts. Everett and Linus, God bless 'em, always had a plan for a good time. It took me a long while to recognize the darkness in Julianna because it was so unlike her light-hearted siblings. I don't know why she inherited all the dark genes. But this I can honestly say…and I'm sorry to be so blunt…I never regretted my decision to walk out of that church. I could turn my back on her, you can't. She's your family and you must deal with her. I wish you luck."

As Grant moved towards the door Naomi Ruth stopped him with a hand on his arm. She looked up at him and said quietly, "It's you Julianna wants. You might turn your back on her but I think you best keep looking over your shoulder."

***

That afternoon Ophelia called Alice and asked if she would come over to Merrebanks for dinner that evening. She had a surprise for her. Alice immediately started asking questions but Ophelia just laughed. Alice would have to come to dinner to discover her surprise. Alice promised she would be there promptly at six o'clock.

Ward drove Eggie over to Merrebanks a little before six. Eggie was thrilled with the mobility she now enjoyed because of Ward's presence. She was thrilled to be able to dine more often at Merrebanks. She loved Naomi Ruth's cooking, especially her biscuits. She hoped Ward never moved out of her carriage house.

Ophelia, Sarah, Eggie and Ward were sitting on the river porch enjoying a pleasant late afternoon breeze, sipping drinks when Alice arrived. She stepped out onto the porch and began greeting everyone when she suddenly spied Sarah. Her eyes grew huge. She screamed, "Sarah!", and flew over to hug her old friend and sister-in-law. Everyone laughed with pleasure.

"Phe, is Sarah my surprise?" she exclaimed. "How wonderful!"

Alice launched into a nonstop spate of questions until Robert brought her gin and tonic and she paused to sip it. Conversation resumed with Sarah and Alice sitting side by side talking together. Ward, Ophelia and Eggie sat and talked about the farms.

Dinner was a continuation of conversations started on the porch. It wasn't until dessert that Alice was told that Ward was Sarah's and Linus' son. Alice stared from one to the other. It was the first time she had been silent all night. "Of course," she finally said. "That is where I have seen you." She was staring at Ward.

"What do you mean, Alice?" Ophelia asked. The family was quite used to Alice's skips in logic but sometimes she had to explain herself.

Alice turned to her mother-in-law. "The photograph by your bed. You and Big Linus on your wedding day. Ward looks just like him. I knew he looked familiar!" Alice grinned and then suddenly burst into tears.

"Oh, dear," Sarah exclaimed. "Whatever is wrong?"

"I'm just so happy for you, for us," Alice sniffed into her napkin. She got up and went over and hugged Ward. "Our nephew. How I wish your Uncle Everett were here. How thrilled and excited he would be...and you would have a man to talk with instead of being constantly surrounded by women."

"What am I?" Robert asked. "Chopped liver?" They all laughed.

***

Sarah looked forward to the talks each night in Ophelia's bedroom. Tonight was no exception. They talked at length about Grant's revelation of strychnine in Minnie's wine. They laughed about Alice's surprise when she saw Sarah. They were touched by her response to Sarah's announcement that Ward was her son.

"I hope Ward and Ev become good friends." Sarah laughed remembering Alice's concern. "How old is Ev now? I think he was about three or four when I left."

"Let's see," Naomi Ruth was thinking. "Alice and Everett married the December after Julianna's June fiasco."

"I remember it well," Sarah said. "Tarboro loves a wedding and it was a doozy. Alice's mother made her famous eggnog for one of the brunches. Everyone was snockered! The actual wedding was beautiful and this time there was a happy ending. It was probably a blessing Julianna didn't come."

"The doctors didn't think it a good thing," Ophelia said.

"To continue," Naomi Ruth beat on the arm rest of the chair for attention. "Ev Jr. was born two years later. So he will be twenty-eight this year. Charlotte is a year younger than he is." Naomi Ruth was the Garrett family historian.

"When is Ward's birthday?" Naomi Ruth asked. It was time to add him to the Garrett family tree.

"Ward was born in June. Actually his birthday is next week"

"Well, we must have a party," Ophelia announced. "Start planning Naomi Ruth. You are staying through next week, aren't you?" She looked at Sarah.

"I have an open-ended ticket and I would love to stay a while longer." Sarah smiled.

"Good. That's settled."

"When I left Hope Springs that October I had no earthly idea I was pregnant. I was ecstatic when I found out." Sarah looked down at her hands. "It was bittersweet and totally ironic. Linus and I wanted children so badly."

"But you felt no compunction about not telling Linus." Ophelia looked closely at Sarah.

Sarah raised her eyes to her mother-in-law's. "No. I felt no obligation to tell Linus. I owed him nothing and I was scared he would try and take my baby from me."

Chapter Twenty-Nine

When the choir, the acolyte and the priest processed down the aisle Sunday morning Mildred and Miss Bessie slipped into the church behind them. They took their seat in the same back pew the two usually occupied at St. Andrew's Episcopal church each Sunday morning for they were habitually late.

Mildred hurriedly knelt and said a hasty prayer. Miss Bessie no longer knelt. She could not pull herself back up from the kneeling position. She picked up the hymnal and found the processional hymn. Mildred rose to join her, scanning the congregation as she began to sing. She easily found her sisters in their regular pews. Surprisingly both husbands were in attendance today. The golf course must be closed. Harriet was sitting with her mother and father. Mildred saw Alice with Ev and Charlotte. Alice looked tired. Mildred continued scanning the other pews until her eyes came to an abrupt halt at the Garrett pew. Who was that with Ophelia and Eggie? She recognized the back of Ward's head but who was the woman? Her antennae tingled.

Miss Bessie leaned towards her, "Who is that woman with Ophelia and Eggie?"

It was during the Peace, when the unknown woman turned to acknowledge those around her, that Mildred gasped in recognition.

"Is that Sarah?" Miss Bessie exclaimed and not in her best church voice. Heads turned.

Yes, it had to be. She was older, of course. There were gray streaks in her chestnut brown hair but her delicate skin was hardly wrinkled and she still had those exquisitely chiseled features. Sarah was still a very pretty woman.

When had she arrived? Why had she arrived? What was she doing here? As far as Mildred knew no one had seen or heard from Sarah for over twenty years. Mildred could scarcely concentrate on the remainder of the service. She could not wait to speak with her sisters. She was sure they too had noticed Sarah sitting calmly in the Garrett pew. Their mother certainly had.

Exiting church was a slow process. The aisles clogged with conversation as the spiritual message was quickly replaced by the secular one. Eggie, Ophelia and Sarah slowly made their way down the center aisle stopping to speak as they moved. They were joined by Alice, Ev and Charlotte. When the Garretts finally finished speaking with Father Matt at the door and exited the church the sisters Hatcher and their mother were waiting.

***

There was always good attendance at the country club for the Sunday buffet. The food was good but the gossip was better. The Hatcher clan occupied their usual table by the windows looking down toward the river. Erwin and Joe Allen were already seated and concentrating on their filled plates. Harriet was talking with an old high school friend. Miss Bessie was hovering over the dessert table. The sisters were moving toward their table to queue together for conversation. Food was immaterial. Gossip was the nutrition of choice.

"What do you think?" Mary Hester placed her napkin in her lap and picked up her fork. "Erwin you are eating too fast. Slow down. You don't have a train to catch."

Erwin looked up at his wife with that peculiar way husbands do, seeing them without seeing them. His fork, full of squash, hovered over his plate. There was no need to respond. He turned back to

Joe Allen and they resumed their discussion of the latest property re-evaluation.

"I was totally taken by surprise," Athie answered. "Maybe Sarah is here because she heard of Everett's death but that doesn't make much sense if she didn't show up for her own husband's funeral. This corn pudding is delicious."

"She was very cordial," Mary Hester continued. "She and Ophelia seemed very comfortable with each other. When do you guess she got here?" She submerged her fried shrimp in cocktail sauce.

"After Thursday, obviously, unless they hid her in a bedroom upstairs during the party." Athie commented.

"Cut the sarcasm, Sister," Mildred said eyeing Athie. "I think we are just going to have to ask Alice." She inclined her head toward a table in the corner where Alice, Ev and Charlotte were seated. "She and Sarah were talking as if they were continuing a conversation. Obviously Alice knew she was here." Mildred picked at her salad. "How on earth can y'all eat all that in this heat?"

Harriet approached the table and sat down next to Athie. "Maybe you have the answer, Harriet," Athie looked closely at her niece. "You were talking with Ward after church. What did he say?"

"We were just talking about a movie we both want to see." Harriet looked at her aunt.

"Does he like his new job?" Mildred asked.

"Yes. He's spending a lot of time with Sam learning about the farms." Harriet began to eat her lunch.

Athie tried again. "Does he ever mention the family? Did he say anything about the lady with them in church today?"

Harriet looked up. She glanced at her mother and her aunts. "No, not really." Harriet resumed eating.

"What does 'not really' mean?" Athie asked.

Harriet paused and looked at her aunt. She had dealt with the voracious curiosity of the female members of her family all her life. At an early age she had developed a system of half answers when they questioned her. It served her well but aggravated them no end.

"She didn't come up in our conversation at church."

Miss Bessie interrupted them as she resumed her seat. She had placed her luncheon plate on the table and left to check out the desserts. She now arrived with an apple pie in one hand and a peach cobbler in the other.

"Y'all better go get your desserts. The good ones are going fast."

"I can see that, Mimi," Harriet said to her grandmother and laughed.

"So why is Sarah here?" Bessie was curious, too.

***

Ophelia, Eggie, Sarah and Ward returned to Merrebanks after church. Ophelia had tried to persuade Alice, Ev and Charlotte to join them for lunch but they were going down to the club for the Sunday buffet.

It was a light meal. The heat robbed one of an appetite. Naomi Ruth had prepared chicken salad, tomato aspic, deviled eggs and chilled asparagus and placed it all in the refrigerator before she and Robert left for the Weeping Mary Church. They would not return for at least another hour. Eggie was relieved to see the biscuits nestled in the silver bread tray. She was also delighted to learn there was a lemon meringue pie for dessert.

Naomi Ruth had set the dining room table so Sarah set the food on the sideboard and Ophelia poured tea into their glasses. Everyone helped themselves then sat down for a leisurely Sunday luncheon.

The conversation naturally revolved around that morning's church service.

"Mother, you created quite a stir in church," Ward looked at his mother and smiled. "Some folks looked like a ghost from the past was sitting in the pew."

"Well, that's about the truth." Eggie put several biscuits on her plate. "It's been ages since your mother darkened the doors of that church."

"I guess only the older members of the congregation would even remember who I am. The Hatchers were certainly surprised. They were heading to the club for lunch. I hope Alice remembers to keep mum about Ward."

"She will," Ophelia said. "Alice is quite canny."

***

After the service at the Weeping Mary Church three men stood talking in the shade of the giant pecan tree. "What's goin' on with sweet little Miss Minnie? Mr. Grant came and checked out her car. Took the piece of tire with the nails in it." Ipock Peck mopped his brow for the heat was stifling.

"He say anything?" Hector asked.

"Nope. Did thank me proper for being kind to her, though. Nice man." He paused and looked at the other two men. "That shameless daughter of Miss Ophelia's still trying to do Miss Minnie harm?"

"Afraid so," Robert answered. "Put poison in her wine Thursday night."

"Do tell!" Ipock Peck exclaimed.

"So I heard," Hector said. "My girls are about to drive me crazy. They're like those monkeys…see no evil, hear no evil and speak no evil…'cept they're the opposite. They want to see and hear as much evil as they can and then they want to tell everybody all about it!

"Anyway, they said strychnine was in the wine. That right, Robert?"

"Afraid so," Robert nodded.

Ipock Peck shook his head. "Don't sound quite copacetic. It's right peculiar to me that a fine woman like Miss Ophelia can have such an injurious daughter." He continued shaking his head.

Robert looked at him.

"And how in Pete's name can that bad daughter just perambulate around trying to kill off Miss Minnie? She got a screw loose, sounds like. Miss Ophelia best do something before she succeeds. Yes, sirree."

***

Athie wandered over to Mary Hester's around five o'clock. When she walked through the back door she found Mary Hester and Mildred already drinking a glass of wine. "Starting a little early, aren't we, girls? And without me. Shame. Shame." She poured herself a glass of wine and sat down.

"We were discussing Alice and why we couldn't get much out of her at the club today. Either she really doesn't know why Sarah has appeared in Hope Springs or she has an infuriating knack for misdirection," Mildred said.

The doorbell rang and Mary Hester rose to answer the door. "Erwin has the television going so loud I know he can't hear a thing. Another golf tournament. They're endless."

When she returned Grant Whitworth was just behind her.

"I'm glad I caught you all together," he said after greeting them. "I've come to ask a favor." He pulled out a chair and sat down with them.

"Can I get you something to drink, Grant? We do have red wine."

"Thank you, no. I need to get back to Minnie. She's presenting a problem. I've tried to talk her into returning with me to Durham. She'll be safe there, but she refuses. I can't budge her. She says she has so many things to take care of, legal things like joint checking accounts, safe deposit boxes, insurance…that kind of thing. Also Carter called and the moving van is coming Thursday for his furniture. He can't come back for a while because he has a new job with a bank in West Palm. Minnie must be here to get his things on the truck.

"I don't want to leave Minnie here by herself. I do not trust Julianna for one minute." He paused and looked at them. "I talked with Ophelia and Naomi Ruth yesterday. They were not surprised by the poison in the glass *per se* but they were surprised that it was such a harmful amount."

"Was Sarah there when you talked with them?" Athie asked.

Grant hesitated then nodded.

"Do you know why she's showed up in Hope Springs now after nearly thirty years? You know she left a couple of years after you did." The sisters looked at Grant.

"No, there was no mention of why she was here. She sat with us while we discussed Julianna but she did not say much."

The sisters looked disappointed.

"I'm glad for Ophelia," Grant continued. "She needs a diversion."

"How did you and Ophelia leave things?" Athie asked.

"Ophelia is a realistic woman. We have talked. She and Naomi Ruth will decide on a course of action and soon. In the meantime I must protect Minnie...and that's why I'm here."

The sisters looked at him in a puzzlement.

"Apparently while she was attending that college in South Carolina Julianna became quite engrossed in acting." He looked at the sisters.

"Yes, that's true. Supposedly she was quite good at it," Athie said.

"We thought she was headed for Broadway," Mildred added.

"It was certainly a profession that suited her," Mary Hester chimed in.

"There was some speculation that the accident where the young man was killed while she was driving turned her off the theater... think he was in drama, too. Then there was also talk that Big Linus wasn't too keen on her being an actress. He didn't think ladies should follow that profession," Athie continued. "She went on to Chapel Hill and never acted again."

"Until now," Grant added.

"What do you mean by that?" Athie asked.

"Ophelia thinks that's why Minnie and I didn't know she was watching us. She used all she learned in her drama training to spy on Minnie and me and not be recognized."

"Oh, my Lord!" said Mary Hester.

"Is there no end to Julianna's mischief?" asked Mildred.

"But why have you come to us ? What can we do?" Athie asked.

"I've decided that until this is settled…and I hope Ophelia will do something fairly quickly…I'm going to live here in Hope Springs and commute to work. The company helicopter will pick me up each morning at the air field. It can land on our building in the Research Triangle Park. It will fly me back here in the afternoon. The problem is during the day. I need you and anyone you trust to watch Minnie for me. There is no doubt in my mind that Julianna will try again."

"Us?" Athie was doubtful. "I don't know."

"We can certainly do that." Mary Hester drew herself up.

"I have a golf tournament this week." Mildred hesitated.

"We will do it," Mary Hester looked sternly at her sisters.

"Thank you," Grant said. "Ophelia made a comment that struck me," he continued. "She said that if we had surveillance tapes we would probably not recognize Julianna on them. Well, I have requested the tapes from the Washington Duke and the Angus Barn. They are the only two places Minnie and I have been together since all this started. If I can't find Julianna in them maybe Ophelia and Naomi Ruth can."

"What will you do, Grant, if you discover Julianna on the tapes?"

"The last thing I want to do is hurt Ophelia and the Garretts but I must look after Minnie. I have the piece of tire and the glass fragments but the more proof I have the easier it will be for me to stop Julianna with Ophelia's help. She's hesitant."

The sisters sat quietly digesting Grant's words.

"Is Julianna even aware that you suspect her of trying to harm Minnie? And, if so, will she think you are serious?" Athie looked carefully at the troubled man sitting before them. "Julianna has never accepted the theory of consequences."

"Maybe I will remind her of a day in June thirty years ago."

***

Supper was a quiet affair at Merrebanks that evening. It was just Ophelia, Sarah, Naomi Ruth and Robert. Everyone was preoccupied. Sarah, realizing her mother-in-law was tired, suggested an early evening.

Leaving Robert once again to clean the kitchen after dinner Naomi Ruth, Ophelia, Sarah and Maize treaded their way upstairs. Sarah wished them a good night and made her way to her room.

Ophelia was weary. She sat at her dressing table and removed her pearls, feeling their warmth as she laid them down. She had always known her pearls had life. They were her wedding gift from Linus. They were his mother's wedding gift from her Linus. They graced the necks of Garrett women, a symbol of love, of continuity… and…of servitude. She sighed.

"Mighty heavy sigh, Phe," Naomi Ruth looked at her from the chair by the window. She sat with the Bible in her lap, ready for tonight's devotional. Maize was stretched out on the rug at her feet.

"Sadness just creeps up on me sometimes, 'Omi. Does it you?"

"Yes, and it usually surprises me when it does, catches me off guard."

Ophelia began to take the bobby pins from her hair. "What are we reading tonight? I hope it's something encouraging."

"Why not your favorite," Naomi Ruth replied.

"You are a wise old thing, 'Omi," laughed Ophelia. "Hope, patience, prayer is a good plan." She brushed her blond hair with measured strokes and watched Naomi Ruth open the Bible.

There was a light knock on the door. Maize raised her head. The door opened and Sarah stood there in her nightgown. "I know you are tired Phe but I can't go to bed this evening without thanking you and 'Omi for welcoming my son…and welcoming me…back here. Ward and I rode through the country this afternoon touring Garrett farmland. I shared my memories of my rides with Lady Bess. He showed me newly planted fields and rode me by a farm he hopes to purchase. His pride and passion were a revelation to me. Your Linus talked often of the land…almost as if it were a living, breathing being. His love of it was always evident…foremost in everything he did. He had a certain pride in the dark soil that his son never showed. My Linus saw the land as a means to an end. Your Linus saw it as the end itself. Ward speaks of the land like his grandfather. It is enlightening and humbling. My son is home. Please ride with him one day…both of you. I think you will be proud to be a part of what he sees. Good night. Sleep well. It was a lovely day." Sarah turned and walked down the hall to her room. Her door closed softly.

Naomi Ruth and Ophelia quietly smiled at each other. "Sometimes 'Omi, when the past returns it is a blessing."

Naomi Ruth rose from her chair. "Come on Maize. That's our benediction tonight."

"Good night, 'Omi. Love you."

"Love you back, Phe."

Chapter Thirty

Julianna needed another plan, hence more information, so she called Pansy Perdue. Another tennis match was arranged for Monday morning.

The four women met as usual at the Carolina Country Club. The day was humid and the match competitive. Julianna managed to hit Emma with the tennis ball several times for she well remembered what Emma said about her at the Angus Barn. The four ladies were not in the most congenial of moods when they entered the Grill Room for lunch. Emma ordered her triple martini and the others their white wine. While they were picking at their salads Julianna grilled Emma.

"How was your dinner with Ben's new boss?"

"Fine." Emma was decidedly cool. "Grant Whitworth is easy to be around. I was nervous thinking he might be overbearing or commanding but he was very polite and attentive. He is dating a nice woman. She was with him. Her name is Minnie something. She was quite lovely in a delicate sort of way. I'd say from watching them she might just be the first Mrs. Grant Whitworth."

Julianna bit her lip.

"Actually it turns out she was the reason he was in Hope Springs. She lives there."

Jane Elliott looked up from her salad. "I was telling Mother about our tennis games and who I was playing with. I mentioned why y'all moved to Raleigh, Emma. Mother laughed when she heard Grant Whitworth's name. She went to a wedding in Hope Springs years ago and it seems Grant Whitworth was the groom. He left the bride at the altar, please. Just turned and walked out. Can you imagine? How awful! How utterly embarrassing! That poor bride. Mother said she was a Garrett, but she couldn't remember her name, it was so long ago. The Garretts practically own the whole county." Jane took another bite of her salad.

Julianna felt cold. She never dreamed one of these women would have any connection with her past. Thank goodness Jane's mother had a poor memory but this might be the end of tennis with this bunch. She just needed to get her information.

"Maybe this Minnie is the woman he ditched years ago. Maybe they have gotten back together. She lives in Hope Springs, after all." Julianna threw out a red herring.

"I guess that's possible. It didn't come up but then it wouldn't, would it? I think that would be a taboo topic. Benji said Grant is planning to stay with her in Hope Springs for several days. He'll commute back and forth from Hope Springs on the company helicopter. How cool is that? No I-40 traffic." Emma finished her martini. Everyone was signing their checks and gathering their gear to leave.

"Oh, Julianna, I nearly forgot. Your name came up when we were dining with Grant and Minnie. Grant said he knew you or had met you…'in another life'…I think they were his words. You never mentioned you knew Grant Whitworth."

"He must have me confused with someone else." Julianna forced a thin smile.

***

Ophelia, Sarah and Naomi Ruth were finishing breakfast. "There is a lot going on these days," Ophelia said as she put her fork down on her plate, "but I do not want to overlook Ward's birthday

Wednesday. That's day after tomorrow. How would he like to celebrate, Sarah?"

"That's dear of you, Phe, but he has never been one to want a big whoop-de-do. We have always celebrated his day rather quietly."

"Kinda hard to have a small, quiet anything around here," Naomi Ruth said as she rose and gathered up the dirty dishes. "Everybody gets their nose bent out of shape if they're not included in any kind of celebration being held anywhere."

"Let's just have a few folks over to celebrate. I wish there were more young people. He seems to be fond of Harriet, so let's have her...which means all the Hatchers because you can't have one without the others...and I'm sure they're chomping at the bit to find out why you are here, Sarah."

They all laughed. "At least the Hatcher sisters haven't changed," Sarah said.

"And, of course, we must include Sam and Estelle. He and Ward have grown close and y'all were so close when you lived here." Ophelia glanced at Sarah.

"Yes, I would love to see them again."

"We'll have Grant and Minnie, too, because I have grown rather fond of Grant."

"I always enjoyed being around Minnie and Carter," Sarah said. "I must admit though that this change of partners might take some getting used to."

"Thankfully Julianna has no plan to darken the door," Naomi Ruth said.

Ophelia grew quiet. "What on earth are we going to do about her?"

"I don't know what but I know it's time to do something." Naomi Ruth started putting the plates in the dishwasher.

Chapter Thirty-One

Alice always enjoyed her hair appointments at *Kut & Kurl*. The beauty parlor was a hive of local buzz and she always came away with a good cut and good gossip. Today was no exception. When she entered she realized she would probably put a damper on the conversation.

The ladies were speculating about the reappearance of Sarah Garrett. After several unrewarding attempts to get Alice to tell what she knew the conversation changed to Miss Phe's new farms manager. Anyone with an eligible daughter was trying to find out as much about Ward Covington as they could. Again Alice remained mum, thankful that no one connected Ward's appearance with Sarah's reappearance.

While Alice waited her turn with Norma Sue, she sat at the empty manicure table.

Ramona was not there today. Alice aimlessly picked up the different bottles of polish, reading their titles and the names on the little tags Ramona had attached to some of the bottles identifying the owner. Frances' name was on a bright red Revlon color named, ironically, Demure. Mary Hester's bottle was Tahitian Twilight. An image of plump Mary Hester in a grass skirt briefly floated before Alice's eyes. Mildred's bottle was Mother Road Rose. Bessie wore Cherries in the Snow. Minnie's was Papua Pink Pearl. Mae Rose's name was on Sheer Petal.

Alice went back to Minnie's polish. It was really a lovely shade, soft like Minnie. She unscrewed the cap and painted one of her nails. Very pretty. Then Norma Sue called her to the chair so she recapped the bottle of polish and got up.

While Norma Sue was styling Alice's hair she asked casually about Julianna. "You know, we were classmates in high school. Of course, Julianna was a Garrett and made sure we all remembered it. Say what you will, though, she has had her share of troubles.

"And Grant Whitworth showing up out of the blue must be an awful embarrassment." Norma Sue obviously did not expect any replies from Alice. "Him leaving her high and dry at the altar might have happened a long while ago but I expect that is something a girl never gets over.

"Julianna has been in here a couple of times lately." Alice's ears perked up. "She picked up Mary Hester one morning. I was running behind so she sat over at Ramona's table looking at the nail polishes like you were just doing till I finished with Mary Hester. Then she surprised Ramona by calling for a manicure last Friday morning. Could have knocked us over with a feather. She's never darkened the door. Thank goodness she came early 'cause Minnie had her manicure a little later and no telling what would have happened had they both been here at the same time. Anyway, Miss La-di-da Julianna brought her own polish…oddly enough the same one Minnie likes… and acted like she didn't know Ramona from a hole in the head. Snooty. Julianna has always thought she was the cat's meow."

With that pronouncement Norma Sue picked up a can of hairspray and lacquered Alice's hair to immobile perfection.

***

The Hatcher sisters decided that the best way to keep an eye on Minnie was to be with her. This morning Mary Hester would drive with her on her errands and then they would meet at Slater's drugstore for lunch. Mildred was playing golf so Athie would take the afternoon shift.

Minnie was not too keen on all this but agreed because Grant insisted.

"How long is this going to go on?" Minnie asked Mary Hester as they drove to the bank.

"I don't think it'll be too long," Mary Hester answered. She was thoroughly enjoying riding in Minnie's big Mercedes. "Ophelia is going to do something soon."

***

Ophelia spent the morning painting in her art shed. She welcomed the solitude. It helped her arrange her thoughts. Maize just slept while Ophelia tried to capture the blues and greens of the hydrangea blossoms Naomi Ruth cut that morning. About noon she and Maize wandered back down the path to the house for lunch. She had decided what to do and when to do it.

***

Robert drove Sarah to Newtons Fork that morning. Sarah needed to pick up some things at Belk's. Robert then took her to a gun shop where she purchased Ward's birthday gift. They were already back home when Ophelia and Maize wandered into the kitchen.

Over lunch Naomi Ruth announced she had some very good news. Hobart had called.

He sold his townhouse in Washington and would be passing through this Wednesday on the way there for the closing. He would spend the night at Merrebanks.

"I did not tell Hobart that Sarah was here. Hobart had heard through Carter from Minnie that we had a new farm manager. That is all."

"Oh, I'm delighted he's coming. I'll be so glad to see him again." Sarah was quiet a minute. "I hope he feels the same way when he sees me."

"He will, dear, don't worry." Ophelia paused, appearing deep in thought. "So...maybe Ward's birthday party is the time to announce who Ward really is. He might be a Covington in name but he is a Garrett by blood and it's high time everyone knows it. Everybody!"

She looked at Naomi Ruth.

***

That afternoon Julianna returned home from shopping in Chapel Hill. She had purchased a suit at Fine Feathers. It cost what most people paid to rent a beach cottage for a week but Julianna didn't bat an eye. The phone rang and when Julianna answered Ophelia was on the line. Yes, she could come to Hope Springs this Wednesday. She would be glad to see her brother. She hung up and stood silently thinking. Another trip home at this time was not to Julianna's liking. Her plan was in place and her being there was not necessary. Hope Springs was tiresome, the same people doing the same things their grandparents did. She also had no desire to spend time with her irksome brother. But she could not risk making her mother mad. She smiled to herself. At least now there was the chance the new farm manager would be around.

***

The Hatcher sisters, still in the role of body guards, were having wine with Minnie on her back patio when Grant returned. "Thank you for keeping an eye on Minnie today," he addressed the sisters, "but I wonder if I can ask another favor. If I treat you ladies to dinner at the club could I persuade you to stay with Minnie a while longer? My friend at the SBI sent the surveillance tape to me today and if Julianna is on it she's certainly fooled me. I do not recognize her at either the Washington Duke or the Angus Barn. I want to take the tape to Ophelia."

"Can we see?" Athie asked. There was not a shy bone in her middle-aged body.

They went back into Minnie's den and Grant put the tape in the machine. A black and white picture of the bar in the Washington Duke played. Grant and Minnie entered and sat at the bar. People came and went until Grant and Minnie eventually left the screen. There were also several shots of people coming and going in elevators. The Angus Barn was similar. Grant and Minnie joined an attractive couple. They dined. They left. There was no sign of Julianna.

"Well, I certainly don't see her," Mary Hester said.

"Me either," Mildred said.

"Nor I," said Athie.

***

Robert stepped out onto the side porch at Merrebanks. "We are going to have to postpone supper for a while. That was Grant and he wants to come out here. He needs to ask you something, Ophelia."

Ophelia and Sarah were sitting on the river porch talking while having their cocktails. Ward and Eggie were not joining them this evening as Sam was introducing Ward to evening Rotary at the club.

"I have the feeling we are waiting for the other shoe to fall," Ophelia said. "I guess it's best to get it over with."

Sarah reached over and squeezed her mother-in-law's hand.

Grant arrived about twenty minutes later. He apologized for coming during the dinner hour. "When you mentioned Julianna's acting ability the other day, Ophelia, you added that if I saw Julianna on one of the surveillance tapes I probably would not be able to identify her. You were right. I can't."

Ophelia's eyebrows rose and her pale blue eyes looked surprised.

"I requested the surveillance tapes from the Washington Duke and the Angus Barn...rather I had a friend with connections request them for me. I have the tape here. The two locations are on it so it doesn't take long to go over the footage. Could I ask you...and Naomi Ruth...and Robert and Sarah, too...to look at the tape and see if you can identify Julianna? I cannot."

Ophelia rose. "Sarah, please go get Naomi Ruth and Robert. Grant, the tape machine is in the library. Yes," she added as she looked up at Grant, "it's time to see her at work, because there is no doubt in my mind that she is there."

Ophelia and Naomi Ruth sat side by side on the sofa as the tape played. They both nodded at the same times as the scenes rolled by. The tape ended. Ophelia and Naomi Ruth looked at each other. "She wasted a lot of talent," Naomi Ruth said.

Ophelia turned to Grant. "Restart the tape and when I say 'pause' stop the film and I will point out Julianna."

Grant looked at Ophelia in amazement. "You mean she's there? I can't believe it."

"She's there."

Ophelia asked Grant to pause the film as a matronly woman entered the bar of the Washington Duke Inn. She was well dressed and used a cane, moving slowly. Eventually she took a seat not far from Grant and Minnie. "That's Julianna."

"How on earth do you know? I'm flabbergasted. I have looked at these tapes fifteen times at least and I never so much as blinked at that elderly lady."

"It's her all right," Naomi Ruth agreed. "There are certain mannerisms she just can't hide. She holds her head at a certain angle when she is watching something intently. Things like that."

"Go to the elevator shots," Robert said. When Grant did he noticed several of the matronly lady entering and exiting. "She is getting on and off different elevators," Robert pointed out. "She probably wanted it to look like she was staying there so she came in on a side elevator then down to the lobby on an inside one. I know about those elevators because I had to get Julianna out of there several times when she stayed there after her face lifts."

"Now move on to the Angus Barn. That one is even more

dramatic." Grant advanced the tape until Ophelia said 'pause' as a man walked behind the table where Minnie, Grant and their companions were seated. The man was seated two tables down from them but still in their line of vision.

"That 'man' is Julianna," Ophelia said.

"What?" Grant was staring at the man in amazement. "He can't be Julianna. Can he?"

"I told you she was quite good."

Grant continued to sit and stare as the tape rolled on. He watched the man, whom he had assumed at the time to be some kind of professor or writer, order and dine while seemingly oblivious to those around him. Looking more closely Grant noticed several surreptitious glances in their direction. It seemed harmless.

"I'll be," Grant shook his head in disbelief. "I would never in a million years recognized either of those people as Julianna."

"What now?" Robert asked.

"These tapes are alarming. She's going to a lot of trouble to follow us. I'm going to have to do something, Phe." He looked pleadingly at Ophelia. "This can't continue. The least I will do is get a court order to keep her away from us."

Ophelia steadily returned his gaze. "I want you to know how much I appreciate your patience and your consideration of the Garrett family when you are well aware of the enormity and danger of the problem. Naomi Ruth and I have a plan but when one plots a course in an open sea one is never sure of the destination until one arrives. Handling Julianna is tricky. She's psychologically twisted so we must try and stop her with a 'psychological' plan. Fight fire with fire, so to speak. If we are right it should all end quickly. We may well see some results by tomorrow night, certainly no later than Thursday. Let's hope we have a solution by the weekend. I will need your help at some point, I think."

"You will have it, Ophelia."

***

Since Everett's death Charlotte and Ev insisted Alice dine with them each evening if she had no other plans. Alice did not argue. She hated being at home by herself surrounded by memories of her life with Everett.

Tonight Ev's best friend, William, and his wife, Gloria, were dining with them. William owned and operated, Jeffrey's, the local hardware store. Gloria taught fourth grade. Gloria, like every woman in Hope Springs, was curious about the Garrett's new farms manager. "I think Ward Covington is going to keep tongues wagging in this little town."

"They already are," William said. "He was in the hardware store Friday with Sam Jenkins. They were setting up new accounts for Garrett Farms since Ward will now be in charge. Sam says he can't wait to turn over the reins. We'll see about that. He's run the Garrett operation for an awfully long time. Anyway, every woman in the place walked by the office and it sure wasn't because of Sam and me. Ladies hung around the store wandering up and down the aisles like they were interested in bolts and nails, just waiting for Ward to leave the office. Our sales soared."

"He is nice, though," Charlotte added. "He has beautiful manners. He helped Sarah, Eggie and Ophelia in and out of the car at church Sunday. Actually, I think it's interesting that he went with them. I guess he feels an obligation to Miss Phe. She certainly seems to include him in everything."

Alice sat quietly. She had not told her son or Charlotte who Ward was. She respected Phe's wishes. Alice knew Phe would reveal Ward's identity when the time was right. In her naïve shrewdness Alice suspected Phe's decision had something to do with Julianna. Alice's attention returned to the conversation when she heard Gloria mention Julianna's name.

"Julianna certainly looked good...for someone her age, that is...at the party. And, man, did she ever zoom in on Ward Covington. It was almost embarrassing."

"She's a good-looking woman," William reminded his wife. "She was in the hardware store a few days ago, too."

"Julianna? Are you sure? She's not exactly the hardware store type." Charlotte was surprised.

"Well, she didn't see me but I was watching her through the office glass."

"Shame on you, William." His wife wagged her finger at him and laughed.

"I think she was lost because she was in the industrial pesticide section. No one goes over there except the pest control people."

Alice and Charlotte looked at each other. "When was this, William?" Alice asked as innocently as she could.

***

Grant was home when the Hatcher girls brought Minnie back from the country club.

They pulled up to the back door and parked. It was no surprise that when Minnie got out of the car they did, too. There was not a shred of doubt in anyone's mind that they were not going to find out what happened at Merrebanks.

Grant was sitting at the counter watching television and drinking a beer when the four women entered the kitchen. They all stood silently looking at him. "She recognized Julianna," was all he said. Then they all went into the den and he replayed the tape, pointing out Julianna at the Washington Duke and the Angus Barn.

Mary Hester, Athie, Mildred and Minnie were without words.

***

Dinner at Merrebanks that evening was a distracted meal. Thoughts were on Grant's tape. Ophelia glanced at Sarah. "I hate that you've had to endure all this mess with Julianna while you're here."

"In a very strange way, Phe, I feel as if I've picked up where I left off. Julianna was a problem then, too."

Ophelia, Naomi Ruth and Robert looked up, forks hovering.

"I left Linus because I was scared to stay." Forks were set down on plates and all eyes turned to Sarah.

"Julianna poisoned my marriage." Sarah looked around the table at the faces watching her. "Linus and I were happily married for five wonderful years…years with memories I treasure…memories I have shared with his son. Then we hit the obstacle of children. We both wanted them but for some reason I never got pregnant…or if I did, which happened three times, I miscarried in the early months." She looked up at the surprise on Ophelia's and Naomi Ruth's faces. "I never shared that with anyone and neither did Linus. He saw it as some kind of stigma…a disgrace…a weakness.

"When Ev Jr. was born Linus was terribly conflicted. He loved Ev Jr. of course, but he was so jealous of Everett for being a father and of a son, to boot. He retreated from me, staying later and later at the office, hardly talking. I tried to suggest a marriage counselor but he blew a fuse at that. I suggested a fertility method but he thought that was an affront to his masculinity. Besides, he wasn't at fault. I was. He blamed me for our childlessness.

"He was convinced my horseback riding caused the miscarriages. Riding Lady Bess was the only thing that kept me sane. You know that. When I went out to the Piney Creek farm and rode in the afternoons my head and heart would clear up. Linus didn't understand.

"During all this Linus started drinking…heavily." Sarah looked over at Ophelia. Ophelia nodded. She had suspected. "He hid it well, though. After all, he was a big man so he could hold his liquor…in public, anyway. His law practice didn't suffer. He was elected to district court…and eventually to superior court, I understand.

"I really don't think anyone had a clue about the amount of alcohol he was consuming. It changed his personality completely. A mean streak I never knew existed came out. People talk about physical abuse but verbal abuse is just as brutal. The scars hide inside where no one can see them. The more he drank the more I retreated to the farm and my sweet Lady Bess. Leaving her was the hardest thing I ever did. I always wondered what happened to her."

"Alice went and got her. She moved her to their farm. Lady Bess was well looked after and died peacefully of old age."

"Oh, thank goodness. Alice is an angel." Sarah sighed and dabbed at her eyes with her napkin.

Sarah straightened up. Her face hardened. "When Julianna returned to Merrebanks after her stay in the hospital…mental institution, Linus called it…after the wedding fiasco…she spent a lot of time at our house. I don't know why. Maybe Linus and Julianna recognized in themselves two wounded spirits. I would come home after an afternoon out…riding Lady Bess or bridge or tennis or whatever I was doing…and the two of them would be sitting in the den drinking. Whenever I asked Julianna to stay for dinner, she refused. That I never understood either because we had always gotten on rather well together…after all I was her maid of honor. She just shut me out for some reason.

"Anyway, after she left Linus was always quiet. I would be fixing dinner and he would come into the kitchen and ask me about my afternoon. Eventually he started asking questions about Sam Jenkins. I didn't understand at first but finally it dawned on me. Linus thought I was having an affair with Sam…dear sweet Sam who loved Estelle better than life. Where did Linus get such an idea? I finally realized that Julianna was telling him these lies.

"Julianna knew Lady Bess was stabled at the Piney Creek farm. She knew Sam and Estelle lived on the Piney Creek farm. She knew Sam helped me tend to Lady Bess. She knew I was out there often riding in the afternoons. Julianna looked for trouble, the possibility of conflict…of putting someone down. She liked to roil the waters. I guess it made her feel superior. And innocence was never a possibility with her. She always saw guilt.

"One afternoon Linus was really drunk when I returned home from the farm. I started dinner. He came into the kitchen and said Julianna had seen Sam and me together in the barn the day before when she came out to the Piney Creek farm looking for me. I said, yes, we were in the barn tending to Lady Bess. Then he raised his voice and asked if I was sure that was all we were doing…was I having an affair with Sam? I laughed. It was so absurd. I told him I was definitely not having an affair with Sam Jenkins. He said he didn't believe me. I looked at him and knew our marriage was over.

"That night I moved into the guest room. He followed me, making horrible and hurtful suggestions. I could not believe the man I had loved, and thought loved me, could say such cruel things. I've never repeated them to anyone…and, sadly, I have never forgotten them. They haunt my dreams." She sighed.

Naomi Ruth watched Sarah, pain reflected in her sad brown eyes.

"I locked my door that night and stayed in the room till I heard Linus leave for his law office the next morning. Then I packed and I left. I know it was cowardly of me to just run away but I was scared to confront him and, honestly, I had had enough. My Linus, that sweet man I married, had gone far away. I flew from Greenville to Chicago. My family welcomed me and asked no questions. Then I discovered I was pregnant. My life began again." Sarah smiled.

She looked at those watching her. A sad smile played at the corners of her mouth, "The ironic thing was…Sam Jenkins could not have children. He had a severe case of the mumps when he was a child and he was sterile. Estelle told me that. When Julianna said I spent too much time at Piney Creek, it was true, but it was not with Sam. It was with Estelle. We would have tea in the afternoon after my ride and talk about children…making a life for ourselves without them. Thankfully I didn't have to…I have my son."

She paused and smiled, looking at the three watching her. "I must add that Linus never called my parents looking for me. My parents were never asked where I was. In time I realized I had done the right thing. Linus didn't care enough about me to look for me. He forfeited his right to his son."

Chapter Thirty-Two

Tuesday morning Naomi Ruth and Ophelia were in the midst of calling to invite friends to Ward's birthday party when Alice arrived. She had a bottle of nail polish in her hand.

"May I paint your nails, Phe? I imagine this is not really a good time but…"

"Of course, dear." She looked at Naomi Ruth and shrugged. Then she rose and she and Alice walked together to the sunroom. Maize knew better than to follow.

Alice was on the stool in front of Phe. "This is a new color. I found it at Walgreen's this morning. It's the color Ramona uses for Minnie's nails…Papua Pink Pearl."

Alice began to paint Phe's nails.

"I had my hair done yesterday at *Kut & Kurl.* Did you know Julianna has been in there twice since Everett's funeral? Once to pick up Mary Hester…she had to sit and wait for her…at the manicure table…and the other time she actually made an appointment with Ramona to do her nails. I think that's odd."

Ophelia didn't answer but she agreed with Alice. Julianna had a manicurist in Raleigh. Why was she getting her nails done at *Kut & Kurl*?

"You know Ramona uses the polish her ladies bring her. She keeps the bottles on the manicure table, labeled with their names.

Frances has her own; Mae Rose has her favorite; Minnie has hers. There are lots of labeled polish bottles.

"I had dinner last night with Ev and Charlotte."

Ophelia made the mental leap. She knew Alice was leading up to something. She waited. "William and Gloria joined us. I hadn't seen them since the night of the funeral. I wonder how Hobart is doing?"

"He'll be here tomorrow. He's sold his townhouse and must be in Washington for the closing. He will stop over here for Ward's birthday party." Ophelia tried to blow on the wet nails of her right hand.

"Oh, good." Alice reached for Ophelia's left hand. "William saw Julianna in the hardware store."

"Julianna? In the hardware store?"

"Yes, in the pesticide section."

Ophelia sat ramrod straight.

Alice finished. "Do you think I should go to *Kut & Kurl* and get Minnie's polish?"

"Yes, Alice. I think that would be a very good idea."

***

Athie drove down the block faster than usual. She was returning from the Pig and did not want her ice cream to melt. She glanced at the Harris' house as she passed. All was quiet. Hector and Clara were with Minnie today. They were packing for the moving van's arrival for Carter's belongings. A bicyclist suddenly rounded the corner in front of her, surprising Athie and causing her to swerve to the left. She glared at the young man peddling by. She recognized the dress of a young Mormon. She turned up her driveway. As she was opening her car door she glanced back down the street. The young Mormon had stopped at Minnie's. Athie paused as she reached for a grocery bag. Why was he alone? Mormons always travel in pairs.

She slammed the car door and started running down the block.

She could see the young Mormon standing on the Harris' stoop. The door opened and Minnie stood there. Where was Hector? Where was Clara? Athie moved down the sidewalk as quickly as she could in the heat. The young man was reaching for something. Hector appeared in the door. Oh, thank goodness.

He said something and Minnie went inside. Athie was getting closer. She began to wave her arms trying to get Hector's attention. Hector and the Mormon appeared to have a short conversation then the young Mormon turned, got back on his bicycle and pedaled down the walk.

Athie started calling to Hector. He turned in her direction. A puzzled expression appeared on his face when he saw Athie flying down the sidewalk with arms waving like a banshee.

The young Mormon reached the end of the walk at precisely the moment Athie did. Athie pushed hard. He fell to the grass tangled in the wheels of his bicycle.

Hector rushed up. Minnie and Clara came out of the house.

They all watched as Athie stood over the poor Mormon shouting, "Shame! Shame! Shame on you, Julianna!"

***

When Grant returned to Minnie's house that evening he found Alice Garrett sitting with Minnie and the Hatcher sisters. They all had a glass of wine in front of them but it was being uncharacteristically ignored. The girls were having a serious conversation, huddled together and concentrating so hard they didn't hear him arrive. He poured his wine and joined them. "How was the day?" he asked.

"Very eventful." Minnie glanced at Athie and everyone laughed. "First, Alice has something she wants to show you."

Alice reached into her purse and pulled out a bottle of nail polish. "It's a long story but you might need to get this analyzed. It's Minnie's nail polish from the beauty parlor." She handed the bottle of polish to Grant.

"Nail polish? Nail polish?" he repeated looking puzzled.

"We've been talking, Grant." Minnie turned to him. "I have been having headaches lately. And this morning a few extra strands of hair seemed to be in my brush."

"Damn!" Grant rose and took his phone into the house. When he returned he picked up the polish and put it in his pocket. Then he lifted one of Minnie's hands. "I see you've removed your polish."

"Better safe than sorry."

***

That evening Ophelia, Naomi Ruth, Sarah and Maize sat together in Ophelia's bedroom. Ophelia and Naomi Ruth were in the chintz covered chairs by the window, Maize asleep between them at their feet. Sarah sat at the end of Ophelia's high antique bed, legs wrapped under her.

She would miss these two when she returned to Chicago. This recurring thought grew daily more painful for her. She respected them and she loved them. She was so glad her Ward would have them in his life.

"Are we ready?" Ophelia asked. There was an undercurrent of urgency in her voice.

"Lordy, I hope so," Naomi Ruth answered.

Sarah knew they were not referring to the preparations for Ward's birthday party the next evening. A barbecue on the river lawn was planned. Everything was ready for that. No, what Ophelia and Naomi Ruth were referring to was their plan for Julianna.

"Dr. Bisbo will bring the sedative and syringe tomorrow." Ophelia looked at Naomi Ruth. "He'll give you a quick refresher course if you've forgotten how to give a shot."

Naomi Ruth nodded. She had not forgotten.

"He will also be available if and when we need him. All we have to do is call." Ophelia leaned back in her chair. She looked tired. "It will be complicated. Julianna is defiant when she's cornered. She cannot handle criticism. She gets defensive and can even get aggressive, though it's usually just verbal abuse.

"Grant's reappearance was a dreadful shock. His presence is like a festering wound for Julianna. His preference for Minnie has infuriated her...picked at her. He has insulted her and she aims to get even. They will be at the party...together...a couple...a reminder to Julianna of rejection in her past. Your appearance, Sarah, will be her second shock. She thought she was rid of you. I imagine Julianna always resented you in a way. She never had to deal with another daughter in the family. She was the one and only.

"Then she will find out that Ward is not only a Garrett, but also your son. That will be her third shocking surprise, and it will come fairly soon after the second. How will she react? You never know with Julianna. We thought her behavior after John's death was bizarre. She was almost happy. She never mentioned her brother Linus after he died so suddenly...and now she seems totally removed from these attacks on Minnie...apathetic, blasé."

"John was her third husband?" Sarah asked.

"Yes," Naomi Ruth answered. "He killed himself two years ago. Julianna never mentions him. It's like he never existed."

Ophelia glanced at Naomi Ruth. "Wednesday will lay the groundwork. If all goes according to plan, Thursday will be the major confrontation. The one thing I do not want to happen, Naomi Ruth, is a confrontation with her after everyone has left the party tomorrow night."

"Sarah and I will see to that," Naomi Ruth looked at Sarah. "Besides, Julianna has never been one to hang around after a party. She has a strong aversion to cleaning up."

Chapter Thirty-Three

Hobart arrived at Merrebanks around two-thirty on Wednesday, the day of the party. He greeted Naomi Ruth and Robert then sought out his mother. He found her in the sunroom talking with a vaguely familiar woman. When he realized it was his long lost Aunt Sarah he was very pleased.

"Aunt Sarah, this is the best surprise I've had in ages. I was not happy when you disappeared. I was just out of college and when I came home for Thanksgiving I was told you were gone…that's all. I thought aliens had abducted you or something. Linus told me never to mention your name again. Daddy just turned a deaf ear. Mother said you and Linus had a disagreement but she was sure you would be back soon. All a bunch of malarkey. I won't even go where Julianna said you were. Naomi Ruth was the only honest one. She told me the truth."

"What was that?" his mother asked. This was news to her. After all these years Naomi Ruth could still surprise her.

"She told me that Aunt Sarah and Uncle Linus had come to a parting of the ways. My words here. She said Uncle Linus had taken to drink but it was not common knowledge so not to discuss it. It was a family problem. He hurt Aunt Sarah so much she had to go away to find herself again. Naomi Ruth said she doubted you would return unless Uncle Linus changed, which he didn't…until it was too late, I guess."

***

Ward's birthday barbecue was to begin at six-thirty. Hector had arrived in the wee hours of the morning to set up his pig cooker and begin the slow process of roasting a pig properly. He had enlisted the help of Ipock Peck, who readily agreed when he learned Julianna would be there. Robert wandered over to keep them company. The pig had to be basted at regular intervals and gradually as the day progressed the growing aroma of roasting pig filled the air. It was a delicious, addictive smell, the favorite perfume of eastern North Carolina.

Alice, Ev and Charlotte arrived at four-thirty to help. Ward would not arrive until five-thirty because of farm duties. He would bring Eggie. Ev and Robert set the bar up on the side porch. Alice and Charlotte were in the kitchen helping Naomi Ruth with the huge platters necessary for serving the barbeque and the huge bowls necessary for serving the accompanying side dishes. Naomi Ruth had forgone her famous biscuits for her almost as famous cornbread. Ice cream and birthday cake would come later. Tables were set up on the lawn, covered with checked cloths. Sarah was placing candles on each table. The plates, napkins and utensils would soon be brought out to the serving table. Naomi Ruth had filled Mason jars with bouquets of hydrangeas and placed them on each table. Hobart and Robert lined the drive with tiki torches. It was very festive.

Julianna drove up the drive at five o'clock. She was surprised by the activity she could see on the lawn through the oaks as she passed by to the back parking. She noted with envy the BMW convertible parked there. She knew it must be Hobart's. She was curious about the festivities on the lawn. Her mother did love a party. She wondered what the occasion was this time? Julianna walked around the house towards the lawn.

The first person she saw was Robert bringing the large bucket to the porch that he used to ice down beers.

"Hello, Julianna," he said as he passed.

"Robert could you get my bags from the car and put them in my room." She glided past.

Robert looked at her, shook his head and said, "I'm busy right now, Julianna." He continued on his way.

She wandered on and eventually found her mother on the lawn talking with Alice and Charlotte. "Hello, Mother. I'm here," she announced, interrupting the conversation. Alice and Charlotte gave her a brief nod and walked off.

"I was beginning to wonder if you were coming, Julianna," Ophelia greeted her.

"I didn't know there was any hurry. I didn't realize we were having a party. Looks like quite a to do. What's the occasion this time? Don't tell me another of your old friends has a beau."

"No," Ophelia said. "Come with me." They walked towards two people watching them approach.

"This party is for Ward. It's his birthday."

Julianna stopped. She turned to Ophelia. "The farm manager? Really, Mother, don't you think this is a little over the top? Granted he's cute but I see absolutely no need to have birthday parties for the help."

"Actually I'm looking forward to meeting him, Snobby Sister." Hobart walked up. "I, for one, welcome any excuse for a party...and, actually, we have more than one reason to celebrate. Look who's here." He turned to the woman walking with him.

Julianna turned to the woman. A puzzled look crossed her face, followed by dismay. "Sarah?"

"Hello, Julianna." Sarah did not smile.

"What are you doing here?"

"Sarah is visiting me, Julianna. She arrived Friday and is staying for a while." Ophelia watched Julianna's reaction.

Julianna's eyes narrowed. "How nice." She turned and walked away. Ophelia and Sarah looked at each other.

Hobart just smiled.

***

Ward arrived with Eggie at five-thirty. Ophelia greeted them then led Ward to meet Hobart. She introduced him only as the farms manager. Hobart's welcome was cordial and enthusiastic. Eggie spied Hobart talking with Ward and hastened over. Hobart was her favorite nephew and quite perceptive. She did not want him talking with Ward too long so she corralled him and asked him to get her a drink. Hobart fetched the two of them cocktails and they sat in the rockers on the porch.

"Think Mother hit the jackpot with the new farms manager. He's quite presentable."

"You just don't know," Eggie smiled. "Where did Julianna disappear to?"

"The Mistress of Mischief slinked up to her room after discovering Sarah on the premises." Hobart took a sip of his bourbon.

Eggie nodded. "Tell me her exact reaction. Spare no details."

Hobart looked at his favorite aunt and grinned. "Julianna didn't seem to recognize Sarah at first. She just casually glanced her way. Then there was this look of surprise on her face…shock almost. Of course, she was dreadfully rude to Sarah and then she slithered into the house. Julianna is not at all pleased that Sarah has reappeared."

"No, I guess not. She thought she was shed of her." Eggie grew thoughtful. "My brother ruined Julianna…or maybe I should say he fed the rottenness in her because of his own vanity. Men! Honestly… they have such insecurities. That's what I love about you, Hobart. You air your insecurities with refreshing glee!"

"What you see is what you get, Aunt Eggie." The two clinked glasses and laughed.

***

The lawn was crowded. The men stood telling hunting and fishing stories watching Hector and Ipock slather the pig. The women were in a knot talking. Bessie, Mae Rose, Eggie and Arthur Taylor were rocking on the porch being thoroughly entertained by Hobart with tales of the rich and famous in Palm Beach. Alice and Charlotte were passing *hors d'oeuvres.*

Julianna took all this in when she emerged from the house. She stood on the side porch looking out over the lawn. She frowned. Sarah! Why was she here? First Grant reappears in Hope Springs and now Sarah! What was going on? She didn't like surprises.

She asked Robert for a gin and tonic. She walked down the steps and wandered across the lawn, eyes roaming. She watched Ward break away from the group of men and come over and say something to Sarah. Julianna saw him smile at Sarah before he turned and made his way back to the group of men. She noticed how Sarah watched him as he walked away. Interesting, she thought. She strolled over to Sarah.

"I don't know why you're here but I guess I mustn't be rude," Julianna announced.

"That's magnanimous of you, Julianna," Sarah answered. Her sarcasm was lost on Julianna.

"Mother did well when she hired that handsome young thing." Julianna's eyes watched Ward's broad back as he walked away. She did not notice the fleeting look on Sarah's face.

"Yes, she did."

"I wonder if he is still seeing Harriet Pearson? I see she's here with her parents," Julianna said.

"I think he sees Harriet when he can." Sarah wondered where this was going. It was all she could do to be civil.

"I think he could do better. I am going to get my Meggie over here. Meggie has grown into a real beauty. A Garrett trumps a Pearson any day."

"I expect he can make his own decisions about the girls he goes out with." Sarah was ready to end this conversation.

Julianna laughed. "Maybe he would be interested in a woman."

Bile rose in Sarah's throat. She turned and looked steadily at Julianna. "You're not his type, Julianna." She turned and walked away.

"And I suppose you are?" Julianna called after her.

"Yes," Sarah answered over her shoulder.

Julianna's laughter followed her. Sarah's skin crawled

***

"That daughter here yet?" Ipock Peck leaned over the grill. He mopped the pig with Hector's special barbecue sauce. Run-over hissed off the coals, spreading smoke and a delectable smell.

Hector looked out over the lawn. "Yep, there she is over by the live oak...blue dress...Miss Sarah is walking away from her...and Grant Whitworth is coming toward her."

Ipock Peck looked. He was quiet. "Hmmm," finally hummed from his throat.

Hector looked at him. "Something wrong?"

"Don't rightly know...this is a befuddling consternation." Ipock Peck slowly shook his head. "That lady is decidedly familiar to me, yes indeedy."

"You've seen her in town maybe," Hector said.

"Nope." Ipock Peck looked hard at Julianna then turned to Hector. "Somethin' else...and it wont long ago, neither. I just need to cogitate on it. Yes, indeedy"

***

Grant was standing by himself sipping his Scotch. He watched Julianna approach Sarah. He could tell the conversation was distasteful to Sarah. He saw Julianna laugh as Sarah walked away. He walked towards Julianna.

"Hello, Julianna."

She turned. Surprise and dismay registered on her face followed by a speculative look. "Why Grant, I didn't know you would be here tonight...at Merrebanks again. Mother invited you to another Garrett family party? I can't believe she is so forgiving."

"I'm here...so obviously she is." He smiled and took a sip of Scotch.

"Is little Minnie here too? Maybe you are here to join me for dinner?" She raised an eyebrow and smiled.

Grant's gaze didn't waver. "Minnie is here and I will join *her* for dinner."

Julianna shrugged her shoulders and smiled a twisted smile. She cocked her head. "You and Mother are certainly chummy these days."

"Yes, I guess you could say we have become comrades. You know, I have always admired Ophelia. She's gracious; she's kind; she's loyal. Lot's of things you're not." He took a sip from his glass, watching her over the rim. "Ophelia is also one I would never underestimate. She has a core of steel."

"Are we talking about the same person? Mother doesn't do anything but paint and party."

"Watch out, Julianna. Ophelia may surprise you." He raised his glass in a salute and walked away.

As Julianna stood staring after Grant, wondering what he meant, Ophelia began to tap on her glass seeking everyone's attention. When she had all eyes and ears she stood quietly for several minutes before speaking.

"I wish to welcome you all to Merrebanks this evening to celebrate Ward's birthday. It was indeed a lucky day for us Garretts when he applied to Garrett Farms for the position of manager." She glanced at Ward and smiled. "Robert, Alice and Charlotte are passing out champagne. Everyone please take a glass."

She waited until everyone had a glass of champagne in their hands. She spied Julianna across the lawn scowling.

"Ward is more special than most of you know. Come stand with me Ward." Ward walked up and stood beside Ophelia. He smiled but looked uncomfortable.

"You recognize Ward as Ward Covington. I recognize him as Ward Garrett." There was a murmur from the crowd. "Ward is the son of Sarah and my son, Linus. He has come home to Garrett land. Please, raise a toast to my grandson and welcome him as family and friend."

Julianna choked. She stared in disbelief as Ward hugged Ophelia then walked over and put his arms around Sarah. After a silent moment of surprise everyone started clapping. "Hear, hear!" floated out from the crowd. Robert and Naomi Ruth were laughing. It was obvious they already knew. Something about Alice's face led Julianna to believe she also knew. Julianna watched as everyone converged on Ward. There was laughter, hand shaking and back slapping. She felt dazed. She watched Hobart shake Ward's hand and follow it with a quick hug. A surprised Charlotte and Ev were right behind him.

Julianna saw Sarah standing to the side, watching. There was a look of pride and adoration on Sarah's face that incensed Julianna. She strode up to her. "Well, aren't you the coy one. I guess you have been priming that young man, whoever he is, all these years to come back here so you can get even with us Garretts. Whose son is he really? Sam's? He's certainly not Linus'. You might have fooled my mother, Sarah, but you have not fooled me." With that she turned and walked quickly away. Sarah stared after her.

Grant came up behind Sarah and watched Julianna stride away. "Amazing, isn't she? Forgive me but I heard what she said to you… she wasn't exactly whispering. Pay no attention to her words. They aren't the problem. But I do think we should make sure she stays away from Ward."

Sarah looked up at Grant. "Thank you. She's just so frightfully horrible. I thought I was immune after…never mind. Forgive me, it's just that she zeroes in on whom you care most about when she comes at you with her insinuations and threats. She's heartless, isn't she?"

"Yes." Grant took Sarah's hand and squeezed it. "She dances with the devil."

***

The bell for dinner sounded. Everyone made their way to the serving tables, piled high with barbecue, potato salad, coleslaw, sliced tomatoes and cucumbers, marinated vegetables and baked beans. They filled their plates then made their way to a table. Charlotte and Ev were helping Naomi Ruth and Robert. They brought drinks of choice, sweet tea, water, wine, alcohol. Naomi Ruth brought out baskets of corn bread. Pickles and assorted relishes were on the tables. When everyone was seated Robert blessed the food and conversation began again.

There were three tables. Arthur Taylor, who had just rewritten Ophelia's will to include her new found grandson, was seated at the table with Eggie, Bessie, Mae Rose, Julianna, Hobart, and Ophelia. He was a jovial soul but had difficulty engaging Julianna in conversation. She was to his left but seemed totally uninterested in any polite conversation. She just sat there and pushed her food around. No one sat to her left. Bessie and Eggie were deep in conversation so Arthur leaned towards them. He had trouble hearing what they were saying and they grew tired of yelling to be heard. They finally turned to each other and talked, leaving poor deaf Arthur to his own devices. Mae Rose, Ophelia and Hobart were laughing together at the other end. Hobart was at his best.

Sarah and Ward were at opposite ends of the next table. Harriet was to Ward's right. They were joined by Gloria and William and Sam and Estelle Jenkins. Harriet, William and Gloria were adjusting to Ward's new identity.

The final table was occupied by Minnie, Grant, Alice and the Hatcher clan. Erwin was at one end talking with Joe Allen. Alice, Mary Hester and Minnie on Grant's right and Mildred and Athie on Grant's left were discussing fingernail polish.

It began to grow dark about seven thirty. Ev and Charlotte went around to the tables and lit the candles. It was a lovely evening and everyone was in a genial mood. Laughter and chatter drifted out over the lawn like confetti whispers. Lightning bugs blinked in the shadows under the trees. All of a sudden the strains of "Happy Birthday" floated out as a singing Hector led a parade of Robert, carrying a huge birthday cake lit with twenty-four candles, Naomi Ruth, Ipock Peck, Ev and Charlotte. All were singing. Everyone joined in.

Robert placed the flaming cake before Ward. "Take a deep breath," Robert said, "...right many candles." Ward blew out the candles with one big whoosh. "Youth," Robert said. He took the cake to the side table and Naomi Ruth began to slice pieces and plate them. Robert and Ev took the plates around to each person. Charlotte set down bowls of ice cream at each place.

Ward stood and everyone grew quiet. "This has been a wonderful birthday party...one of the best, I think. I thank Miss Phe... forgive me but I'm not quite used to calling my boss-lady 'Grandmother.'" He looked at Ophelia and smiled. Everyone laughed. "I'm sure that day will come. I thank you all for celebrating with me. Most of all I thank you for welcoming me into your lives and into this community. I am a very fortunate twenty-four year old. Thank you." He sat down to ringing applause.

While everyone was enjoying their ice cream and cake, Julianna rose and went into the house. She did not go unnoticed. Eggie and Bessie were seated directly across from her. She had not said a word to them, or anyone else at the table, all evening. They glanced at each other. It was a knowing look. Hobart noticed his mother watching her, "Don't worry, Mother. Our preening princess has to adjust to another dip into her monetary expectations." Sarah watched from her spot at the end of the center table. Julianna radiated anger and frustration. Sarah knew she was going to lock her bedroom door tonight and she was going to ask Robert to hide Julianna's car keys.

Alice, Mary Hester and Minnie also saw Julianna stand and walk away. They said, "Grant" at the same time and pointed. Grant, Mildred and Athie turned to look.

"She stayed longer than I thought she would," was all Grant said.

"I would certainly barricade my door if I had to stay in this house tonight." Mildred echoed Sarah's thoughts then turned to her cake and ice cream.

***

In the kitchen Charlotte and Ev refilled pitchers of water and tea and made their way back out to the tables. Robert was scrapping the dinner plates and stacking them on the drainboard.

Hector and Ipock Peck were helping Naomi Ruth put the left-over food into containers then into the refrigerator. Ipock Peck took a trash bag out to the garbage and when he returned he asked Robert whose red BMW that was in the drive.

"Julianna's," Robert answered over his shoulder at the sink.

"Aha! Got it, Hector!" Ipock Peck announced so loudly all eyes turned to him. "I am now familiarized with my confabulation of Miss Julianna." He had everyone's attention.

Hector explained to the bewildered expressions. "Brother Ipock is of the opinion that he has seen Julianna somewhere recently."

"Pray tell, Brother Ipock, pray tell," Robert said.

"I got this call…think it was the Thursday before Memorial Day. Rico over at Jessie's Body Shop wanted me to travel out to White Swamp Road to get a car. When I drove up Rico was there… standing with this woman beside his truck. They was arguing…you could tell…lots of finger wagging. The car had a flat tire and the spare was flat, too. Rico won't happy about that…said only a woman would be that stupid. He wanted me to tow the car to his shop… which I did, yes, indeedy. Anyway, the woman didn't say nothin', stood there angry like, arms akimbo. She won't happy, no sir-ee! Then Rico told her to get in his truck and they took off. That's the same car out yonder in the drive…red BMW…hard to forget….and Miss Ophelia's daughter is decidedly the lady arguing with Ricco beside the road. She was mad as all get out." He nodded his head at the recollection.

"White Swamp Road, Ipock?" Naomi Ruth asked. She had been listening carefully.

"Not much used. Don't go nowhere. It's over yonder behind Battle Hill farm near the river,"

"Oh, I know where it goes," Naomi Ruth answered and looked at Robert. "Julianna and Jake Denton lived out there."

***

It was late when the guests at Ward's birthday party departed for their homes. It was one of those nights no one wanted to end. Good-byes were lengthy. Eventually only Hector, Ipock Peck and the family remained. Ward prepared to take Eggie home. He hugged Ophelia and his mother goodnight. Ophelia nearly cried. Sarah did.

Alice and Charlotte promised to return in the morning to take down the tables and chairs. Then they joined Ev in his pick-up truck and headed home. Hector hooked his pig cooker to his truck and he and Ipock Peck headed down the drive, leaving a lingering aroma of roasted pig in their wake.

The kitchen was a mess but Robert shooed everyone away. He would finish cleaning up. He always did. He enjoyed it. First though he went up to Ophelia's room and freed Maize. The two of them went outside. Robert extinguished the tiki torches while Maize sniffed every blade of grass, gobbling droppings when she found them.

Hobart fixed himself another drink and sat on the porch. Sarah joined him.

Naomi Ruth and Ophelia said goodnight and went upstairs. There was no sound coming from Julianna's room when they passed. They could see light under the door. They moved quietly past down the hall.

They left the bedroom door slightly ajar because Maize would be joining them when she realized there were no more treats in store. Naomi Ruth sat in a chair by the window. Ophelia sat at her dressing table. She unclasped her pearls and began to take the pins from her hair. "What a wonderful celebration that was. I think everyone had a grand time." She began to brush her hair.

Naomi Ruth rose and began to turn down the bed covers. "Poor Robert might be spending the night in the kitchen."

The door nudged open and Maize trotted in. She came over to Ophelia and put her head on Ophelia's lap. "You would have liked the party, too," Ophelia said as she rubbed Maize's ears. "There were lots of old people dropping bits of food. Did you hoover it all up while you were out with Robert?"

Suddenly Maize's head jerked around. She turned towards the door and growled.

Julianna stood on the threshold. Ophelia grabbed Maize's collar. Naomi Ruth turned. "Julianna, you startled us."

"That dog should go." Julianna looked at Maize.

"That dog is not the one who's going," Naomi Ruth muttered.

"Is anything wrong, Julianna?" Ophelia was watching her. "Why did you leave the party? I noticed you didn't talk to anyone at the table. That was rude."

"I didn't feel like talking." Julianna stepped into the room. Maize growled again. Naomi Ruth took a step towards Julianna. Julianna stopped.

"Julianna, Ophelia is tired. It has been a long day. Maybe you best wait till tomorrow to say whatever it is you are boiling to say."

Julianna looked from Naomi Ruth to Ophelia and back to Naomi Ruth. Naomi Ruth's brown eyes were hard and steady. Ophelia's blue eyes were cold. What Grant said came back to her. She turned and left the room. Soon after they heard her door slam.

***

Sarah and Hobart entered Ophelia's room when they came

upstairs and saw her door ajar and her light still on. Ophelia was in bed propped up on pillows. Naomi Ruth was in the chair by the window, the Bible on her lap. Maize was asleep on the floor at the foot of the bed. She raised her head briefly when they entered then went right back to sleep.

Hobart sat down in the other chair across from Naomi Ruth. Sarah sat on the foot of Ophelia's bed. "Mother, you had one hell of a party. I am so glad I was able to be here and I am really happy we have Ward here with us and Aunt Sarah back in the fold. You are not going to let her go back to Chicago, are you?"

Ophelia laughed. "Hobart, you are a mess. I don't want Sarah to ever leave us again but that decision is hers." She looked over at Sarah.

Sarah seemed surprised. "Oh, my. This I must think about. Let me talk it over with Ward."

"Sarah and I have been talking on the porch, Mother." Hobart was uncharacteristically solemn.

"Something has to be done about Julianna. It's a bad situation. I knew some of what's been going on because Minnie talks with Carter but I didn't know it all. I have the feeling that if we Garretts don't do something Grant Whitworth will. She's ours. It's up to us." He looked at his mother.

"I've decided to stay," he continued, "…not to leave tomorrow. My lawyer can delay the closing with some legal pretext. I have a gnawing feeling everything is coming to a head. Sinister Sister is hell bent on mayhem."

"Unfortunately, 'Omi and I are aware of that. We'll tend to Julianna but your being here the next few days would be a blessing. I think we'll need you."

Hobart stood. "Good. That's settled. I'm heading to bed. Night, all." He pecked his mother's cheek, then Naomi Ruth's. He hugged Sarah and left.

Julianna just did get back into her bedroom before Hobart

walked out of Ophelia's bedroom. She had heard the laughter coming from Ophelia's room and gone out into the hall to listen. She resented the fact that Hobart and Sarah were welcome when she had been shooed away. She was pleased to realize, however, that she was the topic of conversation though she could only pick up snippets of what was said. What did her mother mean by saying she was going to 'tend' to her? Oh, she could give them so much more to talk about, if they only knew. Maybe it was time to tell them. Then they would realize she got what she wanted, as Daddy had taught her Garretts always do.

Sarah also bid Ophelia and Naomi Ruth goodnight. "Lock your door tonight, Phe. I feel trouble afoot. I'm certainly going to lock mine."

Naomi Ruth and Ophelia sat in silence. "Everyone seems on edge."

"'By the pricking of my thumb…,'" Naomi Ruth began.

"Tomorrow night this time we'll have a direction, at least. It all depends…" Ophelia trailed off. "I'm sad we have to do this to her but I just don't see another way. She's moved out of bounds." Ophelia closed her eyes and leaned back into her pillows. Her brilliant blond hair fell to her shoulders. She looked her eighty years.

She opened her eyes and looked at her friend. "Have we waited too long? What should we have done, 'Omi? What should I have done? It's all about choices…and living with their consequences. I've always felt that if one hangs in there long enough…through thick and thin…always trying to do the right thing…it will eventually work out." She laughed. "Now I just don't know."

"Pooh, Ophelia. What's happened is not your fault any more than it's mine. We have always known she was selfish. She has always put herself first…or been put first." Naomi Ruth looked at Ophelia. They both knew what she meant. "We let her get by with things because we felt sorry for her, I guess…abandoned and all. Or maybe we let her get by with things because we felt guilty for how we felt about her."

"I never could love her like my own," Ophelia said.

"She was hard to love. Still is."

"Yes," Ophelia paused, "I really dread tomorrow."

Naomi Ruth stood up. "Don't worry, I'll be right behind you. Guess we always knew this day might come. Hoped it wouldn't, but it has. Time for a resolution, I guess." She walked over and squeezed Ophelia's hand. "Goin' to bed now but I'm leaving Maize with you. Lock the door when I leave."

***

It was pitch dark in the room. Maize let out a low growl. Ophelia's eyes flew open. She heard it, too. The knob on her door was turning. It clicked then released. Her door was locked. She glanced at the bedside clock. It was two-twenty-three.

Chapter Thirty-Four

Ophelia couldn't sleep. She was up, dressed and outside with Maize when Naomi Ruth and Robert walked into the backyard.

"Problem sleeping?"

"I was awakened at a very early hour. Someone was turning the knob on my door."

"Thank the good Lord you locked it."

"Yes, and at the time I thought it was a silly idea."

They walked up the stairs across the screened porch into the kitchen.

"She tried to go somewhere, too," Robert said. "I heard something when I was walking home...must have been around two o'clock...took me a while to clean up the kitchen. Anyway I came back to see what it was. Julianna was in her car. She didn't see me. Then she got out... no keys. She was cussin'. Miss Sarah asked me to take Julianna's keys out of her car. I did. Julianna couldn't go wherever she was intending to go. Don't know how Miss Sarah thought of that." Robert shook his head and watched Maize eat her breakfast. "Where you reckon Julianna was goin' at that hour?"

"If I had to guess. I would say Sarah was worried about her son. Mothers have a sixth sense when it comes to their children. I would guess Julianna was up to something compromising."

"But then she came up to your room," Naomi Ruth said. "Why?" She started the coffee pot.

"Who knows how that mind of hers works. Maybe she thought I had her keys. I wonder if she tried to get into Sarah's room?"

"It's gonna be a long day…but first thing we are going to do is go back upstairs and fix your hair! It's all over the place. You a sight!" Naomi Ruth was eyeing Ophelia critically.

Ophelia laughed out-loud, her hand flying to her disheveled blond head. "I did the best I could. I just don't have your knack!"

***

Sarah entered the kitchen just before eight o'clock. She poured a cup of coffee. Ophelia asked if she slept well. Yes, she slept like a baby, Sarah replied as she picked up a piece of toast. Her eyes widened when Ophelia told her of her early morning visitor. Sarah grew quiet when Robert told her of Julianna's attempt to leave in the night. Sarah nibbled at her toast, lost in thought. Hobart came in about eight-thirty. He, too, was told of Julianna's late night rambles. "Damn" was all he said. A little before nine Alice and Charlotte arrived and everyone left the cool of the kitchen for the heat and humidity of the lawn to finish clearing what had not been done the night before.

The group was hot and thirsty when they slowly made their way back to the kitchen later in the morning. They found Julianna sitting at the kitchen table placidly drinking coffee.

Everyone paused at the sight of her. "Mighty nice of you to come out and help us clean up, Thoughtless Sister." Hobart walked past her.

She glanced up at them. "Why should I do that, Sweaty Brother?"

"Why, indeed," Hobart said as he removed the iced tea pitcher from the refrigerator.

Naomi Ruth got down glasses from the cabinet as everyone hesitantly joined Julianna at the table. Sarah left the room with a quick excuse. Robert also left, leaving to lock the barn.

Hobart brought the glasses of tea to Ophelia, Charlotte, and Alice sitting conspicuously silent at the table. He then sat down with his own glass.

"How did you sleep, Rude Sister? Do any sleep walking?"

Julianna looked at Hobart. She did not answer.

Hobart just grinned.

Julianna turned to Ophelia, "Mother, while Sarah's upstairs... and it's just the family here..."

"I consider Sarah family, Julianna." Ophelia locked eyes with Julianna.

"Mother, surely you can't be serious."

"I'm perfectly serious."

"Sarah walked out on this family over twenty years ago..."

"Twenty-five years ago this October to be exact." Naomi Ruth walked over and sat down beside Ophelia.

"Yes, well, the fact is she left. She wanted no part of us Garretts then so why is she back here now with Linus' so-called son? I can't believe you are falling for this charade. She's worming her way back into this family with a story that is totally far-fetched, fabricated, bogus...hoping to get money, get back into the Trust."

"She's never been out of the Trust," Ophelia looked at Julianna.

Julianna stared. "What? That's absurd. When she left she forfeited any right to Garrett money."

"I didn't feel that way and neither did your father. Until we found out why she left we both felt she deserved to continue to be considered a part of our family. We never removed her from the Garrett Trust."

"Well, it's high time you did." Julianna slapped her hand on the table. "She's even remarried, for heaven's sake. She is not a Garrett anymore." Julianna looked at the faces of those at the table. "She's not fooling me one iota…and I'm really surprised at you, Mother. Are you losing it? Can't you see that Sarah has prepped her son to take over the Garrett lands to get even with Linus and the Garretts. It is so obvious! Ward is no more Linus' son than Houdini.

"Sarah and Linus could not have children. Sarah was having an affair with Sam Jenkins. Linus found out and kicked her out. I would guess that Ward is Sam Jenkins' son."

"Why are you saying such things?" Hobart looked at his sister.

"Why?" Julianna looked at him. "Because they're true."

"How do you know?"

"Linus told me."

"He didn't tell you, Julianna. You told him." Sarah stood in the doorway. "You told him the afternoon before I left. You told him you had seen Sam Jenkins and me together. It was a bald faced lie but poor Linus couldn't think…he was drunk. You made sure of that, too. You had been enjoying yourself for quite a while visiting in the afternoons with Linus, feeding him alcohol along with lies to poison our marriage…to suggest I was unfaithful to him. Why, Julianna? I always wondered why."

Julianna just looked at Sarah. "Exactly…why would I lie?" The room grew still. All eyes were focused on Julianna.

"It was the challenge, wasn't it Julianna?" Naomi Ruth spoke quietly. "You were bored and envious. You decided to see if you could break up your brother's marriage. Why should he be happy? Could you make him as miserable as you were? You like those kinds of games, don't you, Julianna? You are good at them."

Julianna's head shot around to stare at the woman who raised her. Julianna's eyes narrowed.

"Is that what happened? Was it just a game to you?" Sarah was staring at Julianna.

"I like games, Sarah…I like to win. Linus was easy." Julianna glanced at the shocked faces around her. She leaned back in her chair, propped an elbow on its back and slowly twisted a piece of her blond hair. "Besides, he made me mad. He told Daddy not to give me a car when I came home."

"Let me get this straight." Hobart leaned towards Julianna. "You set out to destroy your brother and his marriage because you couldn't get the car you wanted? Is that what you're saying?"

"Linus was weak…though I must admit he surprised me later when he quit drinking. He actually started ignoring me. He was barely civil. I guess he felt guilty…figured out how spineless he had been."

"Brother trusted the wrong woman," Hobart shook his head. "He paid."

"Oh, he paid all right."

"What do you mean by that comment, Julianna?" Naomi Ruth leaned forward, her elbows resting on the table. There was a curious expression on her face.

"Nothing…nothing important," Julianna answered with a nonchalant shrug.

Naomi Ruth leaned back, eyes narrowing as she gazed at Julianna. Naomi Ruth didn't like what she was thinking, what had just occurred to her, but she knew she was right. Oh, Lord.

Julianna looked around the table. "Why are you all looking at me as if I have two heads?"

"We're astounded by your cruelty, Bad Sister." Hobart looked steadily at her.

"Oh, pooh, get off your high horse, Gay Brother." Julianna's face twisted. "Their marriage was wretched. If they cared anything about each other they would have worked it out. Sarah would not have cut and run…never to be heard of again…until this day when she amazingly appears with the heir apparent." Julianna looked around the table. "Honestly, you people." She shook her head in disgust. "Can't you see how conniving Sarah is?"

"I can't agree with you there, Sick Sis." Hobart leaned back in his chair. "I for one am extremely pleased to have Sarah back here with us. I am quite happy having our nephew operate the family farming operation. I do not think in any way that Sarah is conniving with Ward to take over everything. I don't think Sarah has a conniving bone in her body."

"Well, you are just a fool, Hobart. You always have been," Julianna spat at her brother. "Sarah wants the money. Ward wants the land. It's Garrett money and it's Garrett land. It's not theirs. Neither of them are Garretts."

"Do not judge others by yourself, Julianna." Sarah looked steadily at Julianna. "I am not here for the money. It may surprise you to know that my second husband was an extremely wealthy man. Ward and I do not need Garrett money." Sarah smiled at the expression on Julianna's face. "We have enough of our own. And, as to why I am here…I was invited…and I joyfully accepted." Sarah sat down.

Ophelia held up her hands. "Enough is enough, Julianna. Ward is Linus' son. Ward is my grandson. Ward is a Garrett." There was finality in her pronouncement.

Ophelia turned to Alice who was sitting quietly by her side. "Alice, please go get the photograph beside my bed."

Alice nodded, rose from the table and left the room. Everyone sat in silence waiting for her return.

Alice handed the photograph to Phe when she walked back into the kitchen. Ophelia handed it to Julianna. "Who is this, Julianna?"

Julianna looked for several minutes at the picture. "You, in the wedding gown you would not let me wear."

"And who is with me, Julianna?" Ophelia prodded.

"Daddy. It's your wedding day."

"Ward looks uncannily like him, don't you think?"

Julianna placed the photograph face down on the table and stood. "I'm leaving."

Voices could be heard on the back porch. Robert entered the kitchen followed by Grant Whitworth. Grant glanced at the table surrounded by Garretts and Julianna standing alone. He stopped. He could feel the tension in the room.

"I've obviously come at a bad time, Ophelia. I'll return this afternoon."

"Stay, Grant," Ophelia spoke. "You know this family as well, if not better, than most. And sit down, Julianna." Ophelia's voice was steady. Julianna hesitated for a moment then flounced back into her chair.

Grant pulled up a chair and sat down between Sarah and Alice. He looked at Ophelia. She nodded. He placed the bottle of nail polish on the table.

"The polish is laced with arsenic."

He looked around the table at the faces watching him. Julianna's was not one of them.

She was looking down, her arms crossed over her chest. She projected an attitude of complete boredom and disinterest.

"How quickly it absorbs through the nails or how toxic it is were questions my friend could not answer without more information. I told him not to pursue it. It's just the intent that matters to me. What matters to you, Julianna?"

"Well, this certainly doesn't. Why should I have any interest in Minnie's nail polish?"

"How did you know it was Minnie's?" Alice asked.

"Whose else would it be if Grant has it?"

"Good recovery, Sinful Sister," Hobart observed.

Julianna sat up straighter in her chair. "What is going on here? Since when is Grant so welcome in our home, Mother, after how he treated us? He also turned his back on the Garretts."

"No, Big Sis, he just turned his back on you," Hobart answered.

Julianna glared at Hobart, "I expect more loyalty from the only brother I have left."

Hobart shrugged.

Julianna turned back to Grant. "Why are you here? Are you accusing me of something?"

"Yes," he answered. "Yes, I am."

"What?" Julianna asked, keeping her eyes locked with his.

"I am accusing you of trying to kill Minnie."

A jubilant expression transformed Julianna's face. She threw back her head and laughed. It was the laugh of the thrill seeker. "Surely, you jest. If I wanted to kill Minnie, Minnie would be dead." She looked over at Grant.

"So you just wanted to scare her a little?" Hobart asked. "Is this another of your games, Twisted Sister?"

Julianna's eyes were locked with Grant's. She turned away. "Perhaps."

"Why, Julianna? Minnie has done nothing to you." Grant's eyes never wavered from Julianna's face.

"You embarrassed me once. I saw no need for you to come back to Hope Springs and embarrass me again...and with such a mousy little woman."

The room was deathly quiet. Everyone's eyes were on Julianna. She was uncommonly still, as if frozen by malice.

"It was thirty years ago, Julianna. For heaven's sake, do you hold a grudge that long?" Grant stared at her. "Besides...your embarrassment was your own doing. Actions have consequences."

"What do you mean by that comment?"

"Smythe Hughes."

Julianna's eyes widened.

"I saw you."

Julianna stared at Grant. An odd expression played across her lovely face. It was followed by a twisted little smile. "I haven't a clue what you are talking about." She slowly rose from her chair, turned, and left the room.

***

Hobart, Grant and Ophelia were the only ones remaining at the kitchen table. Naomi Ruth was rattling around beginning preparations for lunch. Robert and Maize had departed to tend to his garden. Everyone else had quickly excused themselves after the morning's uncomfortable confrontation with Julianna.

"I'm sorry, Ophelia," Grant said. "I didn't want to say this in front of Julianna…hate to give her any more satisfaction than she already has…but Minnie has noticed some loss of hair and her joints ache. Dr. Bisbo is treating her for arsenic poisoning."

"Oh, Grant," was all Ophelia could say. Pain etched her face.

"Damn!" Hobart said. "We've got to do something, Mother. We have no guarantee from her reaction whether she'll quit trying to harm Minnie. Hell, Grant, we're not even sure she acknowledges why you left her at the altar. I didn't understand what you said but obviously she did. Of course, I can guess!" Hobart shook his head in disgust. "She's nutty as a fruitcake. Why was she ever allowed to leave the insane asylum, Mother?"

"It was not an insane asylum, Hobart. It was a facility for those who had a mental breakdown."

"What's the difference?" Hobart looked at his mother.

"When was this?" Grant looked from Hobart to Ophelia.

"After you saw the light and hit the road," Hobart answered.

Ophelia frowned at her son. "Julianna had a breakdown after the 'situation' at the church. A much younger Dr. Bisbo sedated her that night but she wasn't any better when the medicine wore off. She just screamed and cried. This went on for several days. She wouldn't eat. She had tantrums. We could not get her to calm down. She was extremely agitated. She wandered around at night. We had to lock her door. Linus and I didn't know what to do. Dr. Bisbo recommended an…evaluation." Ophelia paused. "As a result she was hospitalized for a while."

"'A while' ended up being three years," Hobart added, looking at Grant. "Turns out Julianna had lots of 'issues.'"

"Yes, unfortunately that is true." Ophelia looked at her son. "Finally she was released, though the doctors were reluctant and not very encouraging. She was emotionally scarred…I think that was the term…and should be medicated. Linus couldn't…or wouldn't… accept what they said. We brought her home. She lived here with us until she married Gil Thomas." Ophelia paused. "It was during that time that she ruined Sarah and Linus' marriage, we now know." She looked over at Naomi Ruth.

"Gil was the father of Meggie and Bingo." Naomi Ruth continued the story. "He and Julianna were married for thirteen years. Then one day…I think it was in February…she called in hysterics. Gil had been in a wreck. He was in the hospital in critical condition. He died three days later."

"Thankfully he left Julianna a sizable estate," Ophelia resumed. "Added to her own worth Julianna was quite well off. She began to socialize and travel. She found nannies for the children. She was quite the merry widow…too much so, actually. It was puzzling. Several years later she met John Stafford. They were only married two years when he committed suicide. I have heard that he went through a considerable amount of Julianna's money. She has said nothing about it to me and I have certainly seen no change in her life style. Julianna has always been extravagant. Julianna rarely mentions John. She has never been the grieving widow. There was more a sense of relief than grief."

Grant sat quietly.

"You dodged a bullet when you turned your back on her, Grant," Hobart said.

"It would seem so." Grant stood to leave. "I'm sorry, Ophelia."

Ophelia looked up at him.

"I will be at Minnie's if you need me."

Chapter Thirty-Five

Mary Hester picked Athie up just before noon. They drove downtown and parked on Main Street. When they entered Slater's Drug Store they were relieved to see there was a booth available. The sisters wanted to talk. They slid into the booth and ordered an iced tea and a diet Pepsi when Lula came over. They were waiting for Mildred, who was at the dentist.

"I could hardly sleep last night," Mary Hester told her sister. "Discovering that Ward was Ophelia's grandson was a total shock. I asked Harriet if she knew and she said, 'no,' she hadn't a clue. Of course, she doesn't think it's a big deal. She knows nothing of the history of Sarah and Linus third. Sarah was always just a mystery woman, mentioned occasionally but no longer in the picture. Harriet knew Linus, of course, but only as a grumpy lawyer who was a friend of the family. I think she can't really accept that Ward is that man's son."

"Most of us can't…Linus changed so much. If you think back though he was a handsome man in his own right, though not dark like Ward, nor built like him…thicker. Yes, this is a big surprise." Athie sipped her Pepsi.

They saw Mildred enter the drugstore. Mildred paused to speak with someone at the lunch counter then eased towards them. She slid in beside Athie.

"I always hate to eat or drink after I come from the dentist. My teeth are so squeaky clean." She looked at her sisters. "What y'all discussin'?"

"Three guesses and the first two don't count," Athie said.

"Come to any conclusions?"

"Nope, we're still in the rambling stage."

"Have y'all ordered?"

"Not yet," Mary Hester answered. "We were waiting on you. I'll go get Lula." She slid from the booth and walked to the counter. She spoke to the small red-headed woman behind it then returned to the booth.

"She's coming," Mary Hester reported.

"Good, I'm starving,..squeaky teeth or not," Mildred said and turned to Athie. "So, what do you think?"

"Well, anyone with a heart…which probably let's Julianna out… is happy for Ophelia. After all, she has found a grandson and some-one to run the Garrett farm operation all rolled into one." Athie paused as Lula appeared beside the table to take their lunch orders.

Lula wrote then announced she was mighty happy to hear about Miss Ophelia's grandson. "And he's easy on the eye to boot." Lula winked, laughed and walked away.

"Guess the tom-toms have been beating this morning," Mary Hester said.

The sisters continued their conversation until Lula brought them their lunch. Mary Hester was just taking a bite of her chicken salad sandwich when she looked up to see Frances pushing through Slater's front door.

"Oh, law, look who's coming."

Frances made a bee line for the sisters booth. She slid in beside Mary Hester. "Erwin said y'all were here."

"What brings you home from the beach?" Athie asked her, grilled pimento cheese sandwich in midair.

"Had to come. Didn't want to. Lost my glasses…couldn't see a thing. Walter worked me in yesterday afternoon. Then while I was home I called Norma Sue about a haircut. That's where I was this morning. That's how I know Ward is Ophelia's grandson. How does Sarah look? Fill me in. Know y'all were at the party. We weren't invited."

"It was mainly just family," Mary Hester said.

"Well, y'all aren't family...yet."

"Don't be snide, Frances," Athie turned and looked at her. "But Harriet is probably the reason we were invited."

"It was a nice party. Everyone was completely surprised by Ophelia's announcement...stunned even...but happy about it...for her." Mary Hester continued to eat.

"Not, Julianna, I'll bet." Frances answered.

"No, Julianna was definitely not happy." Athie took a sip of her Pepsi.

"What's been happening with Julianna and Minnie? Is Julianna still trying to 'off' her?"

"'Off' her? Frances, you've been looking at too many gangster movies." Mildred laughed.

"You know what I mean."

"Yes, Julianna still has Minnie in her sights. Sometime or other Julianna put arsenic in Minnie's nail polish down at the beauty parlor."

"What? I would think it would be another way around. I would think Ramona would put arsenic in Julianna's nail polish."

***

Lunch was a quiet meal that day at Merrebanks. Naomi Ruth insisted they eat in the dining room and she and Robert would not join them. Truth to tell she needed some distance from Julianna.

There was a minimum of conversation at the table. Everyone just pushed their food around. Hobart attempted to start a conversation with his mother but Ophelia was obviously preoccupied. Sarah sat silently, toying with her food. Julianna said nothing and no one said anything to her. Hobart and Sarah were surprised she was still at Merrebanks. They thought she would get in her car and leave after the morning's confrontation. They did not know that Ophelia had asked Julianna to remain. She wished to talk with her later this afternoon.

Julianna had indeed intended to leave after walking from the kitchen that morning. She felt unwelcome in her own home. She felt like they were judging her, questioning her, belittling her. She was angry and resentful. Her mother had come to her room while she was packing and asked her to remain at Merrebanks as she wished to talk with her in the afternoon.

Julianna had no choice but to acquiesce. As much as she hated it she had to stay on the good side of her mother. She controlled the Trust. At times like these Julianna missed her daddy. He realized how special she was.

After the uncomfortable lunch everyone went their separate ways. Julianna told her mother she was going for a drive, got in her car and drove away. She needed to think. Grant had shocked her this morning when he mentioned Smythe Hughes. It was so long ago she almost didn't recognize the name. But then she recalled the night before the wedding. It was a hazy memory. Bad luck to be seen by Grant. She never had a clue. If she had known that was all it was that turned him away she could have explained it beautifully. It was just a foolish mistake. She was filled with remorse, She could have begged forgiveness. She could have convinced him, she was sure, had she known. After all, she was a great actress. Why in the world would Grant give her up for something as trivial as a moments infidelity? It made no sense.

And why did Ophelia want to talk with her this afternoon? She was tired of being questioned. She was tired of surprises and unexpected problems. Life had been going so smoothly. She needed to reshuffle, re-plan. Let Grant have little Minnie. She had bigger fish to fry.

She drove into town and pulled into the parking lot of Jeffreys Hardware. She purchased a small cooler, a trowel and gardening gloves. Back in her car she drove out to the Battle Hill farm.

***

When Julianna returned to Merrebanks she walked past a silent Naomi Ruth in the kitchen. She made her way down the hall toward the staircase.

"Please join us, Julianna," Ophelia spoke when Julianna passed the library door.

Julianna strolled silently into the room and sat in one of the wing chairs beside the fireplace. Ophelia was seated in the other. Hobart was sitting in Big Linus' leather chair behind Big Linus' antique desk. Julianna frowned.

"I expected to talk with just you, Mother. Why is he here?" She turned to Hobart, "And why are you sitting at Daddy's desk?"

"Mother asked me to read something that was in one of the drawers."

Naomi Ruth entered the room and stood behind Ophelia's chair. Julianna looked sharply at her. "Ah," she finally said, "your faithful shadow."

Silence reverberated around the room.

"Apologize to Naomi Ruth, Julianna." Ophelia's voice was steely.

Julianna was startled by her mother's tone. She glanced at her in surprise. Ophelia sat coldly regarding her, as if cast of stone. It unsettled Julianna.

"I apologize, 'Omi."

The expression on Naomi Ruth's face did not change. She stood watching Julianna with the weight of great sadness reflected on her face.

"Who are you, Julianna?" Ophelia quietly asked.

"Why, Mother, you...and anyone who matters...know quite well who I am. I am a Garrett from Chinquapin County."

"Does being a Garrett give you license to be cruel?"

"Being a Garrett gives you license to be anything you want." Julianna smiled.

Ophelia's eyes did not leave Julianna's face but her hand rose to touch her pearls.

"I do hope to have those pearls one day, Mother."

Ophelia was silent. She watched Julianna as her fingers played with a pearl.

"Julianna, I have failed you. If I had been honest with you, honest with Linus, perhaps we would not be here having this conversation today." She sighed and placed her hand in her lap.

"What you did to Sarah and Linus was unconscionable…unforgivable. You knowingly lied and seem to have no remorse about it."

Julianna leaned back in her chair and looked at Ophelia. "Oh, is that what this is all about?"

"Yes, and more…so much more." Ophelia spoke quietly, never taking her eyes from Julianna.

"You have a totally distorted sense of your self-worth, I'm afraid. No one has the right, no matter who they are, or think they are, to harm another person. Your arrogance, your destructive behavior is no longer acceptable in this family."

Julianna sat silently regarding her mother. A fleeting expression of surprise was instantly replaced by a hard cynical expression. "So, you are kicking me out of the family, Mother?" Sarcasm oozed from Julianna's voice.

"I can't kick you out of the family, Julianna, but I can tell you that you are no longer welcome at Merrebanks."

Julianna was silent. Shock played across her face. Then barely suppressed fury changed her demeanor. She sat bolt upright. She did not take her eyes from Ophelia. Her hands lay balled in her lap, clenching and unclenching.

"I will, of course, continue to receive my share of the family Trust, however. You can't take that away from me. Garrett money stays with Garretts. You, Mother, however, are only a Garrett through marriage. So unfortunate."

"You will continue to receive your share, Julianna, rest assured…as long as you do as I say." Ophelia looked at her. "I might be only a Garrett through marriage but I do control the Garrett Trust… and its disbursement."

Julianna's eyes narrowed.

"I will expect you to leave Minnie be. What you have done to her is inexcusable…even criminal. You could have caused her death. You put those nails in her tire; you put strychnine in her wine; you put arsenic in her nail polish."

Julianna laughed. She settled back into her chair. "I'm so glad you recognize my efforts. Creative, don't you think? I just wanted to scare her a little."

"You know, Sick Sister, I think you wanted to scare her a lot," Hobart spoke from behind the desk.

"Maybe. Her presence is bothersome. It's absurd that Grant can't see the difference between a Garrett and…whatever Minnie is. But, if I wanted to get rid of Minnie, I would have."

"So, Toxic Sister, if someone bothers you, you just 'get rid' of them? Is that what you're saying?"

Julianna shrugged her shoulders. "I suppose."

"Well, now you have piqued my curiosity," Hobart teased. "Who have you 'gotten rid' of, as you say? Is it anyone we know?" He laughed.

"Oh, yes. You actually know them all." Julianna began to twist a strand of her hair.

Hobart's face registered astonishment. He looked at Ophelia and Naomi Ruth. They were both staring at Julianna.

A wave of apprehension washed over him.

"Would you like to share with us? You seem so proud of what you have done." He looked at Julianna.

"Gil was first."

"Gil? You mean your husband Gil? The father of your children?" Hobart asked.

Julianna looked at him with disdain. "Of course. What other Gil would I be talking about?"

"Are you telling us you killed Gil?" Hobart was leaning forward in his chair.

"I had help. I don't know anything about cars. Rico fixed Gil's brakes for me so they would fail. It worked perfectly...though he took three days to die."

Astonished silence filled the room. Julianna continued to twist her strand of hair.

"Rico Sessoms...over at the body shop? Why would he do that for you, Julianna? Did you pay him?" Hobart prodded.

"I paid him a little money. He was more interested in me, though." She laughed. "He has drooled over me since high school. He was easy."

"So while he serviced Gil's car, you serviced him!"

"Don't be crude, Hobart. It was a business arrangement."

"Okay, but why kill poor Gil? He was a nice guy."

"He was boring. He never wanted to go out. All he wanted to do was play golf and watch television. I was bored to death. Besides, he didn't appreciate me. He never complimented me. He never said I was beautiful."

Hobart was appalled. He could not believe what he was hearing. Looking at his mother and Naomi Ruth he could tell they were amazed as well. If it weren't so horrible it would be almost funny.

"So poor Gil left us...because he never drooled over you? Dreadfully high price to pay for ignoring you, I would say."

Julianna just gazed at her brother and shrugged.

"Pray tell us who was next?" Hobart continued.

Julianna studied the nails of her left hand.

"John went through my money without batting an eye. He seemed to think what was mine was his. He even forged my name on my Merrill-Lynch account. I was furious. He had to go."

Silence filled the room.

"How did you manage that? Everyone thought it was a suicide."

"It wasn't too hard. I just doped him up then fixed him a few really strong drinks. He passed out and I shot him." Julianna sat up straighter. She smoothed her skirt. "I put the gun in his hand and called 9-1-1. I was very believable as the hysterical wife discovering her dead husband."

"I'm sure you were Academy Award material." Hobart was disgusted. "Is there more to this recitation of bodies in your past? You are quite the Lady Blackbeard."

Julianna looked at Ophelia then Naomi Ruth. She was silent. She looked over at Hobart. "No, that's all," she said in a quiet voice.

The Grandfather clock in the hall struck five. There was not another sound.

Naomi Ruth looked at Julianna. She placed her hands on the back of Ophelia's chair as if for balance then quietly said, "But it's not, is it, Julianna? You said, 'all' not 'both.' There is another person who displeased you...another person you decided to 'get rid' of...as you say...isn't there?"

Julianna looked at Naomi Ruth in defiance. Their eyes locked. "Yes," Julianna replied without looking away. "Yes, there is.

"He was the worst of them all. He should have known better. He insulted me. He said I was worthless. He said I was an ugly person.

Me! Ha!" Julianna's eyes swept over those present as if daring them to disagree with her.

Naomi Ruth watched her steadily. "So you dressed up one afternoon as a middle-aged woman and went to the hospital and murdered him. You were the unknown woman last year who visited Linus in the hospital just before he died. You killed your brother."

Hobart groaned and placed his hands over his face. Ophelia was ashen. Naomi Ruth's eyes bored into Julianna. Julianna laughed.

"Good for you, 'Omi. Somebody finally figured it out. Yes, it was me playing the frumpy old classmate of Linus'. He hadn't a clue who I was, he was so doped up. I brought my own pillow to the hospital, of course. I took it from my bag and just held it over his face. He didn't even fight. Then I replaced the pillow when the machines started making a fuss...and when the nurses rushed in I eased out. Amazingly simple."

"Why, Julianna?" Ophelia spoke softly. Her hand moved back up to her pearls.

"Linus asked me why I killed John. It surprised me...just out of the blue, like that. Linus just stood looking at me as if I were trash. He just shook his head in disgust and turned his back on me. Him... so high and mighty! We were right here in the library having a drink before dinner...just the two of us. He was by the mantle and I was on the sofa. You were in the kitchen helping 'Omi. It was a couple of days before he went into the hospital.

"A friend of his in the district attorney's office in Raleigh sent him John's postmortem report. There were questions...discrepancies. Linus said he had taken care of it. He was not going to have the Garrett name dragged through the mud by the likes of me. He said I did not deserve the name...I had not earned it. I was an interloper...a fraud...an embarrassment! He was very cruel and callous. I did not appreciate being talked to in that manner, let me tell you. Daddy would have been furious with him for speaking to me like that. Linus said he was going to keep the report, though, and in a safe place. He might need it later. He actually grinned at me when he said that. It made him curious, he said. Maybe Gil's accident wasn't an 'accident' either. When he got out of the hospital he might do a little investigating. Linus was enjoying toying with me.

"I just laughed in his face. I knew he would do nothing that would bring shame to us Garretts. My name would keep me safe. I was a Garrett. I was above the mundane laws that affect common people. Daddy taught me that very early on…and I told Linus so.

"Then Linus went and sat behind Daddy's desk. That made me mad, very mad." She looked at Hobart. "No one should try and take Daddy's place.

"Linus reached into a drawer of the desk and pulled out a sheaf of papers. He waved it at me. 'Be careful, Julianna,' he said. 'Maybe the Garrett name doesn't apply to you.'

"I guess he was referring to the fact I had kept John's name." Julianna shrugged and looked around the room. She reached up for another strand of hair. "Then he said that irritating saying of yours, Mother, 'Blood will tell.' It was like he was insinuating something. I was getting madder and madder with him about then. He was acting so holier than thou. I just told him my blood was the same as his and he had the gall to laugh at me. That's when I decided he had to go. I am not an object of ridicule."

Julianna glanced at Ophelia and Naomi Ruth standing squarely behind her. She twisted her strand of golden hair and smiled. "I had the last laugh."

There was a ringing silence in the library. The only movement was the lazy twisting of Julianna's fingers around and around the golden strand. The sound of a door closing upstairs floated down into the room. Footsteps traveled down the stairs. Sarah walked past the door. She stopped when she saw the group in the library.

"Come in, Sarah," Ophelia said.

Sarah glanced around at the faces when she entered the room

then took a seat on the sofa. She knew something momentous had happened. She felt the tension. Only Julianna appeared to be relaxed. Even Maize was alert. Sarah said nothing.

Ophelia turned to her. "Sarah, we have been talking of Linus, your husband and Ward's father. Julianna has just related the truth of his death. Unfortunately, it was by her hands."

Sarah's eyes grew wide. Her head jerked towards Julianna. "You killed Linus? You murdered your own brother?" Shock registered on Sarah's face.

"Oh, please, spare me. Like you care. You had long since left him…never bothering to tell him he had the son he so badly wanted…if Ward really is his son."

"But why? How could you?" Sarah's eyes were sad.

"Julianna was just explaining it to us." Naomi Ruth spoke. "Linus suspected she had killed her husband John. And when he got out of the hospital he was also going to look into the death of her husband, Gil. Actually Linus was right. She killed them both."

Sarah sat speechless.

"What confuses me, Julianna," Hobart spoke from his seat behind his father's desk, "is your rationale. If you knew Linus wasn't going to do anything because he wanted to protect the family name where's the threat? Why kill him?"

"What else did he say to you? What did he say that drove you to kill him?" Ophelia looked at Julianna.

Julianna turned towards Ophelia, a look of defiance on her face.

"It was heretical…and heresy is punishable by death." Julianna leaned forward. "He said I had no Garrett blood. He said I was not a Garrett."

Ophelia cocked her head, never taking her eyes from Julianna. She spoke quietly but firmly.

"Linus was right. You have no Garrett blood. You are not a Garrett."

Ophelia watched Julianna's reaction to these words. Julianna's demeanor grew rigid. Her eyes squinted, her nostrils flared, her mouth was a harsh line. "How dare you say those words to me, Mother."

"I am not your mother."

Sarah and Hobart stared at Ophelia. Shock registered on their faces.

"You, Julianna, are the illegitimate daughter of a manicurist."

Julianna blanched. She reached over and picked up the book beside her chair and threw it at Ophelia. It sailed past her chair. Hobart jumped up and moved from behind the desk. Naomi Ruth stepped from behind Ophelia's chair. Maize growled and stood. Ophelia waved them off and reached for Maize's collar.

Julianna was gripping the arms of her chair. Her eyes were blazing. Ophelia sat calmly, her hand holding Maize's collar. A wry smile tilted the corners of her mouth.

"Yes, I thought it ironic you chose to harm Minnie with nail polish. A good example of that irritating saying, 'Blood will tell,' don't you think?

"For a while my Linus was quite smitten with your mother. She did his hands. He had an indiscreet liaison with her. Her name was Nellie, in case you are interested." Ophelia was watching Julianna closely. Julianna's face was splotched, her mouth ajar. She was breathing rapidly.

"Nellie was not maternal," Ophelia continued. "She also knew a good thing when she saw it. She told Linus her child was his and he could raise it in a finer manner than she ever could. Very noble sounding but what dear Nellie wanted was money. Linus paid her for you...and continued to pay through the years...until she was found murdered. That too is ironic, don't you think?

"Linus believed you to be his child until he died. He never realized Nellie had fooled him. Lord knows who your father really was... but it wasn't my Linus. I found that out when we did that genealogy chart with DNA testing. You did not match any of our children in any way. To make absolutely sure, two years ago I took the curl from

Linus' baby locket his mother gave me and asked Arthur Taylor to have Linus' DNA compared with yours. It was not a match. Linus was not your father.

"So you see, Julianna, you have no Garrett blood. My son Linus was right. You are a fraud; you are an impostor. You are not a Garrett."

Julianna rose from the chair and lunged. Her arms stretched out towards Ophelia, her hands curled as claws. She screamed, "I'll kill you, too! I am a Garrett! I am a Garrett! Daddy was my father. You lie, you bitch, you lie!"

Hobart stepped between Julianna and Ophelia, grasping Julianna around the shoulders, pinning her arms. Naomi Ruth moved quickly, jabbing the syringe into Julianna's arm. Julianna went limp. Hobart dropped her to the floor.

"Oh, my goodness," Sarah said, hovering beside Ophelia.

"I guess you just can't make a silk purse out of a sow's ear," Hobart said as he looked down at Julianna's limp form sprawled on the carpet. It was not a pretty sight.

***

Hobart and Robert managed to get the unconscious Julianna up to her bedroom. Naomi Ruth settled her into bed. Ophelia called Dr. Bisbo. Hobart came downstairs and made a beeline for the liquor cabinet.

When Ward and Eggie arrived for dinner they were told what had happened. Dinner was a somber affair.

***

Ophelia was propped up on the pillows of her bed. Hobart was in a chair by the window. Sarah sat on the dressing table stool. Maize was asleep on the floor by the bed. Naomi Ruth was with Julianna. Robert was once again downstairs washing the dishes.

"I don't think I shall ever forget this day," Hobart said. "In a strange way, though, Mother, I'm relieved to know the truth about Julianna. It explains a lot."

"I should have told her the truth years ago," Ophelia was tired, "and you children. Honestly, though I'm not sure it would have made any difference. She has such a narcissistic personality. Her ego is so exalted...and yet so fragile. She did inexcusable things and yet we excused her. She kept getting by with things...which made it easier to do worse things the next time. I blame myself. Poor Linus only saw the good in her. I didn't."

"What good?" Hobart snorted. "I would say Daddy was suffering from some kind of guilt trip. Remember, he thought she was his. He just couldn't admit she was a mistake...in more ways than one. You were a saint, Mother, to agree to raise Daddy's child by another woman."

"It seemed the right thing to do at the time." Ophelia leaned back into her pillows. She closed her eyes.

"So what happens now?" Sarah looked at her mother-in-law. "There's no way she's staying here with you."

"Her days at Merrebanks have come to an abrupt end," Hobart said.

"I agree with Dr. Bisbo." Ophelia opened her eyes and looked at them. "I explained some things to him...not all, of course...but then...he is treating Minnie and he was here thirty years ago...so he can put two and two together. Julianna will have to go to another facility for mental disorders. He's looking into it. She'll have to stay here for the next day or two, though, till she can be admitted to one. He has recommended a sitter who will come in tomorrow. Naomi Ruth will sit with her tonight. Julianna is heavily sedated. I think that will be all right. Don't you?"

"I suppose, but Sarah will stay with you until Julianna leaves." Sarah nodded in agreement. "You did the best you could, Mother. None of us realized Julianna was as sick as she is."

Sarah rose. “Well, it’s to bed for me. I’m spent. I’ll leave my door open for Naomi Ruth in case she needs help with Julianna in the night.” She hugged Hobart, kissed Ophelia on the cheek and left the room.

Hobart sat in silence with his mother. “I hate that the lawyers insist I come tomorrow but I will be back as soon as I finish in Georgetown. It shouldn’t take but a day.” He sighed.“Maybe things will settle down now. We Garretts could use a little peace.”

“If only…” Ophelia sighed. “Thank you Hobart for being there today. Naomi Ruth and I knew we could count on you.”

“I hadn’t a clue what y’all were asking me to do. ‘Sit there and say whatever comes to mind. We are going to have a conversation with Julianna.’ Very strange and open-ended directions.”

“You have always been the best at challenging Julianna,” his mother said.

“It was all so strange,” Hobart said. “I heard her words but they had no meaning because what she was saying could not possibly be true. To think she had no compunction or remorse about taking the lives of her two husbands and her brother. That was brutally shocking. Poor Linus.” Hobart shook his head. “He was a conflicted soul but he didn’t deserve that.”

“I think she became progressively off balance as she aged,” Ophelia said from her pillows. “Her looks…appearances…money… all the shallow things she worshipped…were fading away.”

“She was still a Garrett, though. That she clung to. That was her constant…till today. Teflon karma…till now.” Hobart rose. “Goodnight, Mother. Love you. Sleep tight.” He pecked his mother on the cheek. “Night Maize,” he said as he walked from the room.

Chapter Thirty-Six

While Ophelia, Naomi Ruth and Robert were having breakfast the next morning Dr. Bisbo arrived to check on Julianna. Sarah had relieved Naomi Ruth. Hobart was still asleep. "I have found someone to sit with Julianna until we hear from the hospitals I have contacted," he announced. "Hopefully we can get Julianna into one here in the state but right now I think we should consider any appropriate available bed. Julianna is a sick woman. If we have to we can put her on the mental health hall at the hospital. That is not the best option, however." He sat down for a cup of coffee.

"The person I have found is a young woman in the nursing program at the community college. She has worked for me since high school. She's quite competent. Very smart. She can administer the sedative and handle Julianna if anything happens...which I don't expect, by the way. Her name is Flora Grace Wright. She'll be here after lunch."

Dr. Bisbo rose and excused himself to check on Julianna. He knew the way.

He had barely left the room when Alice walked through the kitchen door. "Good morning, everyone."

"You are certainly on the move early this morning, Alice. Is anything wrong?" Naomi Ruth looked at Alice.

"I don't know." Alice poured a cup of coffee and sat down at the kitchen table. "I had the strangest dream last night." She took a sip of coffee. "I don't remember much about it other than you, Phe. Someone stole your pearls."

Alice looked from Ophelia to Naomi Ruth. "Why is Dr. Bisbo here so early? Is someone sick? By the way Julianna needs to move her car. It's blocking the walk."

"I'll move it." Hobart spoke from the doorway. "Julianna won't be needing it for a while."

***

Bessie got out of the car with amazing speed and flew up the steps to the back porch. Hector had not seen her move that fast in years. She had been about to burst with excitement when he picked her up from *Kut & Kurl*. "Drive with all speed," she instructed him. "Wait till the girls hear this."

He was a mite curious himself so he followed her into the kitchen after parking the old Lincoln in the garage.

Bessie was ensconced at the kitchen table. Clara was on the phone with Mary Hester. "Yes, your mother said come over right this minute." Clara hung up, dialed and was soon talking with Athie. "Your mother wants you over here right now. She's busting at the seams with some kinda news."

"Hector, holler to Mildred upstairs and tell her to come downstairs immediately." Bessie's red head was swinging in every direction.

Clara looked at Hector and shrugged, palms lifted up in bewilderment. "You feelin' all right, Miss Bessie?"

"Never better, Clara. I have news."

Mildred arrived downstairs the same time Athie and Mary Hester walked through the kitchen door.

"What's the bee in your bonnet, Mother?" Mary Hester asked.

"This better be good. I was baking a pound cake," Athie said.

"Must be major gossip at the beauty parlor to have you in such a dither, Mother," Mildred said as she sat down.

All eyes were on Bessie...Hector's, Clara's, Mary Hester's, Athie's and Mildred's.

Bessie savored the moment. She spoke. "Julianna has gone crazy...again." Then Bessie sat back in triumph. Her news had the proper affect.

***

When Alice stood to leave Hobart walked outside with her. "I'll move Julianna's car. It will be easier for you to turn around."

Alice nodded and continued toward her car.

Hobart opened the door of Julianna's red BMW. "Whoa! Alice come back here. What's that smell?"

Alice retraced her steps, took one whiff and also stepped back from the car. "Phew...not good...rank."

"I'm going to get Robert," Hobart announced and turned back to the house.

Robert returned to the car with Hobart. "Nasty...but there is something familiar about it," he said after leaning inside Julianna's car. "Open the trunk, Hobart."

Hobart cautiously opened the trunk and stepped back quickly. Then the three of them slowly moved closer. A small cooler sat there. Slowly Robert lifted it out onto the pavement.

He nudged the lid off with a stick and the three looked inside. A small wad of greenery lay at the bottom.

"Damn," Hobart said.

"*Cicuta maculata*," Robert said. "Not good," He and Hobart looked at each other.

"What is it?" Alice asked.

"Hemlock," Robert answered.

"Battle Hill farm," Hobart said. "Guess it still grows there."

"Crazy old Beecher...great science teacher but a tad eccentric. I always worried about you kids during those field trips."

"He wouldn't let us near it. Obviously made an impression, though, on all of us. Julianna still remembered it, unfortunately. But then, she did end up living there with Jake and obviously it's still growing out there. Who you guess was going to get a toxic salad?"

Robert looked at Hobart and Alice. "I do not think Ophelia needs to know about this." They nodded.

Chapter Thirty-Seven

Grant saw Alice coming up the driveway. He met her at the back door.

"I can tell from your face something has happened. Sit down. Minnie's at the beauty parlor. Can I get you some coffee or tea or a coke?"

"No, thank you. I've had enough coffee this morning to float a ship." Alice paused. "Ophelia asked me to stop by on my way home." Alice paused again. "This is so difficult...so unbelievable." Alice paused once again. Then she took a deep breath and looked at Grant.

"Julianna tried to attack Phe yesterday afternoon. Thankfully Hobart and Naomi Ruth were there...even Maize stood between them."

Grant looked down at his hands clasped together on the table. Ophelia had made her move. He looked up. "Is Ophelia all right? What happened Alice? Do you know?"

"Yes, she's fine. She looks tired, though...and dreadfully sad," Alice answered. "All I know is...Ophelia, Naomi Ruth, Hobart and Julianna were all in the library yesterday afternoon having a conversation. I think Sarah joined them at some point. Ophelia told me she would tell me everything in time, but not now. Whatever was said sent Julianna into a tailspin. Oddly enough, Naomi Ruth had a tranquilizer syringe, which is telling." Alice looked at Grant with her innocent eyes questioning. "You must know something from the look on your face."

"Ophelia said she was going to do something about Julianna," he answered her. "I didn't know when or what. I just hoped it would be soon. Julianna was growing more and more psychotic."

Alice nodded. "I had a dream last night about Ophelia and her pearls. It was worrisome so I drove over to Merrebanks this morning to check on her. Dr. Bisbo was there. He's tending to Julianna. She's heavily sedated. They are moving her to a mental facility as soon as they can find one to take her." Alice again looked at Grant. "Ophelia asked me to let you know that."

"I'll see what I can do." Grant was quiet. "It's the best thing."

"Dr. Bisbo is sending someone to sit with Julianna until she can be moved. " Alice continued. "Ophelia also wanted me to ask you to come visit her but she thinks it best to wait till Julianna is out of the house."

Grant nodded. "Of course."

"Hobart is going to D.C. today for his closing but Sarah is staying with Phe." Alice rose to go. "Poor Phe. She has been through so much. It just breaks your heart."

"Ophelia is tougher than one thinks." Grant walked Alice to the door.

Alice paused, "Also…just now when I was leaving Merrebanks, Hobart came out to move Julianna's car to the back barn. There was a funny smell coming from it. Hobart, Robert and I opened the trunk. There was a cooler inside…with hemlock in it."

Grant stared at Alice.

"Tell Minnie I'm sorry I missed her." Alice walked slowly to her car.

Alice stopped by Charlotte and Ev's house. Ev was at the boat works but Alice knew Charlotte would be in her studio. She tapped on the window and apologized when she entered. Any aggravation at the interruption was quickly forgotten when Alice told Charlotte the news. When Alice left, Charlotte called Gloria.

***

Frances stopped at Mary Hester's. No one was home. She then went to Athie's. No one was home. She was swelling with impatience when she burst into the kitchen at Bessie's. There was everyone. "Julianna has lost it again," she announced with triumph.

"Mother beat you to it, Frances."

***

When Minnie returned home from *Kut & Kurl*, she found Grant in the den on a conference call. She went into the kitchen. She would start fixing lunch while she waited for him to get off the phone. She could hardly wait to tell him what she learned at the beauty parlor. Mercy. What a distressing mess the Garretts were in.

***

Flora Grace Wright arrived at Merrebanks shortly after lunch. She was a stocky young woman with a round pretty face. She exuded a sense of stalwart competency. She had a small suitcase with her. Naomi Ruth led her up to Julianna's bedroom and gave her a bell to ring in case she needed anything. Then she left Flora Grace Wright to sit with Julianna, who was still very heavily sedated.

Chapter Thirty-Eight

At five that afternoon the Hatcher sisters met at Bessie's. It was wine time and there was much to discuss. Thankfully Frances had returned to the beach and Bessie was watching television.

"I was not able to find out anything new," Mildred said as she poured white wine into the glasses. "No one at the Club has a clue what happened to Julianna."

"Neither was I," said Mary Hester. "Just speculation and gossip at the Pig."

"Nor I," added Athie. "Still a hot topic but without a solution at *Kut & Kurl*."

"If this is anything like the last time Julianna went over the edge we'll never know the 'why' of it either. Garretts are good at keeping secrets." Mildred sipped her wine.

"Well, I do think it is rather ironic that the major players in the first fiasco are on the scene again." Mary Hester glanced at her sisters.

"Yep," Athie agreed, twirling her wine glass, "they've retaken the dance floor but with different partners."

"Minnie obviously knows something. Maybe we can wheedle it out of her," Mildred said.

"I wouldn't count on it," Athie replied. "She's pretty tight lipped, too. No one knew about Carter."

"So all we know is what Cora spilled this morning at *Kut & Kurl*." Mildred was thinking.

"Yes. I wonder if Dr. Bisbo knows his wife gossips so much. They don't call her 'Bis-by Body' for nothing."

"And all she knew was…he was called out to Merrebanks late yesterday afternoon. Julianna had a 'spell'…as Cora politely put it… and is heavily sedated."

"I wonder if Grant knows anything?"

The sisters looked at each other. They sipped more wine.

"I guess we could go ask him," Mary Hester ventured. "He has stayed in town the last few days. I think he was expecting something."

***

"Oh, Lord, here come the sisters," Minnie announced from the kitchen sink. She could see them out the window marching in single file up the drive. She turned and looked in dismay at Grant.

He laughed. "I'll head them off. We know why they're here. Let's endure the inquisition on the patio." He went out to greet the sisters.

Minnie brought a chilled bottle of white wine and three glasses out to the patio. She returned to the kitchen for Grant's and her glasses of red wine while Grant poured the white wine for the sisters. Minnie returned, handed everyone a cocktail napkin, and sat down. She was ready.

"You can blame it on pure-T curiosity but we wondered if you knew anything about Julianna and her condition?" Athie made quote marks in the air with her fingers.

"Probably the same thing you know," Grant replied, choosing not to reveal Alice's visit that morning. "Minnie came home from the beauty parlor with the news that Julianna had a breakdown late yesterday afternoon. Apparently Dr. Bisbo's wife Cora likes to share what's going on with his patients."

"But what happened? What…or who…caused haughty, high-and-mighty Julianna to lose it? She's usually the one causing the trauma. What happened Thursday…yesterday…at Merrebanks that drove Julianna over the edge?" Mildred was puzzled. "It must have been something pretty awful," she added.

"Do you think it has anything to do with finding out Ward is a Garrett? Or maybe Sarah was the cause. Julianna found out about them both Wednesday…just the day before." Mary Hester wondered aloud.

"I can't help but think it's connected to last time," Athie said. "You caused the breakdown last time when you left her at the altar, Grant, though of course we have no idea why you did that." Athie paused and glanced sideways at Grant.

"I can assure you I am not the cause this time," Grant smiled and took a sip of his wine. "Maybe you should look closer to home," he hinted.

"Well, you did say you would give Ophelia a chance to curb Julianna before you did anything," Athie mused.

"But what on earth could Ophelia possibly have said or done to Julianna that would cause this catastrophic collapse? After all, Ophelia is her mother."

***

Dr. Bisbo returned to Merrebanks in the early evening, checked on Julianna and administered another sedative. He informed Phe and Naomi Ruth that Julianna would be moved to a hospital in Durham tomorrow. Grant Whitworth had arranged it. Ophelia was indeed fortunate to have such a man as a friend.

***

As was the custom since the arrival of Sarah and Ward everyone dined that evening at Merrebanks. Eggie enjoyed it immensely, telling everyone she was as fat as a happy pig because of Naomi

Ruth's biscuits. Conversation was easier this evening though Julianna's presence upstairs hung like a cloud over the dinner table. Ward shared news of Sam and Estelle's plans to leave for Yellowstone National Park next Thursday. Ward would be on his own but Sam was a good teacher and he felt comfortable.

Sarah surprised everyone by saying she had driven out to the family cemetery. She wanted to visit with Linus. Ward squeezed his mother's hand. "I'll bet it was hot, Mother. Next time I'd like to go with you. I haven't a clue where it is."

They all rose together, plates in hand, and put them on the drain board. "Y'all expectin' dessert?" Naomi Ruth asked in jest. She always fixed dessert and they knew it. Everyone just grinned at her. Robert uncovered the large bowl of banana pudding and Naomi Ruth started helping the plates.

Eggie took one look at the homemade banana pudding set before her and exclaimed, "Oh, 'Omi, I am so happy." Everyone laughed.

***

Sarah and Naomi Ruth sat in the two chintz chairs by the window with Maize at their feet. Ophelia sat at her dressing table. She unclasped her pearls and laid them on the dresser. She removed the pins from her hair and began to brush it.

"Phe, if you were serious, I would like to come back to Hope Springs." Sarah looked at Ophelia's reflection in the mirror.

A smile broke out on Ophelia's face as she turned on the stool towards her. "Oh, Sarah, what wonderful news! I am thrilled."

Naomi Ruth clapped her hands. Maize looked up to see what the hullabaloo was all about. Seeing nothing unusual she settled back down to sleep.

"I have talked it over with Ward. He thinks it's a good idea, says he needs to keep an eye on me. I think I will look for a little house in town. I do not want to live with Ward. He needs his independence."

"Well, you know you can come live here, if you wish."

"Thank you but for the time being I think I need my own home. What would I do with all my furniture?" She laughed. "I'll fly back to Chicago Sunday or Monday. I'll make the reservation once I'm sure Julianna is situated. I'll settle things as quickly as possible and be right back." Sarah smiled and looked from Naomi Ruth to Ophelia. "I'm happy to think I'll be here with Linus' family...and Ward's."

"And yours, too, Sarah," Ophelia added.

***

Ophelia was awakened suddenly by a blood curdling scream. She sat bolt upright. Then she threw off her covers and slid from her bed. In her haste she forgot to turn on the light and felt for the door. When she stepped into the dim hall Sarah was standing there wide-eyed.

Down the hall a light was coming from the open door of Julianna's bedroom. They hurried towards it but stopped when they saw Flora Grace Wright standing at the top of the stairs.

Her hands were over her mouth. Her eyes were huge. She turned towards them. "It's my fault. It's my fault. I'm so sorry." Then she turned and pointed.

Sarah and Ophelia moved slowly to the head of the stairs and looked down. At the bottom of the stairs lay the crumbled form of Julianna. Her head was twisted at a most peculiar angle.

Chapter Thirty-Nine

By the time the sun rose in the east Julianna's body had been carried away to the mortuary. Flora Grace Wright had gone home. Dr. Bisbo had departed and the police had asked their final questions. The household at Merrebanks returned to its usual morning routine. Ophelia, Sarah, Ward and Robert were sitting at the kitchen table with coffee and Naomi Ruth was fixing a very big breakfast. It had been a long night.

"Poor little Flora Grace," Sarah said. "This will haunt her the rest of her days. Julianna was sleeping soundly. Flora Grace nodded off. Julianna woke up and got out of bed. Flora Grace didn't hear her."

"Flora Grace almost got to her," Robert said. "The police certainly asked a lot of questions," he added.

"They have to come when there is an unnatural death," Ward said. He had hurried over when Sarah called him immediately after calling Dr. Bisbo. She then called Naomi Ruth and Robert. They had been the first to arrive.

Everyone sat lost in thought.

"Another funeral," Ophelia finally said.

After breakfast Ward left to go to work, promising Ophelia he would check on Eggie and bring her over at lunch time. Ophelia had called Eggie early and told her about Julianna. Eggie had little response. Ward would also tell Sam Jenkins when he saw him later in the morning.

Sarah called Alice and told her of Julianna's death in the night. Alice called Charlotte and Ev. Charlotte called Gloria and William.

Ophelia called Grant. After telling him of Julianna's death she asked if he might come over later in the morning. She then called her old friends Mae Rose and Arthur Taylor.

Mae Rose called Bessie. Bessie was having breakfast with Mildred. Both women were surprised when the phone rang. Clara handed it to Bessie. "Miss Mae Rose," Clara said with raised eyebrows. One did not telephone before nine.

"Hello, Mae Rose. Is anything wrong?" Mildred and Clara watched as Bessie's eyes widened, her red curls quivered and her mouth formed a perfect *O*. Finally she handed the phone back to Clara.

"What in the world has happened, Mother?"

"Julianna Garrett is dead."

***

Grant arrived at Merrebanks just before eleven. He found Ophelia, Sarah and Naomi Ruth in the kitchen with Father Matt. "Please sit down, Grant. We are going over one or two things with Father Matt. It won't take long because everything is rather fresh in our minds." A wry smile twisted the corners of her mouth.

"I'm sorry, Phe," Grant said and took his seat. Naomi Ruth brought him some iced tea.

Ophelia and Father Matt discussed the details of Julianna's funeral. There was a surreal quality to the whole conversation. Ophelia changed the hymns then discussed the Committal at the family cemetery.

"It will be dreadfully dusty if we don't get rain between now and then. And it will be unbearably hot," she added.

"No doubt," Father Matt agreed.

Going to be hot where Julianna's going, too, thought Robert to himself. He and Maize had just walked in from watering the garden. Maize was lapping water from her bowl.

The time of the funeral was decided. It would be held Monday at eleven o'clock. Father Matt would contact the ladies on the funeral food team. It would be the same group present for Everett's funeral. They had the month of June.

Father Matt finally took his leave.

Sarah also left. She was going over to Alice's. They had a list of people to call.

Ophelia led Grant into the library. They settled into the two chairs on either side of the fireplace. Ophelia looked at Grant. "You and I were the only two people I know of who ever said 'no' to Julianna. You said, 'no' when you turned your back on her at the altar. I said, 'no' when she asked to wear my wedding dress. Do you mind telling me why you refused to marry her? Please be honest."

Grant looked at Ophelia. "I saw her with Smythe Hughes the night before the wedding. They were in your art shed. Let's just say they were in a rather compromising position."

"Smythe Hughes...I see," Ophelia said. "Yes, so like Julianna... irresponsible...hedonistic...thinking only of herself in the moment."

"Why did you say 'no'?" Grant asked.

"Only my daughter would wear my wedding dress. Julianna was not my daughter."

Grant's eyebrows rose. His face registered complete surprise.

A little smile played across Ophelia's face. "Yes," she said, "my Linus had a brief affair one summer." She paused and glanced towards Linus' desk. "Linus was quite particular about his hands. The woman was a manicurist here in Hope Springs.

"Shortly after his indiscretion the Navy called him to California for some kind of intelligence work. It was the end of the war. The boys and I joined him. I was pregnant when we left for the west coast, which, of course, everyone here knew. Sadly I lost my baby boy." Ophelia briefly paused. "Nellie…that was the manicurist…appeared two days after the death of my child with her baby…a daughter…over a month old and she still didn't even have a name. Nellie just called her, 'Baby.'" Ophelia stopped and shook her head at the memory.

She drew a deep breath and continued. "Nellie told Linus the baby was his. Linus asked me if I could accept her…for him…and for love of him, I did. She was a beautiful little baby girl…so unwanted. It tugged at your heart strings. The boys were too young to understand and everyone back home just assumed she was ours. It was July and we were living in Santa Ana, hence Julianna. Years later I found out Julianna was not Linus' child. He never knew."

"A well-kept secret, Ophelia." Grant looked at her. "I'm sorry." He was silent for a few seconds then said, "And I must assume Julianna did not know any of this."

"Not until Thursday. When I told her she was not a Garrett, she broke into pieces. It was alarming and tragic to watch."

"Yes, I would imagine so. Being a Garrett was everything to Julianna…her identity…who she was. If she wasn't a Garrett she was nobody." Grant looked at Ophelia.

The two sat together in silence.

"I am not proud of myself for what I did but I saw no other way…and as it turns out it was probably the best way." She looked steadily at Grant.

"I must tell you a few more things that came out in our confrontation. I do this because I might need your help in the future in case any of it comes to light…which I sincerely hope doesn't happen."

Grant nodded.

"Julianna also revealed to us…Naomi Ruth, Hobart and Sarah were here with me, though Sarah joined us late…that she killed both her husbands, Gil Thomas and John Stafford."

Grant sat up in his seat, a stunned expression on his face.

"She had the brakes tampered with on her first husband, Gil's, car...done by a local mechanic, I might add, but I won't tell you his name right now. She shot her second husband, John Stafford, after she drugged him, and made it look like a suicide."

Ophelia stopped for a second. A look of pain swept over her face. "My son Linus was going to look into the deaths of Julianna's husbands. There had already been questions raised about John's death. Linus told Julianna this just before he entered the hospital for his gall bladder surgery last year. He also intimated to her, unfortunately, that she was not a true Garrett. He was his father's executor so I guess he found Julianna's adoption agreement among my Linus' papers. That insinuation did not sit well with Julianna so she went to the hospital and smothered him. Julianna killed Linus."

Grant could not speak. He just sat and stared at Ophelia.

***

The Hatcher sisters could talk of nothing but the death of Julianna Garrett. Neither could anyone else in Hope Springs. When Mary Hester, Athie and Mildred walked into Slater's Drug Store they were bombarded with questions. After sliding into their usual booth there was a steady parade of people coming by to find out what they knew. It was very frustrating, for the sisters, too, knew nothing.

Lula came to the table with their usual order of hot dog, pimento cheese sandwich, chicken salad sandwich, all with a pickle and potato chips. "It's just terrible 'bout Julianna," Lula said. "She won't the most popular horse in the barn but still..." Lula eased away.

"I called Frances," Athie said. "She was beside herself. Then she called back. Father Matt called her. It's still our funeral food team. Can you believe it? She...we...have June. Two Garrett funerals in one month! People have barely gotten their funeral clothes back from the dry cleaners." Athie glanced at the luncheon counter and waved at a friend. "The funeral's Monday at eleven. It'll be hot as Hades."

"I don't think as many folks will show up for Julianna's service," Mary Hester said as she crunched a potato chip.

"Then we won't have as many dishes to wash," Mildred said.

***

Sarah excused herself early from the night's usual conversation in Ophelia's bedroom. She apologized but she was tired. She kissed Ophelia and Naomi Ruth on the cheek and departed for her bedroom.

"Meggie and Bingo will be here late tomorrow afternoon. Meggie is staying with Harriet and Bingo will stay with Ev and Charlotte." Ophelia was sitting at her dressing table. Her tired face looked back at her from the mirror. She rose from her seat and wearily started to prepare for bed. Naomi Ruth turned back the bed and helped her into her nightgown.

"What's our reading tonight," Ophelia asked sleepily from her pillows after settling deeply into the covers.

"I thought of Linus' favorite in Matthew," Naomi Ruth said. "Seemed fittin'."

Ophelia laughed. "You are a wily old soul, Naomi Ruth."

Naomi Ruth smiled and began to read from the gospel of Matthew. When she finished she slowly closed the Bible.

"Yes," Ophelia answered, "the perfect parable for the Garretts. Do you think, 'Omi, that this was a favorite of Linus' because he recognized the 'weed' in the Garrett 'field'?"

"Don't know, Phe. It's possible. He wasn't a stupid man…just hard-headed."

"Well, they all grew up together…under the same roof and at the same table…but a weed can only be a weed." Ophelia sighed.

"The 'weed' is gone, Phe. It's no longer in the 'field.'" Naomi

Ruth stood…and the 'weed' will surely burn, she thought to herself.

"Yes," Ophelia read her thoughts, "the weed will burn." They had been friends for a long time. "Do you have a minister tomorrow at Weeping Mary?" Ophelia asked.

"Yes, we can go if you want."

"Yes, I would like that." Ophelia closed her eyes.

"Good night, Phe. Love you. Come on Maize."

"Night, 'Omi. Love you back."

Chapter Forty

Robert drove down the rural road at the usual sedate speed. Naomi Ruth sat up front with him and Sarah and Ophelia sat on the back seat. They made appropriate comments on the sad state of the crops in the fields. When would it rain again? The air conditioning hummed. They were in a state of suspension lumbering along through the heat of the summer day.

Robert parked the Cadillac in the shade of the huge pecan tree beside the church. He helped the ladies from the car. They began a small stately procession across the grass, moving slowly because of Ophelia's high-heeled shoes. As they neared the church Ipock Peck spied them and wobbled toward them with his unusual bobbing gait.

"Miss Ophelia, it is a dee-light to have you here today. Yes, indeedy, a dee-light. I was remorsed to hear of the passing of your dear daughter. I am sure the switchboard in Gloryland lit up with the news of her arrival." He made a slight bow to Ophelia.

"That is a kind thing to say, Mr. Peck. May I introduce Ward's mother, Sarah. I don't know if you had the opportunity to meet her at the birthday party."

Ipock Peck made another courtly bow to Sarah. "So very pleased to make your acquaintance, Miss Sarah. Your husband rented me the land my business is on till I could buy it and then he helped me with all the legalese. He was a fine man. Yes, indeedy, a fine man."

"And a 'good-morning' to you, Sister," Ipock beamed at Naomi Ruth.

“Mornin’, Brother Ipock,” Naomi Ruth responded.

The three women then made their way towards the steps of the church where Eggie and Ward stood waiting to join them. Robert and Ipock Peck watched them go.

Ipock Peck removed a handkerchief from his coat pocket and wiped the rounded beads of sweat peppering his brow. “How’s Miss Ophelia doin’, Brother Robert? That daughter was a rotten one, yes, indeedy.”

“Ophelia holds it all inside. Hard to read her,” Robert said as he watched his family enter the church.

“Hope she don’t pop, like a blown up paper bag. She’s had a lot of misery heaped on her,” Ipock Peck said as he, too, watched the Garretts make their way into the church. He shook his head and continued, “My guess is that daughter is not moving in an upwardly direction. She is most decidedly ridin’ the down escalator. Yes, indeedy.”

Ophelia, Eggie, Sarah and Ward were ushered with Naomi Ruth to a front pew. Ophelia settled back. The wood felt cool. She lifted the palmetto fan from the rack before her and began to fan.

Hector marched past with the choir. He smiled broadly when he saw them. Robert slid into the pew. Bishop Ronald, Mother Esther and Deacon Wiggins followed the choir. Deacon Wiggins welcomed everyone. The choir sang. The service began. It ended two and a half hours later.

At St. Andrew’s Father Matt led a sedate, and considerably shorter, service. He noticed how large the congregation was today. He knew why. It was the hope of observing the Garretts after this latest and very bizarre tragedy. It was the barely suppressed, and very un-Christian, curiosity in another’s troubles. When the only family members present were Alice, Ev and Charlotte, the congregation was deflated but undaunted. After the service gossip ran rampant.

Mildred and Bessie drove straight to the club after church,

arriving a few minutes before Athie and Joe Allen. Mary Hester and Erwin dropped Harriet, who said she was dieting, off at home then followed. After the prerequisite conversation with those of other denominations the Hatcher clan served their plates and made their way to their table. All except Bessie. Miss Bessie was deep in conversation with Cora Bisbo. Dr. Bisbo was making his way down the buffet line. He was quite used to eating alone while his wife talked with anyone who would listen.

"Wonder where the Garretts were today," Athie buttered her rolls, "though I'm not surprised they were absent from St. Andrew."

"They probably went to the Weeping Mary with Naomi and Robert. That's my guess," Mary Hester said, emptying a packet of artificial sweetener into her tea.

"Here comes Alice. Ask her," Mildred added, pointing with her fork.

Alice and Charlotte were approaching the table next to the Hatcher's. Ev was not far behind. He had made a detour to the dessert table.

"Hello, everyone," Alice greeted the Hatchers as she placed her plate on her table and sat down. Charlotte nodded and sat down also.

"Sorry about Julianna, Alice," Joe Allen said, leaning around Athie to speak. "Been lots of misfortune y'all's way lately."

"Thank you, Joe Allen," Alice replied.

"Where was the rest of your family?" Mildred asked.

"Think Phe, Sarah, Ward and Eggie went to the Weeping Mary," Charlotte answered. "Phe always finds peace there and, Lord knows, she deserves some." She took a bite of her broccoli salad.

Bessie arrived at the table. She put her plate down. "Be right back. Gotta get dessert before it's all gone. Hello Alice, Charlotte, Ev." She bobbed off towards the dessert table.

Grant and Minnie walked up, spoke to everyone and joined the Garretts at their table.

Everyone returned to talking among themselves.

Athie leaned in towards her sisters. “We’re going to have to whisper because we’re sitting so close to Alice, Ev and Charlotte.”

“Maybe they’ll be talking and not paying attention to us. Or… maybe we should listen to them. Might learn something.” Mildred was watching the Garrett table out of the corner of her eye.

“Here comes Mother. Let’s see what she’s been up to…besides raiding the dessert table.” Mary Hester watched her mother approach with a dessert in each hand.

Bessie sat down and placed a slice of blueberry pie on one side of her plate and a slice of chocolate cake on the other.

“Why don’t you just start with dessert, Mother?” Mildred asked.

“Don’t tempt me,” Bessie said as she lifted her fork.

“What did you rush over to ask Cora Bisbo?” Athie looked at her mother.

Miss Bessie glanced over at the Garrett table, leaned in towards her daughters and whispered, “I wanted to be sure we knew everything she knew.” Bessie smiled. “And we did, except for one small piece of information.” Bessie pushed her fork into a pile of creamy mashed potatoes.

“And what was that?” Mary Hester asked.

Bessie looked at her daughters. “The name of the person who was sitting with Julianna.”

The sister’s forks hovered. “There was a sitter with Julianna?” Athie asked.

***

It was almost two-thirty when Ophelia, Sarah, Naomi Ruth and Robert drove up the drive to Merrebanks. Ward and Eggie were in his car right behind them. They were all surprised and delighted to see the BMW convertible parked in back. Hobart was home. He came out the door with Maize to greet them.

Hobart opened his mother's door and helped her from the car, giving her a big hug. "Another funeral for the Garretts, Mother. Sorry."

"Yes. Hopefully this is the end. The pickings are getting slim."

Hobart gave a short laugh and took his mother's arm.

In the kitchen Ophelia slowly eased into a chair at the table. Hobart got iced tea from the refrigerator while Sarah and Naomi Ruth pulled out selections of funeral food arriving steadily at the back door since news of Julianna's death spread through the community. While they dined on cold fried chicken, congealed salads, ham biscuits and deviled eggs Hobart asked Sarah and his mother to please tell him again what had happened after he left. Memory is fluid, flowing in and out of forgotten crevices, but they were able to present to Hobart a credible recitation of the facts.

When they came to the scream and the discovery of Julianna at the bottom of the stairs Hobart just shook his head. "I hate to speak ill of the dead but that is just so Julianna. It's fittingly dramatic…the sleepwalking Lady Macbeth."

"Who, by the way," he asked, "was the poor soul sitting with her?"

"Her name was Flora Grace something," Ophelia answered. "I've forgotten her last name."

"I think it was Wright," Naomi Ruth said. "Do you know them?"

"No, but I've been gone from Hope Springs so long. I'll ask Carter. He'll probably know who they are."

"I'm sorry for her," Eggie said. "Everyone will remember Julianna falling to her death on her watch. She's jinxed. It's a crying shame. Just like Julianna to be so thoughtless."

***

"And who was sitting with Julianna, Mother?" Mary Hester asked.

"It was a young woman named Flora Grace Wright. Apparently

she dozed off. Dr. Bisbo sent her to help the Garretts and administer a sedative should the need arise in the night." Bessie began cutting her barbecue chicken into small pieces. "Flora Grace worked for him each summer through high school and he talked her into attending nursing school at the community college.

"Cora said her husband thinks very highly of her…and is nervous that this unfortunate incident will make her give up her plans for nursing school. Of course, it's not her fault but you know how people think…and talk. They'll blame her." She began to eat.

"I wonder if she's kin to the greens-keeper here?" Erwin spoke for the first time. "Bobo Wright. Great tight-end…High School All-American. Nice guy. Got the course in great shape." Erwin went back to his corn pudding.

"I'm sure we can find out, though I don't know what difference that makes." Athie looked at her brother-in-law.

"Flora Grace Wright. Flora Grace Wright." Mary Hester was repeating, her fork punctuating the air. "I don't know why that name seems so familiar."

Minnie turned in her seat to look over at Mary Hester. "Did you say Flora Grace Wright?"

Mary Hester nodded. "You know her?"

"She's Ramona's daughter…"

"Of course," Mary Hester exclaimed, "Ramona at *Kut & Kurl.* She talks incessantly about her daughter Flora Grace…how smart she is…I just turn a deaf ear. Even had to look at all the wedding pictures."

"To Bobo Wright?" Mildred asked.

"Yes," Minnie answered and turned back to her table. Grant looked at Minnie. "What was that about?"

"Mary Hester couldn't figure out who someone was. I don't know what they're talking about but I knew the girl so I helped them out."

"Very charitable of you," Grant said and laughed. "And if I know them they are talking about the Garretts."

"Well, I don't know what the daughter of my manicurist has to do with the Garretts." Minnie looked at Grant.

"Manicurist?" A speculative look crossed Grant's face. He put his fork down. "Whoa…is this one of life's little ironies?"

He looked at Minnie. "Tell me more about this daughter of your manicurist."

Half way through her explanation Minnie paused, "Oh, dear, Ramona was Jake Denton's baby sister. Do you think…?"

Grant looked at her. He turned towards the Hatcher table. Athie was closest to him. He tapped her on her shoulder. When she turned to him he simply asked, "Was Flora Grace Wright the person sitting with Julianna when she fell?"

Athie cast a cryptic glance at Grant and nodded.

***

Food continued to arrive at Merrebanks at regular intervals Sunday afternoon. Sarah and Naomi Ruth cleaned out the refrigerator after lunch to make space for new arrivals. Ophelia went up to her room for a nap. She said she just could not face the parade of the curious this afternoon. Ward and Eggie returned to Mayfield. They would be back for supper.

***

Both Meggie and Bingo called when they arrived in town. They would see their grandmother later. Robert and Hobart once again removed chairs and tables and the whiskey supply from the barn. Even though the funeral might be smaller the ritual was the same.

Frances made an appearance at four o'clock. She told Naomi Ruth once again the ladies who would be helping in the kitchen. She told Naomi Ruth once again what they would need in the way of plates and platters. She told Naomi Ruth once again that the ladies would arrive while the family was at the church. She told Naomi

Ruth once again that everything would be ready when the family and friends returned from the cemetery. Naomi Ruth once again turned a deaf ear. Sarah listened respectfully. Then Sarah ushered a reluctant Frances out to her car. Naomi Ruth knew what to do. Sarah would learn.

At five o'clock Ophelia came back downstairs. Robert fixed her a gin and tonic. Sarah and Hobart appeared and joined her. They moved to the side porch where a warm river breeze was blowing. Alice, Ev and Charlotte drove up the drive about five-thirty, bringing Bingo and Meggie, whom they had picked up from the Pearson's. Eggie and Ward arrived shortly after them. They all sat together on the porch with their cocktails engaging in stilted conversation, fanning the humid air with funeral home fans. Ward was a surprise to Meggie and Bingo. They did not know who Sarah was. Julianna obviously had not shared any family history with her children.

Ev, Charlotte, Ward, Meggie and Bingo left just before seven. They had all been invited back to the Pearson's for pizza. Ophelia felt a great sense of relief when they departed. Julianna's children were tiresome. Like their mother they identified too much with the material world. She imagined that after the funeral tomorrow she would hear less and less from them, unless they wanted something.

Alice stayed for supper. Ward would return after pizza at the Pearson's and take Eggie and Alice home.

Alice was telling them about the crowd at the Sunday buffet at the country club. "I always enjoy going because you see everyone in town. Of course, everyone asked about you, Phe."

"No doubt," Ophelia gave a brief laugh. "I'm sure it was more curiosity than concern."

"The Hatchers sat beside us. Bessie ate three desserts! Can you believe that? She started with two then went back for a third!"

"Bessie has always had a voracious sweet tooth."

"Grant and Minnie joined us. Grant was quite curious about

the girl who was with Julianna when she fell."

Ophelia turned and looked closely at Alice. "Why?" she asked.

"He was startled for some reason because her mother is a manicurist."

Ophelia put down her fork. "Her mother is a manicurist? Please don't tell me she is Ramona's daughter."

"Why, yes. Ramona at *Kut & Kurl* is her mother."

Ophelia stared at Alice. "How...very...odd," she said.

"That's exactly what Grant said...then he added something about life's ironies." Alice looked puzzled.

"Are y'all saying that the girl who was sitting with Julianna was Ramona Sessoms' daughter?" Hobart leaned across the table. His fork hovered in midair.

"Yes, that's right. Minnie knows because she was in Ramona's class and Carter, Jr. was in Flora Grace's class. That's the sitter... Flora Grace Sessoms Wright."

"I was in the class right behind Minnie and Ramona," Hobart announced. "How well I remember." He turned to Ophelia. "Mother, Ramona is married to Rico Sessoms. Her older brother was Jake Denton."

Ophelia stared at her son. "Yes, I know."

"What a strange coincidence," Sarah said.

"I don't believe in coincidences," Hobart looked at Sarah.

"Coincidence is God's way of remaining anonymous," Eggie announced as she placed her fork on her empty plate.

***

"What do you think?" It was evening. Ophelia and Naomi Ruth were in Ophelia's bedroom. Sarah had gone to her room. Maize was lying beside the bed. Naomi Ruth was sitting by the window. Ophelia was pacing. She had just finished reciting the connections between Flora Grace Wright and Julianna.

Naomi Ruth looked at Phe. "What you gonna do? You know something isn't exactly right…too many coincidences."

"Yes, and I wish I could ignore them," Ophelia looked at Naomi Ruth. "It's the irony of it all that gets me. I had no idea that child was Ramona's daughter…and Rico's." She stopped pacing and sat down on her dressing table stool. "Surely you don't think…," Ophelia trailed off.

"The mills of God grind slowly…" Naomi Ruth stood. She turned to look at Ophelia. "If the girl pushed Julianna, how do we prove it? And do we even want to?"

"No," Ophelia answered. "What would it serve to stir up a hornet's nest? Nothing. Julianna's dead. So be it. Amen." Ophelia removed her pearls and began to take the pins from her hair.

"Retribution," she quietly said.

Naomi Ruth moved toward the door. "Long day tomorrow. Come on Maize. Night, Ophelia. "

"Night, Naomi Ruth. Love you."

"Love you back."

Chapter Forty-One

The day of Julianna's funeral promised to be quite hot. Naomi Ruth rose early. She took her cutting shears and a bucket of water and set off in the cool of the morning to collect greenery and flowers for fresh arrangements in the house. Maize trotted along with her.

When Sarah came downstairs there was a remarkable arrangement of hydrangeas, delphinium, Queen Anne's lace and poet's laurel on the dining room table. Naomi Ruth was in the kitchen working on an arrangement for the entry hall. Sarah offered to start breakfast while Naomi Ruth went to help Ophelia. Robert walked in. He had Ophelia's car in place. Wilbur and Willard Womble, the funeral home directors, would arrive at ten to get the family into the black funeral home cars. Once again Phe declared she would ride in her own black Cadillac.

Ward and Eggie arrived at nine-thirty. At nine-fifty Alice, Charlotte and Ev rushed in apologizing profusely for running late. Meggie and Bingo arrived at ten on the coat tails of the Womble brothers. Julianna's children had inherited their mother's sense of punctuality. "Well, it isn't like they're going to start without us," Meggie threw out nonchalantly.

Wilbur and Willard shepherded everyone to the waiting limousines…all except Ophelia who got into her car with Naomi Ruth. Robert was behind the wheel.

A slow procession made its way to St. Andrew's for the funeral of Julianna Garrett Stafford. When the service ended family and friends returned to their cars and followed the black hearse and black limousines once again down the rural roads through the fields of Chinquapin County. The earth was bone dry. The crops were drooping from the heat. There had been no rain in twenty-four days and the heat was brutal. Dust filled the air.

The hearse and limousines turned down the dirt road to the Garrett cemetery. Stunted cornstalks stood as sentinels lining the road. Dust swirled from the passing cars, engulfing each car in the line behind. When the cars stopped the dust settled, blanketing them, creating a dull line of khaki automobiles. No one dared exit their car until the dust completely settled or they, too, would be covered in dust.

Father Matt stepped from his vehicle. The pallbearers climbed from the big black Suburban. They walked the casket to the grave. The family exited their limousines and once again followed Ophelia, Robert and Naomi Ruth in a slow procession to their seats. The friends trailed behind. No air stirred.

It was noon. It was hot. Father Matt raced through the Committal.

After the final Amen he encouraged everyone on behalf of the family to return to their cars and proceed to Merrebanks. This they did with alacrity. It was too hot and too dusty to tarry and talk. They were as parched as the corn surrounding them. They could talk at Merrebanks with a drink in their hands.

The church ladies had platters and trays of food ready. They had pitchers of tea and lemonade poured. They would once again serve, wash and gossip.

About four o'clock everyone had hugged Ophelia, commiserated with family members, had several drinks and departed. The ladies of the church were finishing up in the kitchen. Naomi Ruth was biting her tongue. Ward took Eggie home and Alice, Sarah and Minnie moved to the rockers on the side porch to talk. Ophelia and Grant went into the library. Ophelia asked Hobart to join them.

"I imagine you know about Flora Grace Wright," Grant said to Ophelia. "I just want to be sure we know the same things." He and Ophelia sat in the two wing chairs beside the fireplace.

Hobart sat facing them on the sofa.

"Yes," Ophelia answered. "There seems to have been quite an interesting number of coincidences surrounding Julianna's death."

"I assume we are doing nothing about those 'coincidences,'" Grant said, eyebrow raised.

"That is my inclination. Do you agree…or disagree?"

"I heartily agree," Grant replied. "It serves no purpose that I can see to bother that family."

"Julianna has bothered them enough," Hobart added. "Do you think she even remembered that Ramona was Jake's little sister?"

"I doubt it," Ophelia answered. "When Julianna was at the beauty parlor getting her nails done, she would have had no interest in Ramona as a person. Ramona was there to perform a service for her. I doubt if she even remembered that Jake had a little sister."

"Besides, I imagine she was busy trying to exchange the nail polish bottles without Ramona noticing. I wonder how she did that?" Hobart added.

"No telling," his mother shrugged. "Julianna was quite resourceful."

"Minnie told me that Ramona was married to a mechanic over at Jessie's Body Shop. Rico Sessoms. I assume he was the mechanic Julianna used when she 'fixed' her husband's brakes." Grant looked at Ophelia.

Ophelia smiled. "Very good, Grant, and you are right. Another coincidence?"

"I am curious as to why Julianna didn't have Rico 'fix' Minnie's brakes," Grant said.

"Maybe he realized he was being used. Or, maybe he was found out," Ophelia said.

"You think Ramona knew about Julianna and Rico?" Hobart asked.

"Hope Springs is a small town," Ophelia said. "If she didn't know, I'm sure her daughter did."

"So daughter Flora Grace stepped in to avenge her mother…or her family?" Hobart questioned.

"Oh, I don't think this was premeditated, by any means," Ophelia answered, looking at her son. "I just think the opportunity presented itself and she took it. I imagine Ramona shared Julianna and Jake's history with her daughter. It never was a secret. Everyone in town knew Linus was instrumental in getting Jake drafted…to keep him away from Julianna…or because Julianna asked Linus to do it. I always suspected the latter."

Ophelia paused and glanced at Grant. "His tragedy was his love for Julianna."

Grant was quiet. "I, too, once loved Julianna…or the person I thought Julianna was."

"That was Julianna's tragedy. She was given so much love…but she kept it all for herself." Hobart rose from the sofa. "You were lucky, Grant. The Queen of Mean did not ruin your life…or even end it, for that matter. I still cannot believe what she did. She murdered two husbands. She murdered Linus, our brother and your son, Mother. And, honestly, I have my doubts about poor old Everett. We were all together at Nags Head over Memorial Day weekend."

"Oh, Lord, Hobart…please…," Ophelia looked in shock at her son.

"Sorry, Mother, forget I said that…just rattling." Hobart noticed Grant looking at him with a look of surprised speculation.

At the door Hobart paused and turned. "It might sound terrible but I cannot shed a tear for Julianna. If Jake Denton's niece lent a hand, so be it." He looked from his mother to Grant. "Let's just say she experienced a fall from grace, and leave it at that." He grinned and left the room.

Ophelia and Grant stood. "Thank you for your patience with the Garretts, Grant...today and thirty years ago." She smiled up at him as he stood beside her.

"Your family is special, Ophelia. Back in the day you were all very accepting and welcoming to me. Your family could have been my family. You have been gracious and forgiving. If Julianna had been more like you wild horses could not have dragged me from that altar."

Ophelia laughed. She took his arm and they walked from the room in search of the rest of the family.

***

The Hatcher sisters returned to their mother's kitchen after the funeral. Mildred poured three generous glasses of white wine. "I'm so glad we didn't have to spend the afternoon in the kitchen," Mildred said as she poured. "I'm just not in the mood to be bossed around by Frances." The three sat in companionable silence lost in their separate thoughts, sipping their wine.

"I just can't believe Julianna is dead," Mary Hester finally spoke.

"Well, she was the first to get up from the table the night of Everett's funeral," Mildred reminded her sisters.

"Oh, law, I completely forgot about that! Eerie." They grew quiet again.

"She certainly gave us a lot to talk about through the years," Athie spoke.

"She had a sad life if you stop and think about it," Mary Hester said. "There was Jake Denton dying in Vietnam. Then Grant walked out on her. Gil died because of a car wreck and John committed suicide. She lost two brothers early. It's almost too much to believe that all that could happen to one person."

"It's like Julianna was the Angel of Death," Mildred said.

"I don't believe 'angel' and 'Julianna' have ever been used in the same sentence," Athie said.

The three sisters sipped.

"I still wonder...," Mildred broke the silence then trailed off.

"Doubt we'll ever know what happened." Athie sipped her wine. "The Garretts are tight lipped."

"Maybe Mother learned something from Eggie this afternoon," Mary Hester said. "They had their heads together sitting in the corner."

"I said something to Hobart," Mildred said. "He just looked at me and quietly told me Julianna got what she deserved."

Athie turned to Mildred. "He said that? Rather an odd thing for a brother to say when his sister has just tragically died."

"I never thought there was any love lost between them...especially lately." Mildred looked at her sister.

"Yes, but why did Julianna *deserve* to die? That's harsh. A comment like that is very telling, don't you think? Hobart has that cutting sarcasm, which is usually right on target, but he is not a mean person. What did Julianna do that was so terrible her brother declares she deserved death for it?" Athie looked at her sisters.

"Maybe he was being Biblical," Mildred added.

"I feel so sorry for little Flora Grace. This will stay with her forever. And don't you think it's beyond ironic that Flora Grace is Jake Denton's niece? Do you think she knew who Julianna was?" Mary Hester looked at her sisters. "And why was Grant so interested in the fact that her mother is a manicurist? What does that have to do with anything?"

"I'm sure Flora Grace knew exactly who Julianna was," Athie looked at her sisters. "It's common knowledge. She could have pushed Julianna down the stairs for all we know and who would blame her."

"Oh, my! What a thought." Mildred looked appalled.

"Maybe that's what Hobart meant," Mary Hester said.

"Y'all are totally missing the point." Athie stared at her sisters. "What happened Thursday? That's the question that needs to be answered. That is the mystery."

The back door opened and Bessie sailed into the room. Hector followed her. "I learned absolutely nothing more by staying at Ophelia's. Total waste of time on my part...and Hector won't share anything he knows...which I'm sure is a darn sight more than we know." Bessie glared at him. She turned and pushed through the dining room door. "I hope I haven't missed my program."

"What pot y'all gonna stir now that Julianna has passed on?" Hector asked. He looked at the sisters with a jaundiced eye then turned to leave.

"Hector, wait," Mary Hester called after him.

"Now, you girls know better than that." He grinned at them and went out the back door.

***

At Merrebanks late that afternoon the back screen door banged and Ward walked into the kitchen. He smiled at his family sitting around the table.

"We're having a little libation while we wait for you, Nephew," Hobart said. "Want to join us?"

"Think I'll wait till we return. We probably ought to go now because unless my ears were deceiving me I heard a rumble of thunder when I got out of my truck."

"Rain would be a blessing," Robert said as he rose and picked up the keys to the Cadillac.

***

Fifteen minutes later the big dusty Cadillac turned once again down the dirt road to the Garrett family cemetery. Large gray clouds were forming in the northeastern sky. There was a distant roll of thunder. Robert brought the car to a standstill and waited for the dust to settle.

Then he helped Ophelia out of the rear seat while Sarah,

Hobart, Ward and Naomi Ruth slid from their seats. Maize jumped down from the floorboard and led the way into the cemetery. Everyone slowly made their way toward the mound of flowers covering Julianna's grave.

Knotted together the family stood silently looking down at the withering pall. Ward turned and wandered over to his father's grave. He stood quietly looking at the gleaming marble tombstone. Sarah watched him.

Hobart and Maize walked among the tombstones.

Robert handed Ophelia and Naomi Ruth the large trash bags and they slowly began stuffing them with withered foliage. When they finished Robert carried the bags back to the Cadillac and Naomi Ruth and Ophelia wandered over to Big Linus' grave. Ophelia's hand played with the pearls at her neck as she looked down at the dried grass covering the grave.

"Wonder if he knows what happened?"

"He might," Naomi Ruth answered. "The past sure plays with the present. Don't know why the dead can't stay with the living."

"You may be right but I'm hoping he doesn't. He would be so disappointed in himself."

"He loved you but he didn't have a clue what his decision to adopt that little unwanted girl cost you. You hid it well."

"Did he call her, Naomi Ruth? Did he call Nellie to bring that baby when mine died?"

"Yes, Ophelia, he called her."

"He knew about her baby?"

"Nellie called and told him she was pregnant. She wanted money. He paid her to keep it from you. Then when William Gregory died he called Nellie and told her to bring the baby to him. He paid her a huge sum of money. I don't know if he did it for you…or for himself."

"I always suspected," Ophelia said. "Her arrival was just too much of a coincidence."

Naomi Ruth looked at her. "Why did you agree?"

"It was a simple choice. I knew how important it was to him… family and land. That was his creed. He thought she was his. He thought she was a Garrett. He died believing that. The fault lies with me for not taking action when I discovered she wasn't."

"Guess we're both at fault for that," Naomi Ruth agreed. "We knew what she was…and what she wasn't…but I don't think telling her the truth then would have made any difference."

Ophelia looked at Naomi Ruth. "It was too late," Naomi Ruth added.

The two old friends stood shoulder to shoulder lost in thought. Naomi Ruth reached out and hugged Ophelia's shoulder then turned and walked towards Robert.

Ward walked over and stood at his grandmother's side. "Wish I could have known him," he said, looking down at his grandfather's grave.

"You are like him," Ophelia said, "in your love of the land. I think, however, you are a better man in your love of the family." She smiled up at her grandson.

Thunder rumbled. Everyone looked at the sky. Fat grey rain clouds were marching toward them. It had grown cooler. The air smelled of rain. The family moved together at the foot of Julianna's grave.

"Well, I guess the Queen of Discord got what she wanted in the end, Mother," Hobart said. "She's deep within Garrett soil, resting for eternity with Garretts."

"No one need know she wasn't one. We'll keep that…and everything else…within the family." Ophelia looked at the faces of those around her. Heads nodded.

A raindrop fell. Naomi Ruth and Ophelia turned towards the car. They moved with slow dignity because of Ophelia's high-heeled shoes. Maize trotted at their heels. Hobart and Robert followed with Ward and Sarah. They moved over the dry earth toward the dusty Cadillac. They made it into the car just as the heavens opened. A drenching rain poured down, drumming a staccato beat on the roof of the Cadillac, washing away the dust in thick rivulets. Robert started the engine and slowly turned the big car around and headed back down the dirt road. Rain drops popped in the dust. As they neared the county road Ophelia turned and looked back. She could not see the cemetery. A curtain of rain hid it from view.

She turned and saw Naomi Ruth watching her. She smiled. "I have an odd sense of peace, 'Omi."

Naomi Ruth took Ophelia's hand and smiled. "It's time, Phe."

"It's time, all right." From the front seat Hobart raised his voice over the beating rain. "It's time for a drink! Has this old car ever been over thirty-five, Robert? Let's see what she'll do."

Robert laughed. "She'll do what she should."